INSIDIOUS MAGIC

MODERN MAGIC - BOOK TWO

NICOLE HALL

For Pocket, this tech god is for you

1

RYAN

THE LAST THING Ryan Nolan wanted to be doing was tromping through the Wood looking for a wayward fairy that refused to be found. Zee hated being called a fairy, so he did it as often as possible. A bare branch caught his long-sleeved shirt, and he slapped it away. December in Texas wasn't exactly frigid, but he figured the less holes in his clothes the better.

"Stop playing with the trees and pay attention." Sera frowned at him again.

"They were playing with me. The grabby branches are getting worse. I think they're doing it on purpose." Ryan took a few more steps away from the forest they'd just left and toward the safety of the road, tightening the fleece he had tied around his waist.

Jake snorted. "I thought you liked grabby things."

An image of Maddie clinging to him in the Wood flashed across Ryan's mind, but making a joke about Jake's sister was in poor taste, even for him. "Can we not talk about this in mixed company?"

"Since when do I count as mixed company?" Sera asked.

"Since I don't want to get punched again, and you're a handy excuse."

She crossed her arms and gazed past him into the trees. "That's fair. Also, the trod is gone again."

Ryan glanced over his shoulder. "It always disappears when we leave the Wood."

"Yeah, but this time it was disappearing as we were walking on it, and did you notice the sprites?"

Jake swatted at a glimmer of golden light floating around his face. "What about them?"

"There were only a few on the trod. Usually there are enough to light the way for us."

"It's daytime, in the Wood *and* out here. Maybe we didn't need as many since we could see fine."

She shook her head. "That's not how the sprites work."

Ryan resisted rolling his eyes. Ever since he'd given Sera access to the Fae database, she'd become the de facto expert on magic and didn't mind lording it around a bit. Admittedly, there was a lot of useful information in there, but Ryan had never wanted to know more than was necessary. Magic, in the wrong hands—*in any hands*—was dangerous, and the lure to use it multiplied exponentially. A quick glamour here, a little help there, and one day, the magic becomes necessary to everything.

Ryan could feel his mood getting darker as the sun went down. "Zombie bunnies." It was their safe word. Sera stopped lecturing them on sprites immediately. "Did we learn anything new this trip?"

Sera pulled her ponytail over her shoulder. "Same as all the last times. The trods are basically closed to us. Whatever happened when I brought down the Fae barriers did something to the Wood, and until we can find Zee to find out what, I can't get it to cooperate."

"What if we asked really nicely? Have we tried that?" Ryan turned to the trees and spread his arms wide. "Oh, great and mighty Wood, have you seen Zee? We could really use her to explain some stuff."

Jake snickered behind him, followed by the distinctive sound of Sera smacking him in the shoulder. Ryan wasn't expecting an answer, smartass was his default personality, but then the light changed deep in the trees. The smirk dropped off his face as he lowered his arms. He took a step forward to get a better look, and a path appeared between the pines, dotted with tiny glowing sprites. He glanced over his shoulder, and Sera shook her head, eyes wide. Jake shrugged. *If neither of them had called the trod, then who had?*

He didn't have to wait long for his answer. One second, they'd been watching the sprites float around, the next, a statuesque woman wearing wispy, trailing scarves, complicated Viking braids, and not much else, was propelled from the path. She didn't have a weapon, which was good for Ryan because she slammed right into him.

She was damn near his height, tall for a woman, so they nearly ended up sprawled in the road. Ryan managed to quickly shift his balance and keep them upright, but reflex had his hands splayed over the smooth bronze skin of her back. Apparently, her sheer top tied around her neck and didn't cover the back half, a style Ryan decided he heartily approved of. Add some wrist cuffs and a lasso of truth, and she'd be starring in some of his better fantasies.

Her body was pressed against him from shoulder to knee. If he didn't do something, in a few seconds, she was going to find out exactly how much Ryan liked her top. And the scent of her skin. *Not helping.* He set her firmly away from him and removed his hands from her person.

Her green eyes were wide with panic, but recognition crept in as she straightened and studied the people around her. Ryan felt the weight of her gaze as she lingered on him. Absently, she looked down and noticed her clothes, then did a double-take. Her eyes narrowed in annoyance. He'd recognize those eyes and that look anywhere, even if the body attached to them was new.

They'd finally found Zee.

———

ZEE

Dammit, Chad. Zee was not happy. The trods had never been her favorite form of transport. They were draining and made her vaguely nauseous. Chad had assured her his newest trinket would speed the journey through the magical path, but it appeared to have changed her form and made the trip unbearably long instead. She'd left the Glade to join the battle against Torix, and at the time, she'd been wearing enchanted leather armor.

That had been hours ago.

She was definitely going to neuter him when she got back. The ridiculous dress she was wearing tied in a halter around her neck and flowed down into strips of fabric for a skirt. Not bad for movement in combat but terrible for protection. She could still feel the heat from Ryan's hands on her back when he'd caught her. Another thing to be embarrassed about. Fae warriors were *not* flung from the Wood to stumble about.

Ryan cleared his throat, and Zee met his eyes. He gestured at her. "This is new."

Sera piped up from somewhere behind her. "I've seen her like this before. New outfit though."

Zee considered the dream they'd shared and silently admitted it may have been Sera's vision that called the dress instead of Chad's mistake, though no one should have been able to change her form against her will, and certainly not from outside the trod.

She studied the area around her again, more carefully this time. The humans stood outside the Wood, on the edge of a neighborhood street. Bare trees stretched high above them in front of the tidy houses across the road. Nothing like the cottages in the Glade, and not like anything she'd seen inside the Wood.

"Where am I?" Her voice was rusty, like she hadn't used it in weeks.

"The outskirts of Mulligan. Across the street from Jake and Sera's place...and Evie's place, I guess." Ryan watched her closely, shoving his hands in the pockets of his cargo pants.

The others were wearing pants and coats, and to her surprise, she had goosebumps breaking out all over her. She was *cold*.

How could she be cold? Fae could regulate body temperature with magic. She crossed her arms over her chest and shivered as a chilly wind blew right through the filmy dress. Everything was wrong, and she didn't know where to start in order to fix it.

Ryan wordlessly untied his fleece and handed it to her. She slipped it on and immediately felt better. It carried his warmth and his scent, which was surprisingly soothing but also made her feel tingly and weird. Zee frowned. All three of the humans were watching her like she'd disappear if they blinked.

"What happened?" At least her voice was starting to sound more normal.

Sera and Jake shared a look, but it was Ryan who took the lead. "We'd been searching for you, then I got sassy with the Wood, and it tossed you at me."

Zee blinked at him. "How long have you been searching?"

"Since Halloween, so about five weeks? Not very nice, by the way. We took care of your problem, and you all abandoned us."

Zee's eyes widened. Five weeks? When she'd left the Glade, it had been Samhain, what the humans call Halloween. The trods had kept her walking for hours, but five weeks? She'd never heard of the time difference reaching such an extreme length.

"What about Torix?"

Ryan shook his head. "He got away, but Sera says he's powerless."

"How..." There were so many questions, she had to prioritize. She faced Sera. "What happened on Samhain?"

A soft flush stained Sera's cheeks, and Zee was reminded that humans had silly inhibitions about battle. "I fought Torix, and ended up draining his magic away. It's sort of what I do."

Zee didn't think her eyebrows could get any further up her forehead. "How did you get to him?"

Another flush. "Ah, I may have taken down the Fae barriers."

"The barriers my ancestors placed centuries ago and we've been reinforcing for generations? The ones instrumental in our pact with the Wood?"

"Some new information in there, but yes. It released both Torix and Evie, who is currently stuck in her house because the world still thinks she's dead. We hoped you could help with that."

Zee didn't answer. She pivoted and strode right back to the trees. If she ended up stuck in a trod for several more months, so be it, but if the barriers were truly gone, then the pact was broken and she needed to return to the Glade to check on her people.

She'd taken several steps into the forest before she realized no path had emerged. Zee was crunching over dead leaves and pine straw, but no sprites joined her and she had to weave haphazardly between trunks. Also, her fingers were still cold. She pulled the sleeves of Ryan's fleece down over her hands and tried to use her magic to call on the Wood.

Nothing answered, and she stopped. The humans arrived seconds later. Where were the trods? Warning bells were going off in her head, but Zee remained calm. Warriors did not panic. She closed her eyes to block out the fading sunlight and the brambles, instead picturing the mossy green earth of the Glade. The circle set aside for teleportation. The symbols etched onto the surrounding rocks. She gathered her magic with intention and opened her eyes.

Ryan, Sera, and Jake stared back, waiting.

She was tired, but she should have had enough energy to teleport once. It had to be after-effects from Samhain, but when she'd reached to gather her magic, she'd felt nothing. No corresponding power, no tingles, no sense of purpose. A horrible thought dawned on her.

Zee had left the Glade in her Amazon form, as Sera had dubbed it, but she could change shape at will. When she tried though, her will left her the same as before. The change should have been instantaneous. As soon as she wished to be a small flying creature, she should have been. Instead, she remained a tall woman in a ludicrous dress.

The humans shuffled uncomfortably, and Zee's eyes landed on Sera again. She belatedly remembered Ryan's mention of Evie in his explanation. "What have you done?"

Sera visibly straightened under Zee's scrutiny, and Jake's arms came around her from behind. "I did what I had to do to stop Torix and protect our world." Her eyes glazed over a bit as she stared, and then she gasped. "Your magic is gone."

Zee trembled inside, but nodded. She'd begun to suspect as much. Sera had broken far more than she knew. "I have to get back to my people."

Ryan sighed. "Good idea, but we couldn't get to you *or* the rest of the Fae even before the Wood dropped you on me. After a lot of trial and error, we also think the power surge probably knocked out the Wi-Fi I set up. Honestly, it was pretty shaky to begin with since you boosted it with magic. The surge could have overloaded a capacitor or over-heated a resistor. Either way, it most likely fried the repeater's antenna, so it couldn't send or receive at a 5G frequency..." He trailed off as Zee, Sera, and Jake all stared at him blankly.

Ryan ran a hand through his mussed hair, and a crackle of deep red magic zipped between his fingers like static. "Right. Either way, we need your help before you take your toys and go home."

The lack of trods or technology would make it extremely hard to contact her people, but Zee was relieved she could still sense his power. Like so many other things though, it was twisted from the way it was supposed to be. Ryan's magic shouldn't be visible to normal sight. "I'm not sure I can help you in my current state."

His jaw clenched. She knew what he wanted to talk about, but they'd agreed to tell no one of their deal. Sera and Jake may be his friends, but Zee kept an oath when she took it. The trees, absent of the magic of the Wood, had faded into twilight while they argued. Zee shivered again, and Ryan chose a different topic to be annoyed about.

"It's getting cold and dark. Let's get back to civilization instead of standing around wishing things were different." He didn't wait for them as he turned and started back the way they'd come.

Jake held Sera back, clearly waiting for Zee to precede them. He hadn't said much, for which she was grateful. Sera's eyes lingered on Zee's bare legs for a moment. "Jake might have some sweat pants that'll fit you. They'll be baggy, but better than nothing."

Zee swallowed her pride and nodded, then followed Ryan out of the woods.

Nothing happened when she stepped past the wild grasses and onto the road. Streetlights had come on, and a light was shining in the house across the street. The other loomed in the dark. Intellectually, she knew humans used the road to travel in cars and she shouldn't linger, but she'd never had one under her feet before. The surface was cool and rough, and bits of rubble stabbed into her bare skin. It was novel and painful all at once.

None of her people had ever been able to leave the Wood, except to travel to other Fae villages. The pact prevented it.

In all her training, she'd never prepared for the possibility of being locked out of her home without her magic. Magic was an integral part of her, and the more time that passed, the more she felt bereft. Zee welcomed the pain in her feet as she hurried after Ryan to the dark house.

INSIDE, dressed in Jake's pants and with hot tea in front of her, Zee tried not to gawk. Humans had so many things. Most of the electronics she recognized thanks to Ryan's technological help in the Glade, but the sheer number of comforts seemed excessive. Why were there two rooms for sitting?

She'd seen plenty of media of human homes on the internet, but they never focused on the minutia. The little bits of marvelous convenience and the differences between one house and the next. Jake and Sera's items were a mishmash of new and well-used. She got the sense most of the new was Sera's contribution, and it caused a flutter of pride to know she'd had a part in their coming together.

Exploring the house Jake and Sera shared offered her a respite from her worries over the Wood, but she couldn't ignore it for long. The three humans gathered around the kitchen table, entirely unconcerned, or maybe just humanly oblivious, that decades of magic and tradition had been broken. Zee took the fourth seat and scolded herself. Why would it concern them? They were ancillary to the Wood; she was the one with the problem.

Ryan stared at her hands clasped around her mug, and she wondered what intrigued him so much. Something deep in the house creaked and rattled. No one else noticed, so Zee took her cues from them.

Sera was the first to break the silence. "Okay, obviously something has gone wrong if Zee is sitting here and can't get back to the Glade. It sounds like you were stuck in the trods for over a month. When exactly did you go into them?"

Zee blew out a breath. Sharing information was a good start, even if it went against her instincts. "Samhain night. I was traveling to the clearing to deal with Torix. When did you break the barriers?"

"Right at midnight, when the magic in the Wood was strongest."

Zee nodded. "That makes sense. The barriers were the Fae component of a pact between my people and the Wood. They were built to withstand all challenges." She stared pointedly at Sera. "Apparently, they didn't account for you. When the barriers came down, the pact was broken, and the Wood took action. In this case, it seems it closed the trods as entrance to the Glade and trapped me within one. I should have been in the nexus well before that, but Chad seems to have exaggerated the usefulness of his enchanted rock."

"Who's Chad? Wait, how were you able to survive a month of being lost wandering a path in the woods?"

"Chad is my third in command and the unfortunate Fae who is going to feel my wrath for convincing me to take an untested trinket to a battle." Zee took a deep breath through her nose and continued when she felt calmer. "It wasn't a month for me. The time difference made it so I was only wandering for a few hours, and I wasn't lost. I simply hadn't arrived yet. I sensed the power spike for Samhain, and then something foreign. Stopping would have done nothing, so I kept moving. But the trod never changed."

"Until it did," said Jake.

Zee nodded. "Until it did."

Ryan raised his eyes, and she was surprised to see anger there. "Is the Wood sentient? It released you when I asked it where you were."

Zee shook her head slowly. "We've always treated it as an instinctual entity. Elemental. It hasn't ever responded directly before. More likely your request was an accidental spell that nudged the Wood into reacting."

Sera snorted. "It figures *your* accidental magic is useful."

Ryan didn't look amused. He got up from the table and stood by the window looking out at the trees behind the house. "Magic is dangerous, even more so when it's unpredictable."

Beneath her calm façade, Zee was insulted. Her grip on her demeanor was fragile, but she attempted to respond with compassion for him rather than fear for herself. "That's an argument for another time. The more pressing concern is that the magic in the Wood is chaotic right now. There's no guidance in place to control it. I need to get back to the Glade before chaos takes root. It's possible the Wood could become a danger to my people."

Jake looked incredulous. "You don't think it's a danger now? Why wouldn't the Fae have left the Wood in a mass exodus after such a long time being contained? And what about you? Why would your magic have been stripped?"

"I don't think it was stripped until I was ejected the trod. I left the Wood, and I was deposited in the human world in my human form as powerless as a human."

"Hey," said Jake.

Sera patted his arm. "No, she's right. Humans are pretty powerless when compared to the Fae."

"Says the girl who's half-Fae."

Zee's head shot up. "You know?"

Sera nodded. "I found out on Samhain."

Ryan shifted away from the window, and Zee speared him with a look. "I'd be interested in knowing how you found out."

Ryan didn't back down. "She's a master detective. Sometimes people use their brains to figure things out instead of only relying on brute magic force. Also, the spell broke so I wasn't bound not to and she deserved to know."

Zee glared at him and ignored the last bit, which was entirely accurate. "What would you know about brute magic force?" She ruined the impact by yawning.

Jake shared a look with Sera, then got up to thump Ryan on the back. "I'm sure your brute force is fine, but Sera and I have an appointment. If you guys want to stay here and fight...or whatever it is you're doing, it's cool with us, but we're out."

Sera stood up to join him. "Zee, I'd lend you some clothes, but you're a good four inches taller and in way better shape than me."

Jake grinned at Sera. "I like your shape."

She waved him away. "Not the point. You're welcome to Jake's clothes though, and of course you can stay here as long as you need."

Zee was increasingly uncomfortable with the direction of the conversation. She needed to focus on returning to the Glade, but they had a point. She couldn't walk around among the humans in scarves and sweatpants. It would draw too much attention. Before she could comment, Ryan pushed away from the wall and approached her.

"She's staying with me."

Jake glowered, but Sera only shrugged. "Whatever works."

Ryan met her eyes and offered his hand to help her stand. Zee ignored it. She was capable of standing on her own. She stood, eye to eye with him, and immediately got dizzy, swaying on her feet. Ryan reached out to steady her, and the contact rippled through her in a warm rush. The feeling persisted well after she'd settled herself and he'd let go. She'd known Ryan for years, and she'd always been able to compartmentalize her reactions to him, but her new human body seemed to have a mind of its own. *That's incon-*

venient. It would be a terrible idea to stay with him, even for a short while.

She opened her mouth to refuse his offer, but he smirked, raising an eyebrow in challenge. He thought her weak and afraid. Pride pushed aside common sense, so she straightened her spine and changed her mind. She could control her human body long enough to figure out how to return home *and* fix the mess they'd made without her. *How hard could it be?*

"I appreciate your hospitality, and I accept." Her voice was regal, her mastery of this human form complete. As her first act of control, she chose to ignore the look of triumph in Ryan's mischievous blue eyes.

contest with the driveway. "It's a short drive to my place, and I could do it in my sleep. There's nothing to worry about."

Zee was quiet so long he thought she'd decided to ignore him, but then she spoke quietly. "Thank you. It's disconcerting to know my life could be in danger and I have no power to protect myself."

Ryan scoffed. "I've seen you spar. I wouldn't say you were powerless to defend yourself."

"A sword does little good against an oncoming car."

"You're not wrong about that." Ryan started the engine and pulled out of the driveway with more care than usual. She was right in one respect. A car accident could easily kill her, and it would be his fault.

Less than a minute into the ride, Zee relaxed enough to ask about the buttons on the dash. Ryan explained the radio controls and winced when rock music suddenly blasted from the speakers. She lowered the volume, but left it on.

Her head tilted to the side as she listened. "I've heard this song before."

"It's played a lot. I would have thought you'd be more familiar, or at least comfortable, with the human world once you got Wi-Fi. Wasn't that the point?"

Zee tsked. "We got Wi-Fi because I refuse to let my people wallow in their ignorance, but there's a difference between watching *The Fast and the Furious* and riding in an actual car."

Ryan glanced at her, surprised. "*The Fast and the Furious*? That's what you've been doing with all my hard work?"

Pink tinged her cheeks. "I don't have a lot of time for entertainment, and Lana is a fan of one of the actors."

"Vin Diesel?"

"Yes, she likes his broad shoulders. The name's confusing though. I understand why it was fast, but why was it furious? Most of your human stories don't make a lot of sense to me."

Ryan shrugged and tried not to wonder if she preferred muscle heads like Vin Diesel too. "I'd argue they don't make sense to a lot of people, but it doesn't take much to entertain us. I thought you liked *Downton Abbey*."

"I do, but you have to admit the cars were a bit different in that show."

Ryan grunted. He hadn't seen much of it, but he remembered a Model T Ford, so yeah, a bit different. They turned down Magnolia Avenue, one of their two main streets, and the one he happened to live on. Every once in a while, he was surprised to find himself happy living in Mulligan. It usually happened in early December when the town started putting out Christmas decorations. This year was no exception.

He pulled up to a stop sign, and a soft gasp from the seat next to him made him look over. Zee was leaning forward, her lips parted as she gazed at the lights. Amazement shone on her face, and a tightness developed in his chest. She really was out of her world.

"You haven't seen Christmas lights before?"

Zee didn't look away. He wasn't even sure she was blinking. "Not like this. It's beautiful in person."

Ryan couldn't take his eyes off her face. "Yeah, it is."

Someone honked behind him and made him jump. How long had he been daydreaming like a dumbass? The lights had gone up on the first, but he was still surprised every time he was greeted with the bright, twinkling display. They'd used blue and green LEDs on the trees and soft white on the buildings and the gazebo in the park. Rosie's had changed out their lights to match, but the open sign flashed red as usual. His mouth watered, and he reminded himself that he had chili in the crock pot at home. He couldn't have every meal at Rosie's, unfortunately.

Ryan drove through the intersection and into the parking lot for his building. It was a huge old farmhouse that had been saved from demolition by a local couple that converted it into four two-bedroom apartments. His was on the second floor.

What had he been thinking bringing Zee here when they were barely civil to each other? The short answer was that he hadn't been. He just knew in that moment that he couldn't leave her with Jake and Sera. It was going to be a long couple of nights. At least there were only two weeks left of school. After that, he'd be on winter break, and it wouldn't matter if he missed a bunch of sleep. The kids were crazy at this time of the year, but he secretly loved it. His dad had always said that kids had more passion than their bodies could handle, but it was never a bad thing to be passionate about what you love.

Ryan parked the car and frowned. He hadn't thought about that in years. Zee didn't immediately jump out of the car, transfixed as she was by the decorations, and Ryan wanted to get a few things settled before they went inside.

"We need some ground rules."

Zee glanced at him in surprise. "I'm a guest in your home, of course I'll follow your rules."

Ryan blew out a breath. "That's great. First rule, no magic."

"That one should be easy since I can't seem to access my magic right now, but if I regain access, I make no promises."

"You can't agree to one simple rule?"

"Magic is a part of me. It's unnatural to hide it away." Her hand pressed into her stomach. "I feel like I've lost one of my senses in addition to my home."

Her tone wasn't confrontational, but he felt like an ass anyway. "We've had this argument before. I'm sorry you're locked out, but magic isn't the best path for everyone. In the wrong hands, it's dangerous. Even in the right hands, it causes more trouble than it's worth. Look at Sera."

Zee rotated in her seat to face him fully. "Yes, look at Sera. She was blessed with power and everyone around her spent years hiding it from her."

"Yeah, and when it finally broke through it nearly killed her."

"But it didn't. She learned control, and her life is better for it. Or would you deny her the relationship she's built with Jake?"

Ryan leaned forward. "Are you saying that it was magic that caused her and Jake to get together?"

"The evidence speaks for itself. They were bonded magically, and that bond grew strong on its own. Without magic, they'd likely still be avoiding each other."

Ryan laughed without mirth. "You are so wrong on that one. They were dancing around each other, yeah, but it was only a matter of time before the clothes started flying."

Her brows drew together. "I'm not familiar with that term."

She'd leaned even closer, and he could see flecks of gold in her green eyes even in the darkness of the car. "It means sex. They get naked and nature takes its course."

"Ah, I see." Her voice was low, and he couldn't keep his eyes off her mouth. "And so magic is made."

It would only take a small movement to bring them into contact. Heat washed through him, and his hand itched to dive into those complicated braids to see if they were as soft as they looked. The contrast between the warrior braids and the gauzy top was driving him crazy wondering which side of her would win if he kissed her.

She'd probably pull a knife out of somewhere and gut him.

As he watched, a flash of red stretched between them like static lightning. He reared back to his side of the car, but not before he heard her suck in a breath. His damn magic had a mind of its own.

Ryan ran a shaky hand through his already rumpled black hair. "Are you okay?"

She rubbed her shoulder where the magic had connected them for a moment and sagged back into her seat. "Of course. I'd been worried that my magic was gone, but it's not. I felt it respond to yours a moment ago. It's trapped, but it's still there inside me." She closed her eyes in relief, but panic stirred in Ryan.

"What do you mean it responded to mine?"

"Like attracts like, Ryan. We've discussed this before. It's why so many magical people move to Mulligan."

"This is bullshit," he muttered and climbed out of the car. He waited until she'd done the same then stalked across the parking lot to the building. "I don't want my magic responding to anything. I want it to stay neatly locked up inside me. Better yet, I'd like it to disappear altogether."

Zee sighed. This wasn't a new argument for either of them. "It's not healthy. Your magic is innate, and it can't be separated from you."

He climbed the porch steps and started his ongoing battle with the lock. It never worked on the first try, but he chalked it up to character and rolled with it. "You thought yours was gone all the way up until about two minutes ago. Your overgrown sense of responsibility was all that was keeping you from cursing the heavens."

"I don't curse anything. It's bad for the environment."

Ryan snorted out a laugh, but when he finally wrestled the lock into submission and opened the door, her chin was up and her lips pressed together tightly. She refused to meet his eyes as she tried to sweep past him, but he put an arm across the doorway to stop her.

She jerked to a stop and glared. Ryan thanked whoever was listening that she didn't have access to her power, or he'd definitely be something small and slimy. It was too bad he needed her powers.

"The year is up. It's been up for a couple of weeks now. You owe me a renewal," he insisted.

Her face tightened. "I should have known that was your only concern."

Frustration made him want to shake her. Instead, he dropped his arm and let her precede him up the dark stairwell. "It's not my only concern, but it's a big one. We had a deal. I do your bidding in exchange for you sealing my magic. I've been a good little errand-boy, but the seal is gone. You need to uphold your end."

Zee stopped halfway up the stairwell and spun around. It wasn't very wide, barely big enough for two people, but it seemed half that with her standing above him so close. "I've honored our deal every year for seven years. I disagreed with you even as we struck it, but I have fulfilled my half as you have. I told you in the beginning that it was a temporary fix. Magic can't be contained forever without risking your life. Look at what happened to Sera."

Ryan moved up a step so they were eye to eye. "It's my life to risk."

"Yes, and I'd thought you'd have more time to risk it." She waved her hands in his face. "I can't perform the seal. That option is no longer available. Due to circumstances beyond my control, our bargain is officially broken." A frown crossed her face for a second, but then she shook it off. "You'll have to find some other way to deal with your magic. I suggest you learn how to control it as a first step."

"I have no interest in controlling it. I want it gone."

"And yet you can't have what you want. That must be frustrating for you."

Ryan stared at his clenched fists. It *was* frustrating. Their deal hadn't been exactly what he'd hoped for, and it had required him to stay in Mulligan, but it had been functional. His magic had for the most part stayed under wraps inside him. Now however, whenever he got ornery, he fried all the technology around him. Not a great side-effect for a computer teacher. She was right though. He couldn't make things go back to the way they were. And it wasn't really her fault.

He relaxed his hands and did what he'd been wanting to do since they'd exited the car, pulled one of her braids out of the interlocking layers and let it slide though his fingers. She had a larger braid down the middle, and tiers of smaller braids looped back into it then hung down her back. The plait in his hand was as smooth and silky as he'd suspected.

"I propose a new bargain. I'll do everything I can to help fix things for you, and in exchange, you have to figure out and supply a more permanent solution to my magic."

"What makes you think there's a permanent solution that doesn't involve death and/or dismemberment?" Her voice was huskier than usual, and he wondered if she was as affected by their closeness as he was.

"Because the Fae are tricky on their best days, and you never would have agreed to the first bargain so quickly if it was all you could do."

Ryan expected her to argue more. Despite her battle-sleek muscles, words tended to be her weapon of choice, but instead, she looked away. He thought he'd seen hurt flash in her eyes, but she'd turned her head too fast.

Zee sighed. "Sera appears to have a unique skill. Why not have her absorb your magic?" She was almost whispering, so he had to lean closer to hear her.

He hesitated and she met his eyes again, much closer. For a second, he forgot what she'd asked. Her braid was still in his hand, resting against her shoulder. Her chest rose and fell rapidly, straining against the gauzy fabric tied behind her neck. His eyes followed the movement up to the knot at her nape, and he had the dangerous thought that he probably wouldn't have to pull very hard to untie it. Zee could kick his ass any day of the week, but in that moment, he was sure the risk would be worth the reward. Her eyes dropped to his lips, and he almost closed the distance between them, but then a red glow grew brighter in the darkness.

The hand holding her braid was at it again. Apparently, his magic was triggered by anger *and* arousal. Ryan released her and retreated until his back was resting against the wall opposite her. This had been a terrible idea anyway. He was going to need a cold shower, but at least he'd still have all his parts.

Ryan blurted, "We tried after we couldn't find you for so long. Sera did her thing, but it didn't have any effect. We think it might only work on Fae magic."

Zee nodded, but her eyes were far away. "And you're human."

"And I'm human."

"I have one caveat to the bargain. While we search for a solution, you have to learn how to control your magic." Ryan started to shake his head, but she kept talking. "It's the responsible thing to do. We don't know how long it will take to find a solution, and you won't always have a Fae around to help you. Magic *can* be dangerous in untrained hands. I'll train you."

He wanted to fight it, but it was a reasonable request. He'd learn, and then hopefully he could forget it when their bargain was met. The thought made him strangely sad. "Okay. We'll do it your way. I'll train until you're back to full power and you can fix me up permanently. Then we can part ways for good."

She smiled, but he could see it was forced. "I'll teach you to control your magic, you'll aid in my quest to return to the Glade, and when my magic is freed, I'll create a stronger seal for yours. I agree to your bargain, Ryan Nolan. Together, we'll both get what we desire."

He extended his hand to shake, and she did the same. The moment they touched, wild swirls of red magic wove around their hands, then seeped into their skin and were gone. Zee pulled her hand back and continued silently up the as if nothing unusual had happened. Ryan rubbed his hand as he watched her disappear into his apartment. They'd had their previous bargain for seven years. Once a year, they would renew it, and she would reseal his magic. In return, he'd do whatever tasks she needed from him. Usually it involved tech help, but a couple of months ago she'd used him to summon Sera, which had started this whole chain of events happening.

Ryan chafed under the restrictions. He needed his magic sealed, but he hated that he didn't have the freedom to move away. Whenever Zee texted him, he had to appear for her. He'd resented the power dynamic, and now that had shifted, but at what cost?

The stairs creaked as he followed after Zee. He found her curled up on the couch, asleep. Her long legs were tucked under her, but he could still see Jake's pants peeking out. They'd have to get her some clothes. The traitorous part of his mind reminded him of the flimsy tie holding her top up and suggested they could probably wait a while on that one.

Ryan walked straight past Zee and into his bathroom where he cranked the cold water in the shower. He'd call Sera in the morning to have her take Zee shopping. It was much safer that way.

3

ZEE

ZEE WOKE up in a strange bed. It had happened before, but this time was different. She couldn't teleport herself back home.

The sun streamed through the lone bedroom window. A half-closed curtain blocked part of the light, but a bright swath stretched across where she lay. She threw the covers off and sat up, surprised to see she was still clothed in the thin dress and sweats. *When had she fallen asleep?* The room was unfamiliar, and the last thing she remembered was collapsing on Ryan's couch after agreeing to the height of stupidity.

Magic bound them in the agreement now. Ryan may have thought he was well-versed in the ways of the Fae, but he had a lot to learn about power. Lesson one: don't call on it unless you intend to follow through.

She swung her feet to the floor and let her toes luxuriate in the soft carpet. The Glade had wooden floors. It's not like they had a convenient home goods store nearby, but maybe she could convince one of the humans to do her a favor and bring some luxuries. Her people deserved a little luxury if they were to stay trapped in the same forest forever.

Only, they weren't trapped anymore, were they? And if they were able to leave, why hadn't she heard from any of them? Lana had her phone number for emergencies, but the last place Zee had seen her phone was under her leather armor before the Wood had changed her clothes and ejected her. She had very explicit instructions for contacting the humans should anything ever befall her, and thus far, no one had followed them. Or they'd been unable to follow them.

Zee hoped Ryan was right and it was a matter of communications being severed rather than a matter of... something worse.

She stood up and immediately dropped down onto the bed again. Her head was swimming, and she had to swallow hard against a sudden upsurge of nausea. What in the seven hells was this? She thought back. *When was the last time she'd been to a harvest?*

The Fae didn't eat for nourishment, though they were certainly capable of partaking. Instead, they drew magic from the trees in the Wood as sustenance. The harvest powered them physically and magically. It occurred to Zee that she hadn't replenished herself in a long while. Probably too long if her body was any indication.

A couple of deep breaths later, she tried again and managed to come to a full standing position. The bright window overlooked the park across the street she'd seen the night before. The trees there would have to do.

The door to the bedroom opened to the main room she'd been in before. One door was open to a bathroom, and the other led outside. An appealing smell came from the kitchen, but she couldn't place it. Her stomach cramped again, and she headed for the outside door. Ryan was nowhere to be seen, so she checked for wandering humans before she hurried across the street to the trees there.

The park was beautiful, if somewhat tame. The expanse of grass was crunchy and cold under her feet, but the trees were few and far between. In the middle of the park was the gazebo she'd seen lit up the night before. Concrete paths curved away from it on several sides. To the backside of the little building, away from the paths, was a small copse of pine trees. They grew haphazardly, but Zee was drawn there.

She walked slowly because she didn't have the energy for much else. The sun wasn't very high yet, but the park was mostly empty. The humans she *did* see were strolling next to the businesses that lined the streets around the park. No one paid her any mind. She reached the trees and slumped down next to the closest one.

The rough bark felt the same as the trees in the Wood, but there was no current of magic running through them. At least, not one she could sense. She tried to open herself to the power anyway, hoping that she'd passively absorb the magic she needed, but she was left empty.

Without that magic, Zee was afraid she'd waste away and die alone in a strange human park. Her stomach gurgled, so she rested her forehead against the trunk and tried again. Nothing. A breeze cooled her back and moisture seeped into her pants, but that was all. She didn't understand what she was supposed to do.

Tears slipped out and ran down her cheeks. Her ability to cope was about gone. It was hard to imagine dying, easier to focus on hunger. The knowledge hit her suddenly. That's what she felt. *Hunger.* The kind that came from her stomach. Without access to her magic, she couldn't feed herself, but she wasn't using magic either. Maybe her body needed a different kind of sustenance. It was worth a try, and a sight better than dying in a silly dress with tears on her cheeks.

It took some effort, but Zee levered herself up from the ground with the help of the pine she'd been commiserating with. She'd stopped checking for humans. What did it matter if they saw her? To them, she'd be a sad woman wearing strange clothes and nothing more.

Zee wiped her face, determined to return to Ryan's apartment and keep trying things until something worked. A deep breath cleared her mind and she sensed someone watching her. She raised her chin and wasn't surprised to see Ryan.

He leaned against a lone tree halfway back to the apartment with his arms crossed. Unlike her, he was dressed for the winter day in pants and a thick sweater the deep red color of his magic. She wondered at the choice. It didn't seem intentional, but it looked good on him.

She couldn't read his face this time, but he didn't come any closer. Zee squared her shoulders and approached him. Her body may have been weak, but damned if she was going to come across that way to Ryan.

As she walked, his eyes flitted to her feet then back up to her face. It made her feel strange inside, embarrassed maybe, that she could be judged inept by her appearance alone when she had no control over it.

"You shouldn't be wandering around out here without warmer clothes, or at least shoes."

He was worried about her comfort? Relief trickled through her, but she pushed it away. "I don't appear to have any other options."

He shrugged one shoulder. "You could stay in the apartment."

"I'm not a pet, and I was hungry."

Ryan nodded slowly. "The trees aren't doing it for you?"

"I often forget how much you know about my people."

"Keep your friends close and all that."

Zee wrapped her arms around herself to ward off the chilly breeze. "You consider us enemies? That seems harsh considering all the years you've worked with us."

"*For* you. 'With' implies I had a choice."

"There's always a choice. You refused to see any side but your own so you built your own prison."

Ryan straightened. "Think what you want, but I know the price paid for magic, and I have no intention of paying it again." He tossed a small paper bag at her, and Zee caught it. "I thought you'd need some energy. You've been asleep for over a day."

"A day?" As a Fae, she didn't need as much sleep as a human, but she still slept. She'd just never gone that long before.

"You were breathing and making yourself into a blanket burrito, so we decided to let you rest. Sera dropped some clothes off for you, but you'll need more." He ran a hand through his already messy hair. "She said that fell to me since she and Jake are busy at his worksite today, but she's not the boss of me."

Zee's lips twitched. Ryan sounded put out at the thought of shopping, but she appreciated the effort. And everything else he'd done. He may be cranky, but he'd been doing his best from the moment he'd caught her outside the Wood.

"Thank you." She opened the bag and sniffed. The smell of yeast and sugar made her mouth water. Inside were two donuts. She recognized them from somewhere, and like the scent from the kitchen, it made her stomach growl. Human food or not, it was a better option than withering away and dying from starvation.

She pulled one out and took a tentative bite. Her eyes closed and she moaned involuntarily. She could feel Ryan watching her still, but she didn't care. The sweetness exploded across her tongue as she chewed, leaving a delicious tingle behind even after she swallowed. *My people turned up their noses at this? Maybe we were stupid after all.* She'd had sugar before, in her tea, but all it did was temper the bitterness of the leaves. This was a whole new experience.

She took a much bigger bite and couldn't help the little happy noise she made in the back of her throat. If she was to live as a human, she wanted donuts every day. The grass crunched as Ryan walked toward her, and her eyes popped open. She'd momentarily forgotten he was there. His eyes were hungry, but he wasn't looking at the donut.

Zee swallowed hard as he stopped right in front of her. Immediately, she felt warmer, like she'd come out into the sun. His eyes dropped to her mouth, and for a crazy moment, she thought he was going to kiss her. Instead, he cupped her cheek and his thumb stroked across her bottom lip.

She watched him lift his hand to his mouth and lick his thumb where he'd touched her. Everything inside her clenched. Without thinking about it, she mirrored his movement, swiping her tongue across her lip. It came away sweet and sticky from the donut. If this was how humans ate, the Fae were definitely missing out.

The weakness she'd experienced earlier was fading, replaced with heat and longing. Fae weren't shy with their bodies, but she'd never wanted someone the way she wanted Ryan right then. The all-consuming need burst through her after having been suppressed for so long. Zee wanted him even more than she wanted that second donut in the bag. *What did they put in those things?*

She was moments away from giving in to the urge to see if the sweet taste lingered on his lips like it lingered on hers when Ryan blinked and backed away. It was like coming out of a trance, and Zee was no longer sure if she wanted out. Without his body next to hers, goosebumps popped up all over. She rubbed the chill from her arms and willed herself to return to reason. Ryan had a strange effect on her, but that didn't mean she had to succumb to it. There could be no future between them, so it was better to keep things platonic. That meant she needed to get herself back home before her willpower ran out.

Ryan seemed to have the same idea. He nodded his head at the bag hanging almost sideways in her grasp. "Eat your other donut if you want, but come inside for clothes at least. It's too cold out here."

He turned and walked to his building without looking back. Zee had the distinct feeling he was running from her, and wondered what he'd do if she chased him. She waited until he went through the door to dig the other donut out and eat it in three bites.

Her toes were so cold she couldn't feel them, but she was hesitant to go back into the apartment. Partly because Ryan had told her to and she didn't respond well to orders, but partly because she missed her forest. She'd lived outside Mulligan all her life, but the town was a strange new world to her. It was a lot to absorb with very little warning.

A couple bundled in coats and boots walked by on the sidewalk, glancing at her curiously, and she was reminded that she was making a spectacle of herself by being obstinate. The park was *not* her forest. Nothing there could help her. She braced herself for sharing the small confines of the apartment with Ryan and went inside.

THE MEAT SMELL had dissipated by the time she closed the door behind her, but her stomach growled anyway. Apparently, two donuts weren't enough food to satisfy her. Ryan was in the kitchen mixing something in a bowl, and she found herself drawn to the play of his arm muscles. It was an inconvenient distraction considering her recent decision to keep her body to herself.

"What are you doing?" Zee asked.

Ryan didn't look up from his stirring. "Making an omelet. You'll need something more than sugar and carbs to power you through the hell of the human world."

His words were mild, but Zee heard the rebuke. She chose not to rise to the bait. "The term 'human world' is inaccurate. We all share the same world, some more so than others. I like humans well enough, but my life has been consumed with the needs of the Fae, as it should be."

"You mean you don't normally waylay men in parks bearing food?"

"*You're* the one who brought me the donuts."

"Yeah. Why do you think I'm making you eggs? It was the only way I could think of to get you to make that noise again." His eyes dropped to her lips, but he forced them back to the bowl.

"There are other ways." Her voice sounded almost hoarse. *Curse my treacherous mouth.* Why couldn't she control herself when Ryan was around?

Fire ignited in his eyes. "I'll keep that in mind." If he'd been running before, he was done now.

She tore her gaze away and took in his living space for the first time. None of the furnishings matched like the rooms she'd seen on television. The scruffy brown couch she'd fallen asleep on sat in front of a large screen on a pale wooden console. A bookshelf held large volumes of books titled with random letters and symbols as well as a small resin figure brandishing a sword. She moved closer and bent to get a better view. It was a male wearing needlessly complicated armor with a large head and small black dots for eyes. He had long white hair and a scar across one eye. *What's his significance to Ryan?*

She chanced a look back into the kitchen, but Ryan was facing the stove with his back to her. The pan in front of him sizzled, and a new delicious smell wafted toward her. Food was definitely proving to be her favorite part of the larger world.

A pile of neatly folded clothes sat on the edge of the couch, and a quick search revealed soft stretchy pants and a plain green shirt with long sleeves. They didn't look like Ryan's style, so she assumed they were the clothes from Sera. Zee grabbed the pile and took it with her into the bedroom she'd woken up in.

She changed quickly and was surprised by the relief she felt when she took the dress off. Humans preferred the form of a tiny, winged creature in a ball gown, but she favored this larger size. Form was more fluid for the Fae, so despite her partialities, she didn't like being restricted to a single shape.

The stretchy pants weren't entirely pants. They hugged her curves but only made it as far as mid-calf. She suspected they came to Sera's ankles and sincerely hoped they returned to their previous smaller size when she removed them. The shirt was boxy but flowed past her hips. It was probably Jake's. The color reminded her of new leaves, and a burst of longing shot through her for her cottage in the Glade. No matter how tempting Ryan was, she needed to stay focused on returning to the Wood.

Thick socks had been wadded up inside the shirt, so she pulled those on as well. She stopped shivering and was once again grateful for Jake and Sera's kindness. The pants were remarkably comfortable, and she made a note to ask Sera where to find some.

Ryan was putting two steaming plates on the small table in the corner of the room when she came out of the bedroom for the second time that day. It was a drastic difference from the first time.

Zee sat down in front of one of the plates and waited for Ryan to take his seat. "Why didn't you do this in the first place instead of going out to get donuts? Not that I'm complaining in any way."

"I had other errands to run. The donuts were an afterthought." Ryan started shoveling food into his mouth, so she followed suit.

While not as good as the donuts, the eggs were warm and savory. She ate for several minutes before she ventured into conversation. "We should start your training today."

Ryan choked then took a long swig of water. "I'm pretty busy today."

"I slept for a full day. You had plenty of opportunities to finish your errands then. I expect you can make time now to fulfill your end of the bargain we made."

He ate in silence for a moment, chewing thoughtfully. "How are you going to teach me if you can't use your own magic?"

"I taught Sera without using magic."

"You were in her head."

Zee smiled. "Ah, but that's not magic." She didn't offer any more explanation, though she could see it was killing him not to ask. It wouldn't be difficult to connect with him enough to monitor his progress. The hard part would be keeping herself from going too deep.

Ryan finished eating and took his plate to the sink. "As much as I hate that I'm still at your beck and call, I'll hold up my end of the deal. Magic practice, then we work on the problem with the Wood, then even though it's Sunday, I really do have some work to do before school tomorrow."

Zee wanted to ask about his job. She'd watched his progress from cocky youth to mentor for other cocky youths, and it sparked a sense of pride in her that he'd chosen to dedicate his life to helping kids like he had been. *Does he enjoy it?* Would he continue down that path if he were free to leave Mulligan or would he choose something else? It had never been the right time to ask because they couldn't help pitting themselves against each other whenever they were together, but she'd wondered.

His reluctant agreement meant it was still not the right time to ask. She finished her food and took the dirty plate to the counter. Ryan was putting the pieces he'd used into what she assumed was a dishwasher. He grabbed her plate last, closed it up, and came around the counter to stand stiffly in front of her.

"Where do you want to do this?"

Zee held in her smile. "Are you always this terrible of a student?"

He met her eyes in challenge, like she'd hoped he would. "I'm an excellent student. I simply don't like the subject."

"We'll see." She gestured to the couch. "Might as well get comfortable."

Ryan settled onto one end, and Zee took the other. They were close enough to touch if they chose, but both kept their limbs firmly on their own sides. "Let's start with something simple. Shield your mind."

Zee's power had been vast before she'd stepped out of the Wood, but limited in that she couldn't reach past the line of trees. Except with her mind. She could connect with unshielded humans even outside the Wood, even without magic. She'd lost all her other abilities, but her mind and her capacity to sense Ryan's power remained strong.

He made a feeble attempt, using force of will to try to stop her, but she was able to push past it easily. Will was fickle and could be redirected with little effort. She spoke into his mind because she was already there. *Lesson one: magic is about faith and visualization. Create the image you want and believe it to be real.*

Ryan jerked back. "Don't do that. I get what you're trying to accomplish, but speak to me out loud."

She inclined her head. "Very well. You have a basic shield already. It protects you from ambient noise, if you will. I want you to build something bulkier. Something that will stop an intentional invasion. Find an image that represents strength and protection to you, then apply it to yourself. Visualization and faith."

He sighed and closed his eyes. Zee could poke around and watch his progress as she'd done with Sera, but his reaction to her mindspeak implied that he didn't want an audience. She took the time he spent concentrating with his eyes closed to look her fill without him knowing. His hair was getting longer. It used to be short and spiky on top, but now it fell in black disarray around his face. He wore an elastic hair band around his wrist, but as far as she knew, he hadn't used it in the last few days. She preferred Nordic braids for her hair, but she'd bet the simpler braids of the Celts would look good on him.

His high cheekbones made her think of Fae ancestry, or maybe a Celtic warrior to go with the braids. At first glance, he was thin, but she knew his clothing hid lean muscle. He sat cross-legged with his back against the arm and his hands resting in his lap. She knew his palms had been coarse against her back, and she wondered how a teacher managed to acquire such calluses. Her mind started to wander to other places she'd like to feel his rough hands, but she reined it in and brought her eyes back up to his face.

He was watching her.

Zee hesitated for a second, then tried to push into his mind. A round shield she recognized blocked her attempt. The same red, white, and blue symbol appeared on his shirt. It made her wonder if both were an attempt to protect himself from her. She nudged it, but it held steady, so she prodded harder. No matter how she twisted and pried, she couldn't get past it. How annoying that he'd learned how to lock her out when she most wanted to know what was in his mind. He *was* an excellent student.

"What next?"

Ryan's voice was low, and it conjured an image of the two of them writhing on the messy bed in the other room. Her cheeks flushed, and a small smile came then went across Ryan's face.

He knows. Somehow, he knew what she'd seen. Her shields were firmly in place, and she'd just smacked into his, so it shouldn't have been possible. And yet, as the moment stretched, they were both struggling for breath again.

"Next we test your magic."

Ryan straightened up from his slouch. The attitude of

playfulness he'd had since breakfast vanished, and he was left brooding. "That's a bad idea. I don't want to hurt you."

She cocked her head. "Then you won't. Magic will obey you as long as you believe it will. Yours is unruly because you expect it to be. Keeping control of it should feel as natural as moving an arm or a leg."

"Should, but doesn't. Nothing about this feels natural."

"I know you can learn to control it, and I know how to guide you. I'm not afraid."

He didn't look convinced. In fact, he looked almost scared. Zee was saddened to think that he'd never been able to feel the joy that came with his power. It was enough to have her shift a little closer and take his hand. He tried to pull it back, but she held firm. Physical touch would help the connection, and he needed to see that she wasn't afraid of him.

"You won't hurt me. Release your shield. I'll lower mine and monitor." It was gratifying that he lowered his shield immediately, but the second he let go, she was inundated with a rush of emotions. Desire, resignation, determination, and at the forefront, fear. Zee couldn't tell if the fear was *for* her or *of* her, but she was intimately involved in the emotion. Her shields eased back up a little to slow the over-whelming flow, and she hoped this would be a quick lesson.

A fleeting image of herself looking over her shoulder with her dress untied almost made her let go of him. Ryan was trying to ignore the image, but it kept circling back in his mind. Zee sighed. It was hard enough to fight her own weakness for him, but it might be impossible if she had to fight both of theirs simultaneously.

She wasn't afraid of his magic, but her reaction to him could prove dangerous in its own right.

4

RYAN

"Nudge your magic into waking, give it a simple task."

Zee said it like it was easy, but all Ryan knew was how to make his magic as tiny as possible. Her presence in his mind was both reassuring and disconcerting. He had to keep telling himself that she knew what she was doing and could handle herself if anything went wrong.

Ryan linked their fingers and opened the door inside him. Zee's hand became a lifeline as his magic surged through him. It was both him and not him at the same time. Memories of the car crash flashed across his mind, and he fought to focus on Zee instead. As afraid as he was, she was his calm in the storm, and he wanted to do this for her. He wanted to prove that he was capable of being in control after all the years of running from it.

The maelstrom died down, but Ryan felt the core of it in his center, waiting. She'd said a simple task, but his mind was purposefully empty of everything but Zee. Naked. He frantically searched for a safer task since he assumed she didn't want to be suddenly nude in his living room, but his magic surged forward at the thought. For a couple of tense moments there, it was a near thing, but he held it back, barely.

Zee chuckled. "Fae aren't embarrassed by nakedness. Even so, I'm afraid it wouldn't have the end result you're hoping for." Her grin was a little too knowing for his comfort.

He was *hoping* for that scene with the two of them in the bedroom, but that had nothing to do with magic. Focus.

The truth was, Ryan had no idea what he was capable of. A simple task could be anything from flying to the moon to starting the dishwasher that he'd loaded earlier. Come to think of it, he really needed to do that.

He'd barely finished the thought when the dishwasher roared to life, startling him. His head jerked toward the kitchen.

His magic had stirred, but not in the uncontrolled way he was used to. He'd set a small portion of the whole on a task, and that little bit had smoothly followed through. He grinned and squeezed Zee's hand when she scanned at the kitchen.

"I did it. I made that happen."

"I know. An unconventional choice for a first spell, but functional. Well done."

She was proud of him. More importantly, he was proud of himself. It wasn't something he'd ever thought he'd associate with magic. Like *ever*. Ryan had to admit, using magic to turn electronics on and off from across the room did seem useful.

His mind started down the rabbit hole of tinkering with magical electronics. What kind of technomancy stuff could he create? When he'd set up Wi-Fi in the Wood for the Fae, he'd had some magical interference that he'd had to work around. Zee had done something to boost and smooth out the signal, and at the time, he hadn't wanted to know. Now the possibilities were intriguing.

"Magic and electronics usually don't mix well together." Zee's voice almost made him jump. He'd actually forgotten that they were still mentally connected. The more time that passed, the more comfortable he became with Zee in his mind. She wasn't obtrusive, and her presence was oddly soothing.

"Has anyone done any testing to figure out why?"

Zee laughed. "And possibly waste what few luxuries we have in this technological age? No. We're careful not to perform complicated or powerful magic around our phones and computers."

"Huh." Ryan was itching to get his hands on some defunct computer parts from school, so he could figure out the interplay. He knew what happened when powerful magic was mixed with a large piece of technology, but what if they could find a way to make it safer? Maybe smaller and more contained? Magic and tech could both act as a check against the other to protect the people using them. Very interesting stuff.

Zee touched his knee with her free hand to get his attention. "I think that's enough for today. Completing a spell is quite a bit of progression for a novice. Given how today went, I don't think you'll have trouble with the more complicated components next time." She smiled and patted his arm. "I *am* going to need my hand back though."

When he focused on their hands, a tendril of dark red magic had wrapped around them both again. Zee wasn't struggling against it, but he could see an indentation where the magic was putting physical pressure against her wrist. He'd essentially tied them together.

Ryan's heart rate picked up, and his eyes shot to hers, hoping she'd have more instructions for him. But Zee only leaned sideways against the couch cushions and waited. He could still feel her in his mind, a quiet presence exuding confidence and faith. She was convinced he could figure it out on his own, and harnessing some of her calm, Ryan wanted to prove her right.

He scowled at the tendrils and imagined them uncurling from their wrists and retreating back into his skin. The image was a little creepy, but it worked. His arm tingled with the power though, so he pulled the magic back and back until it finally settled in his belly.

Zee squeezed his hand then let go. "I knew you could do it. It doesn't take much to manipulate power that's always been inside you. The next lesson is to keep it contained when you don't intend to use it."

"Wouldn't that have been useful for the first lesson?"

She held up both hands like a scale. "It's a push and pull dynamic. Whether you learn to push or pull first, you still have to learn to grip it to make it useful."

Ryan didn't fully understand her analogy, but he'd had about enough cryptic magic talk for the day. *Or year.* At some point, she'd eased out of his mind. He grimaced at the empty feeling left in her absence. His shield was up again as well. It wasn't something he'd done consciously, but the ease of maintaining it placated him a little. Especially since he now knew it wasn't a magical ability.

Zee didn't seem eager to vacate the couch any time soon, and Ryan was acutely aware of the suggestive images he'd been sending her on accident. As it was, he was going to have to think of some pretty complicated code for a while before he could get up comfortably. There was a simmering tension in the room that encouraged him to reach out for her. He ached to twine their fingers again and pull her into his lap.

Magic or no magic, he wanted her. And that was complicated.

Zee clearly had different needs. "I have some thoughts on how to get back to the Glade, or at least contact Lana. Is there a computer I could use?"

While he'd been daydreaming of a lazy Sunday in bed, Zee had been planning her escape. *Of course she had. Couldn't have her dawdling here in the human world with no magic.* Anger made him more sarcastic than usual. "Yeah. I have an extra laptop you can use next to my desk. Should I get it for your highness or do you want me to magically teleport it here?"

She tilted her head in question, but he didn't want to talk about his suddenly foul mood. "I can get it. Where's your desk?"

Her serenity made him feel like an ass. He *should* be keeping things professional, or at least platonic, since she'd be leaving sooner rather than later, but he didn't have to be a jerk. "Don't worry about it. I'll get it."

Ryan needed to get out of that room. He'd always thought like his apartment was spacious, but it didn't feel that way when he was sharing it with a too-compelling, magic-obsessed fairy. The whole situation proved his point that nothing good came from magic.

The worst thing Zee could imagine was a mundane life, but a mundane life was exactly what he longed for.

THE LAPTOP DIDN'T HOLD a charge, but as long as it was plugged in it worked fine. Ryan grabbed it and the charging cable, but then he sat on the bed instead of going back out into the living room. *What am I doing?*

He ran a hand through his hair. Zee didn't want to start something they for sure couldn't finish, and his frustration wasn't fair to her. Jake and Sera and all their nauseating coupleness were messing with his mind. He had no qualms about relationships in general, but damned if he was going to throw himself at a fairy that A, wasn't interested, and B, was going back to Faelandia on the first non-malfunctioning trod leaving the station.

She'd always been hot, but she'd had this air of complete control, like she didn't need anyone and couldn't be bothered. Even in her current predicament, she sometimes had an attitude of superiority. *Haughtiness.* It was the moments in between that were getting to him. He'd assumed her confidence came from her magic and her position. He was fuzzy on the Fae hierarchy, but even without it, she was the strongest woman he'd ever met.

She was going to make it home, probably without needing his help at all, and he'd be hard-pressed to remember that the next time she looked at him with need in her eyes.

As an afterthought, he grabbed an extra mouse and a pad from the stack in his closet. The touchpad was a pain in the ass. At least he could help her with that.

He hadn't been in the bedroom long, a couple of minutes maybe, but she'd fallen asleep leaning sideways against the couch with her hands tucked under her cheek. They didn't know anything about her situation, but he was more than a little concerned about how much she was sleeping. The furrows in her brow smoothed when she wasn't focusing on the problem. Ryan frowned and admitted he'd been a bit blasé about what was happening to her so far, but her need to eat human food was disturbing. *Are all Fae the same way? If their magic is gone, will they be able to resort to more human eating habits? Is she special... or in trouble?*

Ryan put the laptop down on the table next to her. He hadn't been making up excuses when he'd said he had to work. The computer lab mostly ran itself as long as he was there, but he had two classes worth of tests he had to grade. Wisps of dark hair escaped from Zee's braid, and he wanted to tuck them back in, or undo the braid entirely, but he didn't think she'd appreciate him manhandling her hair while she slept.

The oddest urges kept popping up in his head, and Ryan thought it was best to have a blanket policy to ignore all of them. They could brainstorm ideas for getting her back to the Wood later. He managed to leave her be on the couch without touching her like a weirdo. Keeping his hands to himself was harder than he'd thought it would be, so he closed himself up in the bedroom with his tests and his resolve.

———

ZEE

FOR THE SECOND time that day, Zee woke up in a strange place. She assumed it was the same day. At the very least, it *was* day, though much later than she remembered it being. The sun slanted through the window, close to setting. She sat up and stretched, but her neck remained sore from sleeping at a tilt. *Are all humans this tired all the time?* Ryan had left the laptop next to her with a note about a malfunctioning battery, so she carried it to the kitchen table where she plugged it in and booted it up.

Ryan had taught her, and many of her people, how to use a similar model of computer. It had been one of her crowning moments as a leader. She'd brought the Fae, or at least their little enclave, into the future. Unfortunately, she hadn't spent as much time as she should have poring over their historical texts. She'd ordered them scanned and had Ryan upload them to a secure server, but not everything had made it in. Not to mention, the computer that had access was still in the Wood with her people.

Zee blew out a breath as a familiar home screen appeared, willing herself to find a solution to the frustrating circle.

There *were* a few reputable sources on the internet that might have information on what had happened to her. There was also a good source in the apartment with her. She glanced at Ryan's closed door. He was probably in there, and could probably help, but she was more than capable of performing some basic internet searches. Truth be told, she needed a break from him. His constant presence was wreaking havoc on her priorities.

She didn't understand him on the best of days, but his downright fear of using magic was highly unusual. Some of it had come through while they'd been connected, but he'd been actively trying to hold it back. She wasn't sure if it was so he could overcome it and learn to work with magic or because she'd been in his head and he didn't want her to see it. More accurately, to see the cause of it.

Zee suspected it was probably both. Something *made* Ryan afraid of his magic. The laptop chimed, interrupting her musing, and she got to work.

ALMOST A WEEK LATER, Zee closed the laptop with a sigh and stared unseeing out the window. None of her emails or texts home had been returned. Ryan was probably right about the tech he'd installed being blown, not that she'd doubted him. Hope was an entirely different response than disbelief.

She'd claimed the kitchen table semi-permanently during her research marathon, and for the most part, Ryan had left her alone during the day. The trees were pretty with the midmorning sun shining through them, but the view didn't do anything to relieve her frustration, so she got up and wandered into the living room.

Zee picked up an errant sock and returned a plate to the kitchen. Somehow over the last week, she and Ryan had fallen into a comfortable pattern living together. After that first day, they hadn't tried any more magic lessons, and though he'd been feeding her regularly, they just sat side-by-side at the breakfast bar and mostly ate without speaking. She'd once asked why it was called a breakfast bar when they ate *all* their meals there, but he'd only shrugged. She'd had longer conversations with the sprites. At least he kept her well stocked in breakfast pastries.

The second morning, he'd tried to give her his bed, but she refused to kick him out of his own space. What she hadn't told him was that she didn't think she could handle sleeping in a place that contained so much of him. It had taken less than a day for him to find an air mattress for his extra bedroom, and she was thankful she could retreat there when she needed to.

Then there were days like today. She was restless and wasting energy cleaning the messes they'd both left behind. Usually, Ryan was already at work when she woke up. When he was at the apartment, he spent most of his time shuffling papers in his bedroom. That suited her fine. She'd never have gotten anything done if he was sitting on the couch, or worse, trying to help. His presence was distracting enough when he was in the other room.

His presence is distracting no matter where he is. Zee sighed and admitted the truth as she stacked dishes in the sink. She was avoiding Ryan in the hopes her feelings for him would go away, but he was making that hard for her too. When they were around each other, he couldn't seem to keep his distance. The proximity was driving her crazy. He'd brush his hands down her hair when he'd walk past, but ignore her when she turned to look. When they had to share the kitchen, he'd invade her space, not touching, but close enough that she could feel him. She wanted to respond, to bridge the distance that was always there, but being a prudent Fae, she also wanted to proceed with caution.

At least, most of her did. A small part of her wanted to storm his room after dark and see if he slept naked like she suspected. And that part grew stronger every day.

The dishes didn't take long to rinse and put in the dishwasher, and her circuit brought her back to the useless laptop. With or without the distraction of Ryan, the Fae server had been a bust. There was no way she could access it outside of their network in the Glade. After that, the internet had seemed like the best place to find any information. She'd been hopeful when she started her research, but with each day that passed, she was becoming more convinced that humans would be the cause of their own extinction.

Zee shook her head slightly. *How could humans and Fae, and others for that matter, live in the same world and have such completely different experiences?*

She was staring out the window at the sunny park, thinking about going for a walk, when Ryan's bedroom door opened. Zee glanced over, then did a double-take and hoped he hadn't seen it. He wore loose grey pants that sat low on his hips...and nothing else. *Oh my.*

She'd known he was fit. He'd jumped into a Fae sparring match once when he was in the Glade repairing something, and he'd held his own. The broad expanse of chest surprised her though. How did he maintain that level of muscle if he taught children and sat in front of computers all day?

He yawned then stopped short when he saw her. Zee thought for a second he was going to retreat back into the bedroom, but he walked through to the kitchen instead.

"Have you had breakfast yet?" he asked in a husky voice.

"Sort of."

He opened the refrigerator and stared into it before pulling out the orange juice, which he chugged straight from the carton. Zee wrinkled her nose. He didn't even shake it up first.

"Are all humans slovenly?"

He swiped his arm across his mouth and put the container back before responding. "Slovenly. What a fancy word. Sometimes I forget you're not human, then you say something like that and I'm reminded again how different you are."

Zee felt a pang of hurt, but it was true. She *was* different. "You're not at work today."

"It's Saturday. On the weekends, we only torture the really dedicated kids."

"Right. The arbitrary human work week."

Ryan absently rubbed his abs, and Zee valiantly fought

to keep her eyes on his face. "You sound cranky. Run out of donuts?"

Zee leaned back in her chair with a sigh and waved at the closed laptop. "Humans are stupid. They can't even get the simplest of Fae stories right. Instead, they insist on adding in flourishes and taking out relevant information."

"You've been trying to find data in fairy tales?"

"I'm trying to find factual information on the Fae, where would you have me look, Wikipedia?"

He held up a hand. "Wait, start from the beginning. Why are you looking for info on the Fae? You *are* Fae. I'd argue you know more than any human, alive or dead."

Zee clenched her fists in her lap, trying to hold on to her temper. She wasn't frustrated with him in particular, but she was tired of days of useless searching. It should have been a simple matter of research, but her people were infamously close-lipped. When they'd first moved to Texas, the original Fae had made a pact with the Wood which created the barriers surrounding Torix and the Glade. It was well before her time, so all she had was second-hand knowledge of the ritual, and no facts. She needed specifics.

Of course, Ryan wouldn't know any of that because she hadn't told him.

"I want to find out the details of the original pact with the Wood so that I can reverse the consequences of breaking it...somehow."

"I thought you knew the details."

Time to bring him in on a few more secrets. "I'm not as old as you think I am. I've only been leading the Fae for fifty years or so. Before that, we've had other leaders. Most of the originals who came here from Europe have moved on. The trods go many places, and while we weren't permitted to leave the Wood, we could travel to other Fae villages. Some leave and don't come back. Some die."

Ryan sat down next to her. "So you didn't help put up the barriers."

"Correct. I was born in the Glade well after the pact was made." Zee forced her hands to relax. "I know how to renew them, but it never occurred to me that someone would remove them entirely. I wasn't even aware that was possible. When the pact was broken, we entered uncharted territory as far as my experience and knowledge are concerned."

She stared down at her short nails. "I don't even know if I lost my magic because I'm the leader or because I happened to be in the trods when it happened, or because you magically pulled me from the Wood. *And* I can't access our database outside the network, so I can't gather any more information."

"Other than from fairy tales."

Zee rubbed her thighs and tilted her head up at him. "And one prolific conspiracy theorist who believes we may be aliens, but he has a disturbing amount of other information correct."

Ryan perked up at that tidbit. "Are you going to send fairy assassins after him?"

For once, Zee couldn't tell if Ryan was joking or not. It would be like him to think they had Fae assassins, and she couldn't explain *that* truth without risking much greater repercussions than just missing her magic. "No, I'm going to keep an eye on him and pass the information along to other, more suitable parties."

Ryan nodded and smiled. "Yep. Fairy assassins."

Zee rolled her eyes. "Or I could have you hack his website and shut it down."

"Nope. I told you I only do ethical hacking. By the way,

it's hot when you use words like slovenly and hack in the same conversation. Makes me think of a sexy, young school marm." He waggled his eyebrows.

"Well, now you've ruined it with your talking."

His face scrunched up. "Ruined what?"

"All the strutting around without your shirt on." Her eyes flicked south of his face for barely a millisecond, but she glanced away immediately, lifting her chin.

Ryan grinned and flexed his shoulders. "Ruined it, huh? That's too bad. Guess I'll have to make it up to you."

You're not interested, remember? She tried to keep her eyes averted, but failed, and her body flushed with excitement anyway. "What did you have in mind?" Though her voice was bland, she wasn't a hundred percent sure she was going to have the strength to resist.

But he sobered, all joking dropped from his demeanor. "Actually, I have some information you'll find useful, but you have to promise not to punish me for it."

Zee raised a haughty brow. "That promise doesn't sound like it would be in my best interests to make. What did you do?"

Ryan hesitated for a long moment, eyeing her skeptically, but then shrugged. "I guess you can't do much without magic anyway."

Zee was tempted to show him how very wrong he was, but decided to wait until he gave her the information.

"When I configured your network and database, I granted myself admin access."

He said the words like the information was important, but Zee didn't know what it meant or how it could help her. "Can you explain that in simpler terms?"

"Let me first say that I would have told you this earlier if I'd known what you were trying to do, but...I can get into your network. From here." He gestured at the computer in front of her. "I can use that laptop if you want. It was a fail-safe because I wanted some insurance."

Zee looked at the closed laptop then back up at Ryan. "You have access to our database? The one you assured me was secure."

"Oh, it *is* secure. I check it regularly like a good IT monkey."

She'd thought Ryan had been developing more of an appreciation for the Fae over the last week. He'd been kind when he didn't have to be, and he'd been receptive to learning how to control his magic. The change made it more painful to find out he'd made plans to take advantage of them should the need ever arise. Zee recognized that he was now telling her the truth to help her, but his distrust cut deep.

"Why didn't you tell me before? I've been wasting time all week."

"I didn't know what you were doing, and honestly, I had other things on my mind. I wanted to get through this week at school and get some breathing room before we tackled the mounting problems of a pissed off forest and a power-less fairy."

Zee stiffened at the 'powerless fairy' remark and crossed her arms, leaning back in her chair. "Well this has certainly been a day of revelations."

"And it's only mid-morning. If it makes you feel better, you're adapting remarkably well for someone whose life changed in an instant. If I had to adjust to living in a new world, I'd have lost it on day one."

Some of her ire drained away. "The food helps."

Ryan grinned, possibly thinking he was out of danger.

"Speaking of food, Jake and Sera want us to come over for dinner tonight."

Zee's mouth dropped open. "I can finally find some answers and you want to go to dinner like it's some kind of double date?"

"How do you even know about double dates? And no. I want to relax and go visit my best friend after a hard week at work. Best case scenario, I'll drink more beer than I should, eat some steak, and give him shit for letting Sera take over his life. That's what I want to do tonight."

She waved him away and opened the laptop. "Give me access, then go I'll probably get more work done if you're gone anyway." As much as she wanted him to stay away as 'Ryan the temptation', she wanted his help as 'Ryan the tech god', his words. But she was also disappointed in his seeming unwillingness to truly help. *No matter, I'm used to working on my own.*

Ryan shut the lid again. "No can do, princess. They want us both there, and if I give you access now, you won't go."

"Why is it so important that I go?"

"Sera is worried about you, and Jake is smitten with Sera. Your fault, by the way."

Irritation mixed with a strange sense of longing grew inside her. "I thought you liked Sera."

"I love Sera, but Jake's life revolves around her. She's everywhere, and sometimes a guy just wants to sit on the couch without being buried in throw pillows."

Zee glanced at his bare couch. She didn't understand the connection, but she wasn't going to digress further by asking. Ryan was excellent at dangling tangents in front of her during conversation when he didn't want to discuss the original topic.

She shook her head. "I've wasted a week chasing information in circles, and I'm not going to wait any longer. Go without me."

Ryan stood up and leaned into her face from across the table. "You don't get to give orders this time. You're not the leader, and you can't force me with your magic. These people are your friends. They care about you, and it won't hurt anything to spend time with them. It might even help if you told them, and me, what you're looking for."

He was close enough that she could feel his breath. The table really was tiny. "My life is in limbo, and you want me to go and talk about the problem instead of looking for a solution?"

"Yes. I want you to stop acting like the world is going to end if you can't wave your hand and get what you want. We're a team. You need to stop hoarding all the information all the time. We happen to be subject matter experts on the human world and how to do things here. You could've had access to your records days ago if you'd included us." He stood up and planted his hands on his hips.

She stood up so he wasn't looming over her, but she didn't back away. "This goes beyond me and my predicament. The Wood is disturbed, Torix is on the loose, and my people could be in danger."

"I highly doubt the Fae are in danger from some trees. If they were, they'd send out a distress call. Besides, Sera said Torix is magicless. Those are convenient excuses, but they're still excuses. You're obsessed with returning to the Wood because you believe it'll give you back the most important thing in your life. Your magic."

Zee narrowed her eyes. He wasn't entirely wrong, but he had the direction mixed up. She wasn't running *to* her magic; she was running *from* him.

"Come with me tonight, relax, have dinner with people

who care about you, and then I'll give you the access to the database."

The offer was tempting. She enjoyed the company of Sera and Jake, and he was right that the Fae would most likely send out a distress call if they were truly in danger. That eased some of the pressure, but she never made a bargain without knowing all the options. "And if I refuse?"

He leaned back and crossed his arms. "Then you can keep throwing yourself against the wall of human stupidity."

"You win." Zee straightened, carefully stepped over the power cord for the laptop, and went into her bedroom. She could feel Ryan's eyes on her until she closed the door and slumped down against it. There wasn't another option. She was going to dinner.

It sucks to be powerless.

5

RYAN

WINNING that battle should have felt better. He'd never had to blackmail a woman into having dinner with him before. Granted, Zee *always* won, so he was happy to come out on top for once, but it had hurt her. He could see it in the way she wouldn't meet his eyes. Also, in the way she hadn't left her room for the rest of the afternoon.

The whole morning had been a mess anyway. He hadn't forgotten she was there, per se, but he hadn't been fully awake when he'd come out of his room. All he'd wanted was some juice and maybe another couple hours of sleep. The weeks before winter break were no joke with teenagers. They were either not there at all or so zoned out they might as well not be. The next week would be worse. Ryan thanked God all he had to teach were two classes and he could zone out himself in the computer lab the rest of the time.

If his brain had been fully functioning, he might have put on a shirt. Her double-take then lazy perusal when he opened the door almost blew through all the control he'd been practicing. He wanted her hands on him the way her eyes had been, better yet, her mouth. He wasn't sure when it happened, but he was obsessed with her full lips. She'd almost caught him staring the couple of times they'd crossed paths in the last week, and he was supremely grateful she'd taught him how to shield his mind. The last thing he needed was her knowing smirk when she got a headful of his thoughts.

Zee hadn't left the guest room all day. She wasn't making any noise, so Ryan assumed she was asleep. He almost checked on her, but even though Sera had dropped off a few more basic outfits, she hadn't provided any pajamas. Too much of him wanted her to be sleeping naked, so he resisted and worked on some other projects in his room. Sometimes, he was surprised by how easily they'd fallen into a rhythm living with each other. He cooked all the meals, mostly because he didn't trust her with the stove, and often left her a plate on the counter. She ate, sometimes with him, sometimes after he'd left, and cleaned up the mess. They almost never saw each other, like being roommates with a very polite ghost.

It was time she joined the living.

Ryan knocked on her door and yelled without opening it. "Zee, it's time to head out."

He heard shuffling on the other side, then the door opened and Zee barreled into him. "Whoa." He caught her arms before she bounced onto the floor. "Everything okay?"

She frowned. "Of course. The sooner we have dinner, the sooner I can start my research. Let's go." She scooted past him and slipped into the sneakers he'd found the second day, then tapped her foot as she waited at the door.

He shook his head. "Part of the deal was you had to relax."

"I am relaxed." The tension in her glare matched the stiffness in her shoulders.

Ryan shrugged. "Fine." *This is going to be a long night.*

They didn't talk on the way to Jake's place. The sun was setting in a glorious display of purple and orange, and Zee couldn't keep her eyes off of it. He kept sneaking glances at her. At some point since leaving the Glade, she'd changed. She was subdued, smaller than usual. Like the sunset, she was a force of nature, and he missed that aspect of her personality.

———

ON JAKE'S STREET, Ryan passed Will going in the opposite direction. The jerk smiled and waved like he always did, and Ryan's hands clenched the steering wheel. The man was a menace. He hid in his car and tortured Sera, and the cops couldn't do anything about it. Nothing illegal in driving. Tiny red sparks of magic from Ryan's hands danced over the wheel and toward the console. He fought to pull them back in like he'd been practicing, but when he was tired and angry, it took concentrated effort.

He pulled into Jake and Sera's driveway and shifted the car into park, still watching Will's taillights fade into the distance. Zee put a hand over his before he could move. He turned and found her watching him with a smile. "I'm proud of you."

Gratification unfurled in his chest. Not a lot of people had said that to him in his life. His anger drained away, and the magic settled back inside him. "Thank you."

She nodded, and her hand slid away. The side of Zee

that represented her strength and compassion instead of her magic intrigued him. She was so much more than what she could do or be for other people.

Zee didn't go very far once she got out of the car. Jake's place was across the street from the Wood. She stood at the edge of the driveway and stared into the expanse of trees with her arms wrapped around herself. The forest was dark, but sprites were flitting around Jake's porch. A group of them looked like they were trying to get into Sera's house next door through the kitchen window. He guessed Evie was in there blessing people or something.

Sprites were drawn to magic, and as far as he could tell, they didn't do anything other than light up like tiny useless puffs of smoke. Sera claimed they could open doors, turn lights off, clog sinks, and all kinds of other little things, but he was skeptical. Zee ignored them.

She wanted to go home. Ryan could see the longing in the way she leaned forward and wrapped her arms around herself, and he didn't know what to say to ease her pain. Every time he opened his mouth, they started fighting about priorities. *Maybe if you kept your mouth shut...*

Her shoulders stiffened slightly as he approached, but she didn't turn. Ryan wrapped his arms around her from behind and settled her against him, careful not to cross the line from hug into something more. After a second, she relaxed and let him take her weight. Her hand gripped his arm, and they stood together watching an empty forest.

Ryan admitted to himself that he shouldn't have forced her to come out to Jake's. He'd told himself he'd been trying to take care of her, to give her a break, but she was a grown-ass fairy, she could decide when she needed a break all on her own. Standing with her in his arms, he felt like an ass for hiding behind the shallow excuse.

He'd been upset at her rush to go back.

She had this unique chance to try something new, to live a life she hadn't experienced before, and all she focused on was what she'd lost. Ryan wanted her to look around and see the humanity he embraced, to recognize that it had value. *Why is it so important?*

The longer they stood there, the darker the underbrush became, and the scene in front of him finally penetrated his thoughts. The forest shouldn't be that dark. The sun had barely set, and the rest of the neighborhood was still bright enough that kids were playing outside down the street. He couldn't see more than a few feet between the trees.

A chill of foreboding ran down his spine as the neighbor kids screeched with joy, and the red ball they'd been using flew into the woods. Normally, the Wood stayed dormant when non-magic users went into it, but the strange shadows made Ryan nervous. When one of the boys started forward, he released Zee and took off running down the street toward the kids. He didn't glance back, but the silence behind him said she'd stayed put. *Good.*

The kids were a couple of houses down, and as he got closer, he could hear them daring each other to go get the ball. None of them had left the safety of the yard yet. *Thank goodness.* The kids were young enough that a strange man running toward them made them get quiet and back up toward the house. He thought about introducing himself, then decided it would be a waste of breath. They wouldn't care anyway.

Ryan slowed down on the sidewalk and crossed the street at a slower pace. The ball couldn't have gone far, though it had been a wicked throw from way back by the house. He stopped at the tree line and peered into the dim interior. A splotch of red peeked out from some brambles about twenty feet in, but it disappeared in darkness almost immediately. If he didn't know better, he'd say the Wood had been tempting him with a glimpse of the ball, but the Wood wasn't sentient or playful. *Was it?* The wind picked up a bit and the trees swayed madly. Ryan couldn't see the ball anymore among the shifting shadows.

He hesitated.

The whole situation felt off, like he'd stepped into a horror movie. The trees creaked in front of him, but the kids had gotten silent. Ryan squared his shoulders. If he was this unnerved, he definitely wasn't letting the kids do this themselves.

He took a couple of steps into the brush and stopped. The ball was at his feet, clear as day, but the wind had stopped. Ryan stooped down and grabbed it, but when he stood and turned to go back, there were only trees shrouded in darkness.

His first reaction was a mental high five because he'd been right. The Wood *was* dangerous. Or at least suspicious. He wasn't clear on the danger level. The landscape was dark and creepy, but nothing was threatening to eat him or anything. *Yet.*

Movement above him drew his attention up. He didn't feel any wind in the silent forest, but the tops of the trees undulated back and forth. All the branches near him were still, and he was pretty sure he didn't want to find out what happened when they started moving too. He could run, but every way he turned looked the same.

His heart beat wildly. The hand clutching the ball started to glow a darker shade of red as power oozed out. For once, he was glad to see it. Magic had gotten him into this mess, so as much as he hated it, maybe he could use magic to get out of it.

Ryan closed his eyes and leaned into it. With his magic loose, a subtle feeling of comfort and light emerged behind him. Focusing on the impression made it clearer as he turned toward it, but he didn't move forward. He'd spent a lot of time in these woods, so he respected the danger of walking around blind. Branches and crap littering the forest floor would *for sure* impale him if he tripped.

His body warmed and relaxed as if turning toward the sun. A pull from the middle of his chest drew him in that direction. *Screw the debris.* He took a couple of halting steps, then opened his eyes when he was sure it wouldn't break his concentration. The dark, silent forest still engulfed him, but the pull got stronger, and he thought he heard his name.

He took one more step staring into the shadows, but not really seeing them. The pull guided him. When he paused, something grasped the front of his shirt and yanked him forward.

Between one moment and the next, the shadows were gone, and Zee had wrapped her arms around his middle. Ryan craned his neck to peer back so he wouldn't have to let go of Zee. Sure enough, the Wood had returned to normal. No more mysterious shadows or phantom wind.

"What were you doing?" Zee's voice was muffled because her face was buried in his shoulder.

"The woods looked weird." The kids had moved to their porch, but they cheered when he flashed them the red ball. With one arm locked around Zee, he tossed it firmly back into their yard. His magic had receded at some point, thankfully. He'd never tested it to see if non-magical folks could see it the way the rest of them could, and he hadn't planned to start with those kids. Jake didn't count because even though he didn't have magic on his own, he could use Sera's through their bond.

Zee lifted her face. "You disappeared. Literally disappeared. I couldn't see you. I could sense you, though."

Ryan studied her. She was so tempting with her mouth right there and worry in her eyes. "There was something wrong with the shadows, and I didn't want those kids to be wandering around in the woods at night."

"Good instincts. When did you turn into a white knight?"

Just now? Being a white knight was worth it if he got to feel the entire glorious length of Zee pressed against him as a reward. He let his forehead drop to hers and sighed. "Don't tell anyone. It'll ruin my reputation."

Zee patted his chest, but it ended up more like a caress. "Your secret's safe with me." She pulled away, and he reluctantly released her.

"Does this mean you're not mad at me anymore?"

"I was never mad at you. Frustrated by my inability to handle the situation myself, yes, but you were right about the collaboration part. And you were genuinely trying to help."

"How do you know that? Maybe I get off on being a jerk to women?"

She tapped her own chest. "I can feel it. You have your shields up, but I can read the emotions behind your actions."

Ryan was glad he didn't have to grovel, but he also thought her reading might have been clouded by her judgement. As fun as digging through his complicated emotions sounded, it would have to wait. He was pretty sure the Wood had just tried to kidnap him, and that trumped roommate squabbles.

The walk back to Jake's house seemed much shorter

than when he was running to the ball's rescue. "Are we going to ignore what happened back there?"

"I thought we should include Sera and Jake in the conversation."

Ryan shoved his hands in his hoodie pockets. "Good thinking. They're more likely to be eaten."

Zee started. "Did you see a creature in there?"

He hunched his shoulders. "No, but it was dark and creepy. I feel like we should put up a sign or something at least. 'Do not enter, scary shadows ahead'."

She didn't answer him, and when he glanced at her face, it looked like she was considering it. If he hadn't been there, one of those kids would have gone in after the ball. What then? Would the others have even told anyone? How long before that kid's parents noticed that he hadn't come home? Ryan shook his head. He was making jokes, but the situation was seriously messed up.

He stopped Zee in the driveway. "Before we go in there and share our fun little adventure, I want to say something to you. Thank you."

"You don't have to—"

He held up his hand. "I *do* have to. You pulled me out. I don't know what happened, but I know there was no obvious exit from where I was standing. But I felt you. It told me which way to move, and then you physically yanked me out of there. Maybe I could have escaped on my own from dumb luck, but I hope we never find out. Ultimately, it was your hand on me that brought me back."

She slid her eyes to the woods. "You scared me. The Wood has never done anything like that in my lifetime. I couldn't see you, but...I could feel you too." Her voice dropped to a hoarse whisper as her face tilted up again to meet his eyes. Gazing down, he knew this time he wasn't going to resist.

He moved slowly, giving her a chance to back away, but she stood strong, her eyes locked on his. His lips brushed hers, barely a touch, but she opened for him. One of them moved, maybe both of them, and his hands plunged into her much looser braids. She pressed closer and slid her hands up his back as Ryan took her mouth. She tasted like sugar and heat.

He kissed her long and deep, and the world around them faded away. Her skin was soft and warm. He couldn't stop stroking the curve of her cheekbone with his thumb. Their tongues intertwined in a battle for dominance, but Ryan was happy to let her win this one. His hand trailed down her neck, along the side of her breast, and under her baggy shirt to curl into the small of her back. She fit him perfectly, and Ryan would have given years off his life to be anywhere but in Jake's driveway.

He pulled back to take a ragged breath, but Zee didn't release her grip. Her eyes had closed at some point, and he desperately wanted to see his need reflected in the green depths. As if answering his plea, she opened eyes full of desire and smiled.

"You're welcome," she said huskily.

Ryan chuckled. "Jake's probably watching us from his front hallway like a pervert, and no matter how much I'd rather continue right now, I hate giving him a show."

Zee took a deep breath and backed away, letting her hands fall to her sides as she nodded absently. "We should get inside. There's a lot to discuss."

Ryan nodded, but he wasn't going to leave it there. He skimmed a hand down her arm and lifted her fingers to his lips. "We're going to finish this later." He brushed the words across her knuckles, then laced their fingers together to pull her up to the porch. She raised a brow but didn't pull away. He'd gotten a taste of her, and he wanted—no, needed —more.

Jake didn't show any interest in their joined hands when he opened the door, but Sera gave him an arched look from over Jake's shoulder. Ryan couldn't tell if it was approval or censure, but he didn't give a shit anyway. Sera didn't get a say in what happened between him and Zee.

Nobody mentioned that fact to Zee though. After the usual greeting crap, she squeezed his hand and pulled away to go with Sera into the kitchen. Ryan hoped Sera didn't mention the database. He didn't want to explain that particular decision to Zee.

Jake didn't immediately follow. He stood blocking the hallway with his arms crossed.

Ryan wasn't sure he had the patience for Jake at the moment. "What?"

"You sure you know what you're doing?"

"No. Definitely not, but I'm going to do it anyway."

Jake blew out a breath. "Seriously, you need to be careful with her."

Ryan brushed past him into the living room. They were speaking quietly, but Zee had ears like a fox. "I know. It's dangerous for me to piss off a Fae even *if* she's without her magic right now."

"It's not about you, dumbass. It's about her. She's lost everything important to her, stranded here in a strange world, and you're messing around with her feelings."

Ryan flopped down onto the couch. "I'm not messing around. What's between us is exactly that, between *us*."

Jake frowned from the doorway. "It's not going to stay between you two for long if you're making out on the street.

This is Mulligan, Texas, population: something thousand and everybody already knows your business."

Ryan rolled his eyes. "I *knew* you were watching. You need better hobbies."

Zee appeared in the doorway, and Ryan wanted to say screw dinner and drag her home with him. "Sera says dinner is ready." She announced, leaving before either man could move. They both stared after her.

Jake spoke first. "Good luck, man. She's worth at least two of you."

Ryan stayed frozen on the couch a minute longer. He could hear silverware clinking and low voices from the other room, but he needed to get a grip on the mess in his head first. Jake was right. He'd been so concerned about the effect magic was having on his life that he'd glossed over how tumultuous this must be for Zee. There wasn't a good excuse for his over-sight besides willful ignorance. The bargain they'd made tied them together, and if he tried, he could *feel* her emotions with very little effort. Even if he didn't try, sometimes it came through loud and clear. All he had to do was pay attention.

This emotional connection wasn't just a simple attrac-tion, this was something...more. Magic? He turned the idea over in his mind, but no matter how he twisted it, she wasn't Maddie. In fairness, Maddie wasn't Maddie, but Zee wasn't going to turn around one day and use her power against him. She'd used magic *on* him before, but only to protect her people and never in a way that would hurt him. The belief that came with that knowledge surprised him. He hadn't realized he'd started making excuses for magic use.

Zee laughed at something in the other room, low and sexy, and need shot through him all over again. He wanted his hands on her, his lips on her, his—well, the more time

they spent together, the harder it was becoming to
remember why it was a bad idea.

ZEE

Zee didn't know what Ryan was doing by himself in the
other room, but he was missing out on an excellent meal.
Jake had made a giant lasagna for dinner, and by the time
Ryan sat down, half of it was gone. He didn't seem to mind,
but he didn't meet her eyes as he served himself.

"Thanks for making dinner, man."

"You're welcome, but you should know we had an ulte-
rior motive for asking you guys over. Zee specifically."

She forced her eyes away from watching Ryan eat. She
kept reliving the kiss outside and his promise that they
weren't finished. A low hum of excitement at her center had
been slowly building since that moment. As a result, she
was having trouble concentrating. *What's wrong with me?*
Pay attention!

Zee shook her head and faced Jake. "What did you need
from me?"

He glanced toward Sera, and she was the one who
spoke. "Information, as usual. We'd been trying some things
in the trods before you arrived, but Jake didn't want to take
any chances after..." She trailed off, and Jake set down his
silverware to take over.

"How dangerous is the Wood right now?"

Ah, I know the answer to this one. Finally. "Very. I'd advise
you not to go into the forest at all until balance has been
returned." Ryan snorted, but his mouth was full so he

couldn't elaborate. "We need to tell you about what happened when we got here."

It took fifteen minutes of constant interruptions for Zee to get through the story. She left out the part where her heart stopped when Ryan disappeared, and the part where she tried again and again to call her magic to help him. Ryan contributed what he'd experienced when he was inside the shadows, then went in for a second piece of lasagna.

Jake brought two glasses of water to the table and handed one to Sera. "So you're saying the Wood is activating some kind of elemental magic in order to eat people?"

Zee pushed her empty plate away. "What? No..." She shook her head. "Okay, sort of. The shadows were definitely magical, but I'm not sure of the purpose. If one of the children had run into the trees, it might have simply been a forest. But Ryan ran in instead. His magic may have triggered the shadows to activate their own magic."

Sera paled. "Do you think this is *my* fault? Why didn't it do anything to us before now?"

"It did. It trapped me in a trod and led you in circles."

"Yeah, but it didn't try to keep us, and it sounds like Ryan wasn't in a trod."

Zee shook her head again and sighed heavily. "I don't know. I need to do more research. Everything I'm telling you now is speculation at best. I don't know if the Wood is dangerous to humans right now, but I wouldn't risk it." She paused and rubbed her temples. "The trouble started gradually, but the reactions seem to be getting more insidious." Zee sat back and stared out the window, though she couldn't see anything past their reflections in the dark glass. "It's strange. The power in the Wood is supposed to be neutral. That was why my people had to give up something to access it. I wonder if something else is influencing it."

Jake and Sera shared another look, and Zee started to suspect they knew something relevant that they weren't sharing. Sera still appeared queasy, but Jake rubbed her back and nodded.

She leaned forward and clasped her hands together on the table. "I think I know why the Wood is leaning toward destruction. When Evie was declared dead, all her stuff passed to me, including some land north of town that used to be a ranch. It overlaps the Wood pretty heavily, and there are some overgrown places that feel...different. One of the reasons the rancher had to sell was that he couldn't use that land. The cows wouldn't go there."

"Magic," muttered Ryan.

Sera ignored him. "Anyway, Evie bought it, ostensibly to protect the Wood, and these developers started pushing her to sell to them. They want to build a master-planned community there. Now they're pushing *me* to sell. It wasn't a big deal until a little over a week ago when I found out that Will is working with the developers as a consultant." She spit out the last word.

Zee had never met Will, but she sensed the turmoil from Sera. There was fear mixed in with disgust and pity. The jumble of emotions wasn't worth unraveling, easier to simply assume she shouldn't trust the man. In addition, the three humans around the table all looked like they wante to murder him.

"Could they be doing something illegal or something harmful to the environment that's pissing off the trees?" asked Jake.

Ryan pushed his chair back with a scrape to take his plate to the sink. "She's not the Lorax, man. How is she supposed to know what the Wood takes offense to?"

Zee didn't understand his reference, but both questions

were valid. The Fae had sworn to protect the Wood along with the barriers, and they'd failed. *Spectacularly.* If the humans were doing something stupid, the Wood using its power to protect itself made sense. There were too many variables to know for sure, but there was a guaranteed way to find out.

She straightened her shoulders and nodded. "I need to detain Will."

6

Ryan's shocked laugh echoed in the kitchen, but Zee didn't see what was funny. "We can't detain people, Zee. That's kidnapping. What's next, torture?"

She tilted her head. *Not a bad idea.* "I'll rephrase. I need to find out what he's doing. The easiest way is to restrain him and let me look in his mind, but he may not know the details."

Sera snorted. "There's no way he knows the details. He's a front man. Pretty face and words, but lazy when it comes to actual work."

Ryan shrugged. "So, we follow him. He drives by every night around the same time. We borrow a car and see where he leads us."

The others debated the details, but Zee sat back in amazement. She hadn't expected such a response from them. They'd been properly warned of the danger, so there was no reason to help her fix the Wood. Despite that, they were talking about breaking human laws to gather information as if there were no question of their involvement.

"Why are you so eager to help?" Zee blurted out.

They stopped mid-sentence, and Sera answered her. "It's my fault the barriers are gone. Plus, we're all interconnected. The state of the woods affects our homes, and your state of magic affects us being able to help Evie. Besides all that, we're friends too, aren't we?" Sera looked a little unsure, but continued on. "I can't speak for the others, but why wouldn't I help?"

Zee shook her head. "It's not your fault. You did your best to stop Torix, without the benefit of my people, I might add. And if not for you, Evie would have remained trapped in the barriers. You saved her life, and you should be proud of that."

Sera's eyes teared up, and Jake grabbed her hand. "Thanks for saying that. I've been so guilty over what happened to you, and now this, even though I wouldn't change anything if given the chance."

"Evie would have done the same."

Sera wiped her face and took a deep breath. "Speaking of Evie, is there anything we can do to reinstate her in society without your magic working?"

Zee winced. That wrinkle *was* her doing. "Unfortunately, no. Without magic, I can't recall the golem or fiddle with the people in charge of paperwork. If I get it back, I can try, but the more time that passes, the stronger Evie's death will be in their memories. Especially in this small of a community. Everyone knew Evie and everyone mourned her when she passed. Honestly, it might be too late at this point to reverse."

Sera let out a frustrated sigh, but accepted it. Jake, on the other hand, scowled. "Why on Earth would you fake her death if you couldn't reverse it?"

Zee speared him with a quelling look. "As far as I knew, there was no need to reverse it. Evie was trapped behind the barriers. Even if she miraculously emerged, the most I could work with would be a couple of days. Over a month?" She spread her hands helplessly. "Even I have limits."

"I'm going to throttle my sister when she gets back from Europe," muttered Jake.

Sera put a hand on his arm. "It's not her fault either. It's Torix's fault and only his."

Jake pouted. "Can I at least blame Will a little bit?"

She rolled her eyes. "Fine. You can blame Will too if you want, but I think he's getting himself into plenty of trouble without throwing some of Torix's culpability at him."

"I'm truly sorry that I can't help Evie." Zee was surprised at the depth of her sorrow. Evie had been a useful ally, but Zee had tried to keep the humans at an emotional distance. *When had that changed?*

Sera waved a hand. "And I'm sorry that I bulldozed through your protections. There, now we're even."

Her flippant comment started a playful argument among the three of them about who'd done the most accidental destruction. Zee allowed a small smile. She liked Sera's style. This whole mess started when Zee had underestimated the humans. Evie tried to help with the barriers, Sera took the responsibility upon herself of stopping Torix, Jake offered himself as a conduit, and Ryan...Zee watched him banter back and forth with his friends, but she knew he was volatile inside. He'd gone into the Wood with them in the end. He'd tried to use his magic to protect everyone, even as he hated himself for it. They'd all do the same again.

It was time to start accepting that these humans at least were more than just semi-useful people that needed to be coddled and sheltered.

Zee hated to bring up Will again with everyone smiling, but one of them needed to take charge. Sera beat her to it.

"Okay, we're all in agreement that I'm the most destructive, but Will still gives me creeps with his stalker crap. I wish the cops would do something. It may not be illegal to drive down the street, but I *feel* threatened."

Jake's smile dropped right away. "He won't touch you."

Sera dropped a quick kiss on his cheek. "I know, but I have this fantasy where he tries and I kick his ass."

"I could help with that." All three focused on Zee. She hadn't really meant to speak, but it was too late. "I could teach you a few moves that would help you defend yourself if you ever needed to."

Sera considered it for all of three seconds. "Yeah. I'm in."

Jake's brows drew together. "Are you sure that's a good idea?"

She patted his hand. "Have you seen Zee's arm muscles? She looks like she belongs in a superhero movie. Especially with those Amazon warrior braids. This is going to be great." She turned back to Zee. "Can you teach me to kill a man with one finger?"

Zee's smile widened with a predatory glint, but she didn't answer.

Ryan did. "No. Let's keep the warrior princess fantasies to a reasonable level. Sera, even if she taught you that, you'd never use it. You're a marshmallow on the inside."

She scowled. "You don't get a say. Zee gets to decide what she teaches in warrior princess class."

"Now it's a class?" Ryan rolled his eyes.

"You don't think other women in town would be interested in learning how to defend themselves? Look at her, she's a walking advertisement for badass."

"I *am* looking."

Zee's eyes clashed with his, and Ryan's dropped in a slow perusal that caused aftershocks all the way down her body. She tried not to respond outwardly, but inside she was a quivering mess.

"Besides, it's a good way to integrate Zee into the community. You're not going to be able to keep her hidden in your apartment much longer."

The image of them tangled together in his bed appeared in her mind again, and she had to look away from Ryan. They'd never get through an entire conversation at this rate.

"It's fine. There's not much difference between teaching one woman and many."

Sera clapped her hands and stuck her tongue out at Ryan. "Warrior princess classes are a go. I'll talk to the high school, see if we can borrow the gym one night next week. Oh, and I'll bet Mrs. Wilson would let me put up a flyer."

This was spiraling out of hand. Zee'd wanted to help alleviate Sera's anxiety, not start a movement. It was probably too late to ease it back though. Jake gathered the dishes and nodded along with Sera's planning, but Ryan was watching Zee.

From the moment he'd disappeared into the Wood, her senses had become hyper alert. She'd had to reinforce her shields to avoid his emotions washing over her constantly, but even that wasn't working completely. He'd drawn her attention all night. She was beginning to suspect that they'd done more than make a simple bargain that first day.

Glass and metal clanked together behind her, and Sera

got up to help Jake. Alone at the table, Ryan captured her hand and brought it to his lips again. Warmth rushed up her arm to her face.

"Ready to go?" He spoke the words against her fingers, and Zee nodded.

They both stood up, and Ryan released her as Jake turned. She could feel the blush creeping across her cheeks, but she couldn't stop it.

"Thank you for dinner. It was the best lasagna I've ever had."

Ryan chuckled. "It was the only lasagna she's ever had, so don't get all excited." He clapped Jake on the back. "Delicious as always."

Jake flicked water at him. "I see how it is. Eat and run." He lowered his voice. "I'll text you about coordinating to trail Will."

Sera shut off the water. "I heard that. Zee, I'll let Ryan know what time the class will be. Is two hours long enough?"

"That should be fine." All she wanted was to get back to Ryan's apartment, but humans spent so much time saying goodbye. Jake and Sera walked them to the door and waved as they climbed into the car. Once they were on the road and moving, Zee sank back into the seat and closed her eyes. *Finally.*

"I didn't think it was that bad."

Zee peeked at him from beneath her lashes. He'd lost the playful look in his eyes, and his jaw was tight. Had she done something wrong? "It wasn't. I've been on edge since we arrived. I like Jake and Sera, and the conversation was surprisingly helpful."

Ryan snuck a quick glance at her. "On edge, huh?"

She smiled. "Because of the Wood."

He scoffed.

"And because of you."

"Are we talking about this now?"

Zee shrugged as they pulled into Ryan's parking lot. "Why not? We want each other, and neither of us is in a relationship. The problem is that I think we may have bound ourselves together accidentally."

Ryan stopped the car too fast, but the seatbelt caught Zee. He slammed it into park and faced her. "We did what now?"

"I think your magic bound us when we made the bargain." She got out of the car and walked across the short stretch of pavement toward his apartment. He needed a moment to react, and she was more than happy to oblige.

Zee knew better than most that when two people are bound, it doesn't necessarily translate into sexual attraction. The magic enhanced what was already present, but it didn't make anything new manifest. She'd never seen it done without Fae magic and a specific intent though.

Ryan caught up to her on the stairwell. He grabbed her wrist gently and pulled her to a stop. Zee remembered the last time they were this close in the stairwell and braced herself to turn. Blue fire blazed in his eyes. *Not calm yet, then.*

"Why would the magic bind us? We've made bargains before and were free to go our separate ways. Why this time?"

Zee was tired of people constantly demanding answers from her. She wasn't an oracle; she couldn't pull answers out of her ass. "I don't know."

Ryan was still holding her, but he'd loosened his grip so his thumb was resting on the inside of her wrist. He had to feel her pulse racing. More, he had to know she was as frustrated by the bond as he was. *Didn't he?* The longer they spent in each other's company, the clearer she could read him. She'd assumed that went both ways.

"It's not supposed to work this way. I've been saying that too much lately for it to be coincidence. The magic is shifting, and it's beyond my experience or my knowledge."

Ryan's thumb swiped across her sensitive skin, then he released her. "I want you. So much that I have trouble thinking of anything else. I want to back you against the wall and taste you again. I want to see if your skin is that soft everywhere. I want to bury my hands in your braids."

Zee lifted a hand to touch her hair. "My braids?"

"I've never seen your hair down. The point is do I want all that for myself or because magic arbitrarily decided we'd make a good match?"

Her hand dropped back to her side. "Magic can't make you want."

"Right. It's not *supposed* to work that way."

He brushed past her and went into the apartment. Zee stayed where she was. She needed a second to process. There was a chance Ryan was correct, but her reactions to him didn't feel like magic. They felt like long-repressed needs. If she was honest, he'd always affected her in a strange way, but there'd been no point in courting a relationship that couldn't go anywhere.

That hadn't changed. She intended to reclaim her magic and her position among her people. It was what she'd been groomed for, and it was a responsibility she took seriously. Ryan wanted nothing to do with magic, and there'd been plenty of other, less intense, options in the Glade.

But she wasn't in the Glade anymore.

She was in Ryan's world, and he wanted her too. What

would be the harm in testing that intensity? The image of them in bed together flashed across her mind again, and this time she let it linger. Maybe it would release some of the pressure, and then they could focus on something besides each other.

Ryan had left the door open for her at the top of the stairs. Like the first night, water was running in his bedroom. She probed with her senses and knew that if she joined him, he'd welcome her but he'd be angry with himself for giving in. He'd lumped the attraction and the magic together, so fighting one meant he fought both. Zee went as far as putting her hand on the knob, but she backed away before turning it. He wanted a lot of things, but he wasn't *fighting* for any of them.

She was worth more than that.

Zee stared at the door and willed her body to calm down. Ryan was most likely taking a cold shower again, and it didn't seem like a terrible idea at the moment. She returned to the living room and the second bathroom. It had a small shower stall that she'd been avoiding all week. There were tubs in the Glade for soaking, but no showers. Why bother when they could magic themselves clean? The whole process of showering was foreign to her.

The mirror over the sink caught her attention. Zee knew what she looked like. It was a form she'd chosen after all, but she'd never been so disheveled. Her hand came up to her braids again, once intricate and tight, but now hair was pulled loose and sticking out in frizzy loops. She ran her hands over the mess and tried to called on her magic. *Nothing.* All that happened was her hand snagged one of the floppy portions.

Zee sighed. They'd have to be redone. This was why she'd been avoiding the bathroom mirror. So many parts of her had been left behind when she'd stepped out of the trod, but she'd held tight to this tradition. *I earned those braids, dammit.* Though she knew how to fix them, the act of unbraiding her hair made her feel like she was losing herself all over again.

If there was nothing left of the Zee she was before, what power did she have to reclaim her life?

She closed her eyes against the shell of the warrior staring back at her and pulled the band free from the tail. Her head dropped along with her hand. With her eyes squeezed shut, she pulled the hair over her shoulder and began unplaiting it.

"What are you doing?"

Zee's head popped up, and she opened her eyes. Ryan was leaning against the doorframe watching her. His dark hair was wet and hung past his ears. It was longer than she remembered, but she liked it better that way. A slow burn started, and she was glad he'd put on loose pants and a shirt with what she assumed was another superhero symbol.

Part of her had known he was there, but she'd been completely focused on the other parts that were hurting. His close proximity made it harder to care about those other parts.

"I need to take a shower, wash my hair," she finally answered him.

"Then why do you look like you're about to sacrifice someone?"

Zee searched his face. "Why do you care?"

He pushed off the wall and crowded past her into the tiny bathroom. "Good question. I'm not sure I know the answer. I do care, though, for whatever reason. Tell me about your braids."

He stood behind her, not touching, but she could feel his

heat. She met his eyes in the mirror. The only harm in telling him was in baring a part of herself she didn't normally share, but she'd been learning that he wanted to know because he wanted to help. It was his way of offering support.

"I'm surprised you don't already know. You have access to most of our knowledge."

His lips curled into a half-smile. "Yeah, and I'm definitely going to use that access to search for an explanation of Fae braids."

"I try not to make assumptions." She returned his smile as she finished unraveling the main braid and let the hair spread out behind her. "The braids serve two tasks. One is to maintain an unobstructed line of sight when in battle. The other is a visual demonstration of our roles in the community." She broke eye contact to start working through the tangles on one side. Ryan surprised her by threading his fingers through the strands and gently separating the other.

"We were a warrior people once. It was necessary for our way of life because there have always been bigger and stronger creatures who correlate size with strength. Our best warriors, both physical and magical, became what you would consider tribal leaders. Some chose to train for that role, and when a skill was mastered, they were taught the appropriate binding as a mark of honor. Most chose to use it in their hair, I know of a few that wear cords instead."

The gentle tugging on her scalp was calming, and telling the story helped distract her from grieving for what she'd lost.

"Your hair is so soft. I always thought warriors had rough hair from all the time spent outside killing people."

Zee snorted out a laugh. "It's more ceremonial at this

point. My people have a tendency to cling to traditions even when they're no longer useful."

"Does that mean you can't kill someone with one finger?"

She met his eyes briefly and let him read the truth there. "Before, I could kill someone without touching them. Now, I suspect it will take more effort, but I'm not powerless. I've earned my braids through more than magic."

I'm not powerless. The phrase echoed through her head. It was the truth, but at the same time, it felt false. Brute force, useful in certain situations, did no good against her increasing need to lean back against Ryan and let go. Power, though, wasn't what she was trying to maintain. At this point, she wasn't even sure *what* she was clinging to. She'd already lost everything she cared about, what more could she lose? *What more, indeed?*

Ryan's hand spread over her scalp and pulled, unraveling her past along with the knots in her hair. "What if you didn't go back?"

She'd grappled with the same question all week. "Then most likely Lana would take over leadership, unless she was challenged, but I trained her myself and I have faith in her abilities." His fingers trailed over the nape of her neck, and Zee shivered. "The Glade would survive without me, but what would I be?" She hadn't meant to ask that question, didn't really expect a response from him.

"You'd be Zee, warrior princess, trainer of magics, binder of braids ...eater of donuts." She elbowed him in the stomach lightly and he laughed. "You'd keep what you value about yourself and find new things to braid into your hair."

Tears threatened. Ryan believed in his image of her, and she wanted to believe too.

"This side is free." He moved back as far as the confines

of the bathroom would allow. Zee still had a few inches of braids to work through.

She'd never put much thought into her appearance, form was fluid after all, but sharing a tiny space with Ryan made her acutely aware of the details. His eyes traced her arms, her back, her loose hair, and stopped on her face. He clearly liked this strong, capable form, and so did she, but she'd miss her wings. Flight was a thrill all its own.

Zee ran her fingers through the last of her hair. Without the braids holding it back, it was long and wild with waves. She faced Ryan and spread her hands at her sides. "Now what?"

"Now you shower. Don't think I haven't noticed that you've limited yourself to sponge baths all week." He reached over and closed the shower curtain, then turned on the water full-blast. The steam started gathering quickly, but Ryan didn't seem to be in a hurry to leave.

"I think I can handle the rest myself. I promise not to drown my sorrows in your bathroom."

He smiled. "That's not what drown your sorrows means. There's extra soap and stuff under the counter. We can talk more when you're done."

When he brushed by her this time, he had promises in his eyes. She lifted her hand and let it trail across his stomach because she wanted to touch him. The bond flared, and she got a rush of need he'd been holding back behind his shields. He wanted his hands in her hair, wanted her naked and writhing under the hot water. Like his shower earlier, Zee would have welcomed him. The bond went both ways. He knew, but he didn't pause. The door closed behind him, and she was left in the steam alone.

Zee knew it wouldn't have taken much to convince him. Despite the fire in her body, she told herself they both deserved more than a couple of hours of pleasure. She tossed her clothes in the corner by the door, but it offered little relief. Her senses remained heightened, and she could feel Ryan in the other room. The bond kept them connected, and Zee knew he was as aware of her as she was of him.

She found the soaps easily enough, and cleaning herself wasn't hard. The pulse of the hot water loosened her muscles, but she wanted a different kind of touch. She opened herself to the bond and with the image of Ryan locked in her mind, Zee let one hand slide down the slick skin of her neck. She let her fingers trail lazily across the curve of her breast and over her nipple. Her breath caught, and she let her eyes close. Ryan's need joined hers and pooled low in her belly.

She imagined his hand underneath hers, caressing her stomach and slipping lower. One stroke and she couldn't stop the whimper. He urged her on, urged her to find her pleasure and share it with him. Zee leaned back against the cool tile and tilted her hips forward for a better angle. She felt a kiss beneath her ear, a tongue against her collarbone, a pull against her breast, Ryan's phantom touch sent shock-waves of pleasure through her. Her breath sped up with her hand, and she approached climax. She bit her lip as she crested and a wave of satisfaction mixed with her pleasure.

Zee hadn't caught her breath when she sensed Ryan approaching the door, but he stayed firmly on the other side of it.

"The hot water won't last forever. I'm heading to bed." His voice was low and rough. Zee could feel he'd been affected, but disappointment cooled her. What had she been hoping? That their shared experience would bring them closer? *That he'd pick her over his fear.* He'd made his choice on the stairwell.

Zee didn't respond, and he didn't linger. She shut off the water and shivered in the rapidly chilling air. Ryan had retreated behind his shields, and she would be better off if she did the same. Too bad she craved his touch more now that she'd had a taste of the possibilities.

7

ZEE

Z<small>EE DIDN'T SLEEP</small> well that night, and Ryan was gone when she woke up. There were donuts on the counter and a new bottle of orange juice in the fridge. She toyed with the idea of trying to contact him, but after the shower incident, she thought he might need some space. Hell, *she* needed some space.

She took her breakfast to the table and found a note on top of the computer. It had instructions for how to access the database, along with a warning that the message would self-destruct in five seconds, which made no sense. Zee shook her head, and her loose hair tickled her face. She'd forgotten all about the database and their fight before dinner. A shift had happened with all the events of the past day. Her concern had expanded from herself and the Fae to include the effects on the humans in town, Jake, Sera, and Ryan in particular.

The computer instructions were precise, so Zee had no trouble accessing her supposedly secure database of Fae secrets. Several hours passed with her hunched over the keyboard. Eventually, the sun shifted enough to create an annoying glare on the screen that broke her out of her focus. She got up from the table and stretched. The data was searchable, but she didn't know what she was looking for. Centuries of information was a lot to sift through.

Zee checked the clock and frowned. Ryan hadn't been home all day, and it was well past lunch. He was free to avoid her if he liked, but she didn't think it would make much of a difference in the end. They'd been playing with fire last night, and the heavy usage on the bond strengthened it. She didn't need to search to feel him any longer. The knowledge was there in her mind. He wasn't close, but he was content with what he was doing.

Magic or no, they certainly appeared to be rocketing toward something inevitable.

She shook her head. Ryan wasn't ready yet, and he may never be. *I am* not *sad about that.*

Her focus needed to be putting her energy into an outcome she might be able to shape. She'd found the original pact with the Wood. There were no hidden components beyond what she already knew. Zee wandered to the window to stare out at the park across the street.

There was mention of a sacrifice to demonstrate commitment, a requirement to give as well as receive in the interaction. The Fae gave up their freedom in exchange for the barriers around Torix. She'd been born in the Glade, and she'd assumed she'd die there. That's why it had been so important to find a way to connect with the outside world. Evie and her family had paved the way, initiating contact, and Zee would be always grateful for her kindness. Without Ryan though, they'd still be wallowing in ignorance.

The Wood didn't care. It wasn't sentient as far as anyone could tell, but it *was* powerful. To use the magic, her ancestors had to offer something up in return. What had she said to Sera all those weeks ago about her bond with Jake? *A gilded cage.* Without the cage, why wasn't the town overrun with Fae?

What had replaced it?

The information about the Wood before the pact was sparse. An elemental forest, a conduit of magical power, a nexus. If it didn't make conscious decisions, why was her magic locked inside her? The worst case scenario should have been them losing the protections, but Zee suspected more had happened. When she'd stuck her hand into the shadows to pull Ryan back, she'd detected something else. Not anger or anything so direct, but a defensiveness. The feeling was too vague to properly search for in the database, so she'd started looking into magical bonds instead.

Mulligan was full of people with some level of power. The Wood drew them. *Like calls to like.* Unfortunately, the Fae didn't care much about the humans beyond their connection to the world outside the Wood. Magic was magic, but something about the humans made it act a tad differently.

Zee *knew* she and Ryan had been bound. She also knew they'd done it to themselves, but she couldn't figure out how. Her best guess was that without her to guide the magic, his had attempted to follow some convoluted intention between them. Without knowing the specific intention, Zee was uncomfortable removing the bond. *Not that I can at the moment anyway.*

A loud ringing startled her. Ryan had a phone attached to the wall in his kitchen, which she'd thought was decorative until that moment. Someone was calling him. Zee shrugged and answered it.

"Hello?"

"Hey, it's Sera. I set up the warrior princess class for tomorrow evening. I hope it's enough warning, but there's been a lot of interest today and it was the only time the gym was free."

Zee switched ears and reached for her glass. "That should be fine. I assume someone will come get me as I have no intention of driving."

"Ryan is going to take you. I already talked to him. I also made fun of him for having a landline and told him to get you a cell phone if he was going to be avoiding you."

"He admitted he's avoiding me?"

"Of course not, but I know. He's a homebody, and he's spending his day off at the school volunteering to do maintenance on the computer lab? Yeah, right. He likes his job, but he loves his free time. He's avoiding you. Want to talk about it?"

It was strange having someone want to talk about her feelings. Strange, but nice. Zee was grateful, if unwilling to talk to anyone about Ryan just yet. "No, thank you. Maybe some other time. Is there any news on Will?"

Sera sighed. "Not yet. Jake is having a mechanic friend from Kilgore loan him a car, but we can't get it until Tuesday. I've been keeping an eye on the Wood, at least the part I can see from the living room window, but there haven't been any weird shadows or anything."

Zee frowned. She didn't want anyone else wandering into a confused elemental forest, but it was disturbing that nothing else had triggered it. *Could I have done it?* She'd been standing next to Ryan when the shadows emerged. Perhaps the bait had been for her. To be safe, she'd stay away from the Wood until they had more information.

"Zee? You still there?"

She'd almost forgotten Sera. "Yes, I'm sorry. I appreciate your vigilance. Will you let me know if anything changes?"

"Sure, but do you think people are really in danger if they go into the woods?"

"I'm not sure. Ryan wasn't harmed, but he *was* prevented from leaving. It may be that when the Wood returns to normal we'll find a pocket of townspeople who wandered in at the wrong time. Has anyone been reported missing?"

"No, thank goodness, and Jake has been spreading the word to stay away from the forest for now. People trust him, and everyone around here knows that sometimes you don't ask questions."

The sentiment made sense. A town founded on a conduit of elemental energy, next to a Fae village, full of people with varying levels of magic was somewhere that strange occurrences would happen with regularity. A thought slowly took hold. *What if she was asking questions of the wrong people?* She'd have to think on that a bit more. "If that's all, I have studying to do."

"What are you studying?"

"The Fae. I'll see you tomorrow night." Zee hung up without waiting for a response. Knowing Sera, she'd keep asking questions until dusk. She eyed the angle of the sun and debated if she wanted to be in the main living space when Ryan returned. The laptop worked as well in her bedroom as anywhere else.

Her stomach rumbled as she was unplugging it from the wall. She'd skipped lunch and only had juice and pastries for breakfast. If she was intent on doing her own avoiding, she'd better eat something. She dug through the pantry for the cereal she liked and grabbed a couple of bananas. It would hold her over until morning.

When she heard Ryan come home, Zee sat cross-legged on the bed with the computer in her lap, scrolling through advanced spells for gathering the magic of others. Her door was closed, but his footsteps hesitated as he walked past. She willed him to keep walking, and whether through magic or good instincts, he moved on to the kitchen. They hadn't seen each other since they'd unbraided her hair, and she'd hoped the separation would ease the ache. Magic didn't work that way, though.

Zee reinforced her shields in an attempt to concentrate on the words in front of her, but the bond had burrowed underneath. She could sense his every movement as he made himself some food and went into his room. Her body tried to convince her that keeping her distance was the height of stupidity, but she didn't trust the way she acted around him. It was too easy to become distracted and let other concerns fall to the wayside.

She had to admit that human life wasn't so bad, barring the disconnection from the natural world. As the days passed, she became fonder of the vibrant and surprising nuances. The longer she was away from the Glade, the more it seemed like a far-away dream. She'd stopped reaching for her magic as a first response to everything, and she was a huge fan of showering.

Despite all that, she could feel her magic curled up inside her, and the Wood required a sacrifice to maintain balance with the Fae living inside it. Although now that they didn't need to keep Torix and his evil magic contained, maybe that sacrifice didn't need to involve barriers at all. She'd have to consider the human impact as well, but none of this mattered if she couldn't get back to the Glade. As

much as Zee liked aspects of the human world, she couldn't
stay.

───────

IN THE MORNING, Zee found a cell phone at her spot on the
table with another note. *I'll be back at 5 to take you to the
school.* Nothing else. She powered on the phone and scrolled
through the contacts. He'd preloaded himself, Jake, and
Sera, and it came with emergency numbers, not that she
needed them. It was older than her previous phone, heavier
and with no touch screen, but it would do. She left it where
she'd found it, and moved the laptop back onto the table.

Her neck was sore from staring down at it yesterday, and
she felt safe from interruption in the kitchen with Ryan at
work. The abundance of information surprised her with
how much she didn't know about her own people. They had
schools of a sort, but very little was taught that referenced
their history. She'd never considered it important, but
knowing more about the past could have prevented many of
the current problems. It was another change she was going
to have to institute in the Glade.

The rest of the day passed with Zee reading tedious
manuscripts. They'd scanned all the documents, so if the
originals had small script, she had to squint to make it out.
Her head was throbbing, and she wasn't sure how to heal it
without magic. Zee closed the laptop with fifteen minutes to
spare so she could stretch and change into clothes that
moved with her. The jeans were functional, but she
preferred yoga pants.

───────

RYAN

THERE WERE some days Ryan thought about faking his death and living out his life alone on a tropical island. When the kids were too rowdy to listen and the lab had problem after problem, he just wanted a beer and some quiet in his own home. Unfortunately, that wasn't on the menu. Zee was in his home, and the quiet surrounding her was driving him insane.

Ryan admitted he'd been avoiding her, but she was doing the same. After the shower incident, which was by far the hottest thing he'd experienced in his life, he'd tossed and turned dreaming of her. He wanted to believe that what he felt was real, but he couldn't bring himself to trust the magic between them. How could he know? He'd be damned if he became involved with Zee because some outside force said so. He deserved to be wanted for himself. *Great. Now I sound like one of those sappy movies Sera is always watching.*

Ryan came in the door scowling. Zee sat on the couch in the living room with her back to him, and his pulse sped up at his first look at her in days. She'd pulled all that glorious hair back into a single braid, and he wondered if it signified anything. Probably that she wanted to kick someone's ass, and her hair had been in her face.

"Ready to go?"

She grimaced at him. "What do humans do for a headache?"

Ryan went into the bathroom and came back with a bottle of pills. He pulled one out for himself and tossed the rest to her. "Tylenol. Swallow one, it should help." He followed his own instructions and watched her grimace as she tried to down it dry.

He went into the kitchen and filled a glass from the tap,

then handed it to her. "This'll help. Long day?"

Zee chugged the water before she answered. "My eyes feel gritty. Some of the documents are tiny and impossible to read." She got up to put the glass in the sink and rubbed her temples.

Ryan crossed his arms so he didn't reach out and replace her hands with his own. "Have you found anything useful?"

"I can tell you how many Fae it took to build the stone circle and when exactly the pact took place, but that's the closest I've come. There's a lot to sort through still."

She didn't meet his eyes, and he knew she was keeping something back. The Fae didn't lie, but omitting some truth was totally acceptable. He wasn't going to push. These were her secrets, for her people. Besides, he wanted to know about their other problem.

"What about the bond?"

"The best I can come up with is that it was an accidental spell. Magic can't do things on its own, it needs guidance. Yours takes an...unconventional path. We made a deal that we both considered binding, and the magic bound us."

The idea made a kind of sense, but it also reinforced his point that magic was unpredictable and dangerous. "Is there an off switch?"

Zee sighed and rubbed her temples again. "Not that I can see. Without clear parameters, I'm not sure what the bond is tied into. We could take the chance on Sera removing it, but—"

"No. We'll keep looking." As much as he hated another rein, he wasn't going to risk Zee.

Ryan finally gave in to himself and brushed her hands away, stepping close. He rubbed her temples with his thumbs and concentrated on making her head stop hurting, instead of the feel of her skin or the warmth of her body just inches from him. A red glow emanated from his hands where they touched her, then subsided. He hadn't meant to call his magic, but he hadn't fought it like he normally would either. Zee sighed and relaxed almost instantly, leaning briefly into him.

"Thank you." She covered his hands with hers, tilting her chin to meet his eyes. "I know you don't want to hear this, but you have a lot of potential. You instinctively know how to use your magic, when you trust yourself."

Danger Will Robinson. Ryan pulled his hands away and moved back. "I'm glad your headache is gone." Strangely, his was gone too. He didn't want to think too deeply about that. "We really should go though. Can't have you being late for your first warrior princess class."

RYAN PULLED into a surprisingly full parking lot at the school. They didn't have a large lot to begin with, but he hadn't expected *this* much interest in Zee's class. Part of it was probably curiosity at the newcomer, but knowing Zee, they'd learn something useful in addition to gossip fodder. He spotted Jake holding the door open so it wouldn't lock and assumed Sera was already inside with the others.

Zee got out of the car and straightened her shoulders. She'd been distracted since he'd gotten rid of her headache, but now he watched her step into her role of leader with ease. Her body relaxed and she walked with confidence. She was most comfortable here, as the bearer of knowledge and power. Ryan followed her, but hung back and stopped next to Jake at the entrance. Zee didn't notice, her eyes were already cataloguing the women gathered on the bleachers.

It wasn't limited to women either. There were a couple of

teenage boys, and Mr. Hogan was in the back attempting to blend in with the wall.

"How did Sera get so many people in only a day?"

"Turns out gathering people is her superpower."

"Doesn't she have enough of those already?"

Jake shrugged. "I figure she deserves as many as she can get after what she went through."

"Speaking of that, can I ask you some stuff about what Zee did to you guys? The bond thing, I mean."

Jake gave him a searching look. "Sure, but you don't usually ask first."

Zee was starting the class, so Ryan took a couple of steps inside and leaned against the wall. Jake kicked the door-stop down, followed him, and waited.

Ryan took a deep breath. *Now or never.* "Did you ever wonder if your reaction to Sera was because of the bond or magic or anything like that?"

Jake shifted awkwardly, and they both stared straight ahead. "No. All the bond did was make it more obvious. It's harder to deny feeling something if it's obvious to both of you. But was it caused by magic? Hell, no. I've wanted Sera since she was seventeen." He grimaced. "And that sounded creepy, even though we were *both* seventeen. Let's forget that last part and never tell Sera."

Ryan laughed under his breath. He was definitely going to keep it a secret right up until he needed to use it for blackmail.

Jake snuck a glance at him. "Why do you care?"

Zee smiled and demonstrated something with her hands. She held the attention of the audience effortlessly, and Ryan didn't want to look away. Maybe Jake would understand the sentiment.

"There's a solid chance that I accidentally bonded Zee

and me together. Since then…" He was going to say she'd been driving him crazy, but that wasn't accurate. She'd always driven him crazy, but he'd had a better hold on it. It was like Jake had said; the bond made it impossible to hide.

Jake chimed in. "You can't stop thinking about her, you want to touch her all the time, you tell yourself to stay away but then come running back the second she might need you?"

Ryan blew out a breath. "Yeah. That pretty much nails it."

"Sorry, man. That's not magic." Jake shook his head in mock pity, then sauntered over to the group with his hands in his pockets.

Ryan stayed where he was by the door. He told himself it was so he could direct any stragglers, but the truth was he didn't trust himself to be close to Zee. Her confidence was sexy as hell, and he hadn't noticed until now, when she was back in her element, how much of it had drained away while she was dealing with everything.

Her braid swung as she answered questions, and he had to give Sera credit for finding better clothes on the second go-round. The black leggings showcased every muscle in Zee's long legs, and though the top came down to mid-thigh, it skimmed the curves he dreamed about getting his hands on again. She'd even found a green color to match Zee's eyes. Eyes that searched the gym, and flared with heat when they landed on him. She didn't linger, and he felt the loss when she turned back to the assembly to organize them into groups.

If Jake was right and it wasn't magic, then he was in a lot of trouble.

ZEE

Zee had never been inside a gym before. All her previous training sessions had been outside on dirt-packed ground. This place was sheltered from the cold, well-lit, and had mats on the floor to protect the participants. It also had over twenty people excited to learn how to defend themselves. They listened intently as she explained the purpose of the class, to provide protection when needed. She didn't want the moves she taught them to be use offensively for any reason. The boys tittered, but she quelled them with a glare.

After her introduction, she separated them into groups, two pairs each with one larger person matched to a smaller person. It was easier to defend against someone smaller, but she believed people should learn what was useful rather than easy. That meant the smaller people needed to learn how to defend against larger opponents.

There were an even number of people, so she ended up without a partner to demonstrate. Jake had declined to join in the class, and Ryan continued to stand by the door like some kind of sentinel. It didn't matter for the first section. To her surprise, the townsfolk picked up on the basic moves easily. They practiced with a determined focus not often seen in her recent Fae trainees. She supposed the Fae were becoming complacent. Life didn't change much in the Glade, and when it did, it brought Netflix.

She'd planned for the class to be an hour and a half. Twenty minutes of explanation followed by an hour of practice with a couple of breaks. At the first break, she determined that they needed to move on to some more complicated lessons. Ryan had pulled out his phone by that point, but he hadn't moved any closer. She thought Jake might be asleep on the bleachers.

It was nice that they'd come for support, but now she needed at least one of them to participate. She glanced at Ryan, but moved on before he noticed. *Too distracting.* It would have to be Jake.

He was lying on the bench with his arms crossed behind his head and his eyes closed. Zee walked up to him and nudged him with her toe. He popped one eye open.

"Time to go?"

She smiled. "Time to help. I need you to come up here so I can demonstrate the proper way to dislocate your arm."

He got up and stretched. "Well, when you put it that way, how could I say no?"

Zee felt Ryan's eyes on her as Jake followed her back to the center mat. Of course he was paying attention now, when she needed to concentrate on not actually hurting Jake. A benefit to teaching Fae that she didn't have among the humans was that if she accidentally injured one of her own people, they were in the middle of a group of healers. Here, there'd be a lot more paperwork, and questions.

She whistled once to get people's attention, then began the second half of the class.

"Jake has kindly agreed to partner me for this section. You'll notice each pair of you has a size discrepancy. For this series, I'll give instructions to the larger individual, then the smaller, then we'll practice the move."

One of the teenage boys raised his hand. "Is the bigger person going to get to practice?"

Zee smiled. He was lean, but tall, and paired with a tiny woman twice his age. "Of course. After a few iterations, we'll switch the pairs in the group and the bigger people can practice on each other. Like I said at the beginning, it's rare for someone to have to defend against a smaller enemy. Size alone is the best deterrent."

The boy nodded, and Zee made sure everyone else was paying attention. Mr. Hogan, who was working with Sera, still looked like he might puke, but the rest were eager to start.

"We'll begin with escaping a wrist grab." She faced Jake and relaxed her shoulders. "I want you to grab my left wrist with your right hand. I'm going to squeeze and twist. Don't fight the motion for now." She made eye contact with several of the larger people in the class. "That goes for everyone. When they twist your wrist, go with the motion to avoid getting hurt. We'll work up to a strength match later. For now, we're teaching our bodies what the move feels like."

Zee nodded at Jake, and he grabbed her wrist as instructed. "First, you tuck your elbow into your side and pull your arm up so your palm is facing you. His hand is now underneath mine and bent back." She demonstrated a few times and most of them mimicked her movements. Good, they needed to internalize the action to make it the most useful. "Next, you use your other hand to secure the position by placing it around their wrist, palm facing you." Again, she showed them a few times to be sure everyone saw it.

"Here's the fun part. Keep your elbow tucked in, and squeeze with that free hand. You're going to rotate their wrist outward by turning your hips. Don't move your elbow, you'll lose your strength. Turn your hips and look in that direction." She swiveled, and Jake took an involuntary step forward, losing his grip on her wrist. Zee was holding Jake's arm, and he was bent at an awkward angle. She held the pose for a second because people loved drama, then let him loose.

Everyone applauded, and Zee tried not to blush. It was

a simple wrist grab, but they acted like she'd done something amazing. Humans were strange. She showed them a couple more times, both slow and at full speed. No one had any questions, so she had them pair up and start practicing.

Jake headed back to the bleachers, and Zee observed and corrected as needed. Walking around, she could separate those eager to learn from those who'd come out of curiosity. All of them were doing their best, but for some, their best was more intense than others. Sera, especially, was putting her whole body into the movement. She wasn't trying to break her partner's hold; she was trying to break his wrist.

Inside, Zee was proud of her. There was no point in learning self-defense if they were too skittish to make the moves count. Unfortunately, Mr. Hogan was one of the curious ones.

Zee approached them as Sera performed the move and her partner winced. "Okay, Sera. That's good, but Mr. Hogan looks like he could use a break."

"I think you're right. Sera, do you mind if I bow out? I'm afraid I might be too old to be a warrior princess." He massaged his wrist as he spoke.

Sera patted his shoulder. "Don't worry about it, Mr. Hogan. You did great. Why don't you go sit by Jake, he's got the packages of gummy dinosaurs we're going to pass out after class."

But Zee waved Jake over from the stands. "Sera needs a new partner." Jake grinned, and Zee left to check on the other groups. He'd probably be regretting that grin shortly.

They practiced the wrist grab, switched aggressors so the second half could try it, and worked on the same move with the opposite hand. Zee used Jake to demonstrate again, then sent him back to the vicious Sera, if Jake's grumbling was to be believed.

Five minutes before the scheduled end of class, Zee was doing the final debriefing. Almost all the people who'd come had stayed to the end, even Mr. Hogan was still sitting on the bleachers, though he never came back down to participate. She had an odd sense of accomplishment looking over the sweating, smiling people. This wasn't her first training class, but it was the first time the class had been optional for the people taking it. She finished the way she always had, asking if there were any questions.

Sera raised her hand. "Can you show us what these moves would look like in the real world?"

Zee considered it, but didn't think she could make it work. She'd need a partner who knew how to spar or it would be a quick match. She shook her head and opened her mouth to answer, but Ryan interrupted first.

"I can help."

He'd come closer while she hadn't been paying attention, so Zee sized him up. She'd seen him spar with some of her people before, and she knew he was in good shape. Most of the participants had already moved to sit in the bleachers while she talked, and they watched her and Ryan with interest. If she agreed, they'd be more likely to return for the next class, and they'd probably bring more people. *When did I start wanting to do another class?* Sera started passing out little clear bags of snacks. Probably the gummy dinosaurs she'd mentioned earlier.

Zee nodded. "Very well. Ryan and I will demonstrate the moves you worked on tonight." She raised a brow. "If he can move in those jeans." Scattered laughter and calls of encouragement came from the audience.

A slow grin spread across Ryan's face. "Try me, princess."

8

ZEE

A THRILL of anticipation went through Zee. She hadn't had a good training session since she'd left the Glade to defend it against Torix, and Ryan was competent. Then there was the added bonus of having a valid excuse to touch him. Despite all the reasons she shouldn't let him close, she wanted his hands on her.

Ryan toed his shoes off, and they faced each other on the mat. The chatter from the people watching quieted to a low hush. Zee pushed the gym, the class, and the people out of her mind. She focused solely on Ryan and her training.

Their eyes met, and the fire there told her he was looking forward to this as much as she was. She nodded, and they began circling each other. Neither dropped into a defensive stance per se, but they were both ready to move at a moment's notice. Ryan shifted his weight slightly, and Zee decided to let him grab her. She needed to demonstrate some of the moves before having her fun.

He shot forward, and she left an arm within his reach.

As she'd planned, he grabbed her wrist, and she was able to break the hold in the way she'd shown the class. Instead of letting go as they'd been doing, she used his momentum to wrench his arm around and up behind his back. A few of the spectators clapped, but Ryan quickly broke free and tried to grab her legs.

Zee moved back, but not fast enough. He got a hold on one ankle and pulled her off-balance. Instead of toppling to the ground, she jumped and kicked him in the chest hard enough for him to release her other foot, which she landed on. Ryan stumbled back a few steps, then closed in again.

They were within reach of each other, but both were breathing hard and circling. She couldn't stop the smile from spreading across her face. The class was muttering, but Zee shut them out. Ryan was faster than she remembered, and she didn't want to miss his tell.

He shifted his weight again and advanced with a strike at her face. She blocked, but he slid one hand behind her neck to keep them locked together. Her hand wrapped around his wrist intending to break his grip on her neck, but he'd slid his free arm around her waist and yanked her forward. She braced herself against his shoulder, but he'd already twisted his hips. Too late, she realized his plan.

Zee went flying past his hip and onto her back on the mat. That hadn't been a free shot; he'd done it all on his own. His hand behind her neck had shifted to her head and cushioned her fall as he followed her down.

He dropped his full weight on top of her, sliding a leg between hers and pulling her arms straight above her head. In any other setting, she'd be moaning. As it was, she had to bite her lip from making inappropriate noises. He was hard against her thigh, and she thoroughly enjoyed the pressure while it was there. His hair tickled her cheek as he leaned down to whisper in her ear.

"It's not a competition, but I'm winning."

Zee made a husky, non-committal noise and pushed up hard to the side with her hips. Ryan rolled with it, but she was able to break his wrist hold again while they moved. She found her footing and spun around him, holding onto his arm with both hands. His shoulder ended up between her thighs, with one calf wrapped around his neck. It only took a second of painful pressure on his arm for him to concede.

"You win. Let go."

Zee released him and stood, then offered her hand to him. The entire group burst into applause. Ryan jumped up, but didn't let go. He raised their hands and then brought them both down in a bow. Zee inclined her head, then gasped when Ryan's thumb trailed across her palm in a lazy caress. A ribbon of heat pulled taut between her hand and core, but they were literally standing in front of an audience.

Zee drew herself up into instructor mode. "Thank you, everyone, for coming. Remember that this was simply the beginning of what you can learn to defend yourself."

"Will there be another class?" She couldn't see who'd shouted it, but it'd sounded like one of the teenage boys. Sera sent her a questioning look.

"I'll be glad to teach another class if the gym is available and I'm still in town. Sera can keep you updated."

Someone muttered for Ryan to give her a reason to stay, but again, she couldn't pinpoint the voice. It *had* sounded suspiciously like Jake.

Ryan pulled her toward the door. "The secretary said to leave everything here and the gym kids would clean it up in the morning. The doors will lock automatically after us."

"We should make sure everyone else is gone first."

"We will." Most of the others were ahead of them, but a few stragglers were chatting by the mats. Ryan led her past the edge of the bleachers but then ducked sideways into the shadows. He backed her against the wall, grabbing her other hand, and Zee found herself hidden by his body in the alcove under the stands. Their joined hands curled behind her, and he pulled her flush against him. Scorching excitement burst forth with a ragged breath, and she had to lock her knees to keep from melting into him.

"I could make you let me go," she said.

"I know, but you won't." He whispered it across her lips.

Zee waited for him to close the distance, and when he didn't move, she did it for him. The kiss started out soft and sweet, but Zee didn't want sweet. She wanted fire.

She pressed against him, her tongue sweeping across his lower lip, and his arms tightened around her. His head tilted, and he claimed her mouth fully. If she hadn't kept her shields locked for the entire evening, she might have been prepared, but his energy pushed at her until she surrendered and let him in. His mouth plundered hers, and Zee arched against him. This was what she'd wanted since that night at Jake's. Since the shower.

The room around them disappeared, and Zee lost herself in the waves of delicious need crashing into her through the bond. She'd have stayed there all night, but the sound of the door slamming closed penetrated her fog. She tore her mouth away and tried to catch her breath. Ryan rested his forehead against hers and recovered a smidge faster.

"We really should head out now." His voice was rough, and he didn't move.

He was right, but Zee wasn't entirely sure she could walk

straight. Judging by the feel of him pressed against her hip, he definitely couldn't. Their shields were down, and this kiss felt different than the last. He wasn't fighting his reactions.

Zee extricated herself gently and leaned against the wall. The coolness of the plaster seeped into her and slowly calmed her racing blood. "What changed?"

Ryan didn't pretend to misunderstand her, but with both of them open, she knew the moment he chose not to answer her. He shrugged one shoulder then winced. "That was a nice armbar. I wasn't expecting it."

"If you'd been expecting it, it wouldn't have worked. You shift your weight in a particular way when you're about to attack. I can help you with that if you'd like."

He rubbed his shoulder and shook his head. "Maybe next time. All I want right now is a hot shower and some pita chips. Sparring with you was fun, but I'm not planning to enter any competitions or anything." He gestured toward the door with his good arm. "After you."

Zee pushed off the wall and preceded him out of the gym. She didn't think she'd had pita chips yet. The air crackled between them as they approached the car. Ryan walked next to her, and there was a magnetic pull every time his arm brushed hers. She wanted to pick up where they'd left off, but he hadn't mentioned her in his plans for the night.

"What are pita chips?"

"Like potato chips but made with pita bread instead, imagine the love child between a cracker and a chip."

Zee settled into silence. The disparity between the intense longing she was getting from the bond and the bland conversation they were having was confusing. She wasn't sure what to say. They stopped on opposite sides of the car, and Ryan met her eyes.

"I'd love to finish what we started, but I have another responsibility tonight." He frowned, but she could sense he wouldn't compromise his plans. Whatever they were. He must have noticed her confusion because he shot her a wry grin. "It's raid night."

Zee tried unsuccessfully to hide her smile. She knew what that meant. Chad was on the verge of ineptitude because he put all his effort into playing video games instead of his duties with the Fae. Many of her people played games, but Chad was the only one she knew of who had a raid night. Now that she thought about it, his was the same night.

She narrowed her eyes. "Do you play with Chad?"

A laugh burst out of Ryan, and it dissolved some of the tension. "You sound so disapproving. Yeah, Chad and I used to play together, but he's hardcore so he left our group for a tougher one."

"Has he been playing in the last month?"

Ryan stilled as he thought about it. "I'm not sure. We don't hang out much anymore, so I don't track his comings and goings. I don't think so, though."

Zee deflated a little. She'd hoped they'd stumbled on a way to contact someone in the Glade, even if it was Chad. "Can you check tonight?"

"Of course."

They got into the car, and Zee stared out the window. Her body demanded she convince him she was worth skipping raid night, but she respected the act of showing up when other people were depending on it. Especially with a pastime many considered trivial. Chad could benefit from applying that lesson to other aspects of his life.

Ryan turned on the radio, but it didn't mask the electric current running between them. She had goosebumps all over. Unlike the last few times, when the kissing had stopped, Ryan hadn't immediately retreated behind his shields. Something must have happened during class that had made Ryan open himself up to her and stay that way. While she was curious what had changed his mind, she was happy enough to simply accept the benefit. Maybe all it took was a hip throw and an armbar to convince him that their connection was real.

Neither spoke for the rest of the ride, but Zee could feel that he was torn between her and his friends online. She was less torn, but there was a deep-seated fear that if she gave in, he'd expect more of her than she was able to give. It was probably for the best that they both had other pursuits to occupy them at home.

Zee followed him into the apartment, then hesitated. It seemed rude to withdraw to her room without acknowledging him, but she didn't think it was a good idea to prolong the evening. In truth, she didn't trust herself not to try and convince him to skip his raid.

When she roused from her thoughts, he was staring at her contemplatively. She wasn't the only one reconsidering his plans for the evening.

"Are you going to go back to your research?" he asked.

Zee arched a brow. "Are you going to play your game?"

He laughed low and ran a hand through his hair. "Yeah. I think I should, but I'm not hiding anymore. You and I are going to finish this eventually."

"We'll see." She walked into her bedroom without looking back and closed the door. The bond ensured that she knew when he moved to stand on the other side of the flimsy wood. They stayed there, both aware of the other person, both regretting their decisions, until Zee pushed away. She'd work, as she'd said she would, and ignore his presence in the apartment and her mind. Ryan went to his room shortly after.

Zee's lips curled in a small smile. They'd separated themselves physically, but the connection remained open and strong. It was a turning point, an acceptance, and she couldn't wait for what it brought.

RYAN

RYAN DIDN'T SEE Zee nearly as much as he wanted until the last day of school before winter break. The difference was this time he wasn't *purposely* avoiding her for three days. His classes were insane, and the administration decided that the second longest week of the school year was the perfect time to roll out a new policy that involved office time.

He had to be in his office a certain number of hours of the day since he wasn't teaching a full load of classes, but his office was a computer lab filled with desperate students. If he never had to recover another accidentally deleted file, he'd be happy. The constant stress made his day long enough that by the time he got home, all he had the energy for was food, mindless TV, and sleep.

After talking to Jake on Monday night, he'd decided to see what would happen if he stopped fighting the bond. It relieved a great deal of the pressure from always trying to protect himself, but the continual access to Zee added a new kind of pressure. The fun kind that came with imagining her naked almost constantly. Unfortunately, there had been no naked time.

Zee was always there when he got home, and she'd tried her hand at cooking the last two days. They'd ordered pizza the first night after she'd burned the frozen waffles, but the rest of it had been edible. It meant a lot to him that she'd work on learning a new skill to help make his life a little easier.

The highlight of his day was coming home to find Zee in the kitchen muttering at one of the appliances. He loved being able to walk over and drop a kiss on her without being handed his balls. After dinner, they'd talk about anything new she'd found during her searching and try to come up with a game plan. She was still advocating for the 'kidnap Will and make him talk' plan, especially since his raid group hadn't heard from Chad since Halloween. He was personally behind that plan, but he wasn't going to tell her that. The bond probably clued her in that he wasn't totally against it, but she didn't push too hard.

As much as he wanted to chug an energy drink in the evenings and follow through on their promises, he limited himself to enjoying her snuggled against him on the couch. Any time things started to progress, she stiffened up a little. He wasn't even sure she was aware of it, but he wasn't going to make moves when she wasn't ready. Each night, he'd gone to bed hard and aching, but she was getting more comfortable in his world. And he wanted her there, wanted her to stay.

He wasn't ready to share that particular fantasy with her yet.

On Thursday, though, a virus got loose on the school network, and he spent all day chasing it down. When he finally got the infected computers separated, one of the aides from the main office told him they needed him to stay late for an extracurricular. The normal teacher had gone home sick. He'd gotten so fed up, his magic had escaped and fried the computer closest to him, startling them both when it sparked and began smoking. The aide had left in a hurry, and Ryan had considered chucking the damn thing out the second story window.

By the time he got home that evening, he was in a foul mood. He'd spent the rest of the afternoon keeping a tight leash on his power and found that it was easier if he closed his shields completely. As a result, he managed to surprise Zee when he inadvertently slammed the door open in his frustration with the day. She jumped and squeaked, which would've been funny if she hadn't been holding a pot of boiling water.

A splash hit her bare wrist, and she sucked in air through her teeth. Ryan dropped his stuff on the floor and rushed over to grab the pot out of her hands. He set the spaghetti back on the stove and gently rotated her arm so he could look at it.

There was an angry red splotch on the inside of her fore-arm, but it didn't look like it was blistering. She hissed when he got too close and tried to pull away.

"We need to put this under cold water."

She nodded, and he cranked the faucet. He'd been pissed and half-angry before, but now he was filled with guilt. All his worries about hurting people with magic, and he'd managed it with hot water alone. She was clearly capable of holding her own arm under the flow, but he didn't move away.

Zee clenched her jaw as the water hit her, but her shoulders relaxed a bit when his arms came around her. He held her injured arm immobile and wished he could take some of the pain away.

"I made pasta." She sounded both annoyed and proud.

"I see that. We'll keep the burn here for a couple more

minutes then I think I have some aloe in the bathroom. I'm sorry."

"You're forgiven. Besides, this is kind of nice." She leaned back into him, and he kissed the top of her shoulder.

"There are easier ways to get me to hold you than first-degree burns."

She snorted. "Are you sure? We seem to do everything in the hardest way possible."

They stood in comfortable silence for a few minutes, and the stress of his day faded. Zee smelled like coconut. He didn't remember buying any coconut scented products, but Sera was always bringing girly stuff over to his place. The more he breathed her in, the more he relaxed his shields. After having been open to her the last few days, he didn't like feeling the barrier between them.

The red on her arm was slowly turning pink, but he could tell she was still in a lot of pain. He rubbed his thumb over the soft skin of her wrist and willed the burn to fade. As he watched, a dark red wave of magic washed over her arm and sank into her skin. Zee immediately sighed in relief. He wasn't sure what he'd just done, but he was happy that he'd helped.

The magic didn't freak him out for once, and the red mark disappeared. She beamed at him over her shoulder. *Completely worth it.*

"You healed it."

He shut off the water and backed away to reach for a hand towel. "I did *something*."

She dried off her arm and leaned over to kiss him on the cheek. "Healing is one of the tougher skills to learn. It seems you have a natural affinity for it."

Ryan didn't want to talk about magic. He wanted to pull her

back against him, without injuries this time, and see if any parts
of her tasted as good as she smelled. Instead, he shrugged and
backed out of the kitchen. She met his eyes as he sat at the
breakfast bar, and he saw the same need reflected there. Apparently, they were both going to ignore it for the time being.

She tossed the towel onto the counter and picked up
where she'd left off with the spaghetti. He loved spaghetti,
but he wasn't particularly hungry for food at the moment.
Just to torture her a little, he imagined what her skin would
feel like if he trailed his fingers down her bare arm.

Zee's breath got ragged, but she ignored him. He could
feel through the bond that she wanted to finish making
dinner, but where she normally held some part of herself
back, he had access to everything this time. Her reservations
were still there, but she'd moved past them.

"You need another magic lesson."

His attention snapped back to her face. "I thought you
said I had an affinity for healing."

"Yes, so you should practice with it and improve. It was
part of our bargain."

She was bustling around heating up sauce and meatballs, but her enthusiasm came through loud and clear. It
was important to her. Ryan thought about the disaster at
school with the now blackened computer. He'd been frustrated and angry, and not interested in keeping a handle on
it. Worse, he hadn't known how to handle it once the erup-
tion was over. He spent all day near electronics, and his
magic was too much of a risk in its untrained state.

School was out for two and a half weeks over winter
break. It was time he finally did the responsible thing and
learned to control it.

Zee put a plate of spaghetti and meatballs in front of

him, and his stomach growled. "Okay, after dinner. Magic lesson number two."

She smiled and came around the bar to sit next to him. "Good. Now tell me why you were fully shielded when you came home."

Ryan ate and told her about his day. She asked questions and offered suggestions. The bond made it easier to explain because he didn't have to try to put into words his overflow of emotion. She could feel it. He stopped short of telling her that a lot of the frustration stemmed from his desire to get home to her.

The happiness emanating from her told him she already knew. Ryan wondered if this was what it was like between Jake and Sera. It would explain a lot about the way they argued.

When they'd finished, Ryan washed the dishes and they settled onto the couch. He was eager to be close to her, but that wasn't all of it. The idea of harnessing magic for healing hadn't occurred to him before, and it was intriguing. This was something he *wanted* to learn. The ever-present fear hadn't left him, but he'd found that lately, he was able to acknowledge it and put it aside.

"Where do we start this time?" he asked.

Zee faced him, tucking one leg under her. "I want you to relax and let go of the frustrations and guilt from today. When you direct magic, you want to give it clear intentions so that it does only what you want it to."

"You're not going to do anything dramatic like slice your palm and demand I heal it, are you? Because that seems like a third lesson kind of thing."

Zee's lips tipped up. "No. I'd prefer not to bleed during our lessons."

"That's a good policy."

Amazingly, it wasn't hard to let go of the day when he was bantering with Zee, especially when she was curled up next to him on the couch. He couldn't see any remnant of the burn on her arm, and he didn't have to go back to the high school until January. Yeah, the Wood was a problem, but maybe it would eat someone he didn't like.

Zee smacked his thigh and interrupted his daydream about the vice principal disappearing into an alternate universe. "You seem fine now. We can't really practice healing without an injury, so instead, you're going to practice activating and deactivating your magic."

He struggled to keep a straight face. "You want me to try turning it off and then back on again?"

She tilted her head. "I suppose you could look at it that way."

Ryan snickered, but didn't blame her for missing his joke. She'd have to be much more aware of the culture around IT guys, and that thought gave him an idea for something they could do after magic school was over.

She smacked his thigh again. "Pay attention. You're easily distracted today."

"Squirrel?"

Zee opened her mouth but no sound came out, so she closed it and tried again. "I don't always understand you, but I can usually figure out the gist through context. Today? I've got nothing."

Ryan shook his head. "Don't worry about it. I'm good now. I promise. No more tangents unless you start taking clothes off."

"Strip magic lessons. The idea has merit for motivation if nothing else."

His hand shot up. "I'm in. Can we start now?"

She finally laughed, and Ryan felt vindicated. He could

bring joy too, not just pain. They smiled at each other for a moment before Zee cleared her throat. "Not today, I think. In its natural state, magic is dormant. It sleeps inside you until you call it forth. Yours overflows sometimes, and strong emotions trigger it, so that's where we need to begin."

"Turning it on is easy, it's turning it off that's a problem."

Zee focused on his legs and reached out a hand to run a finger up his thigh, raising just her eyes to meet his from between long dark lashes. "Turn it on now."

9

RYAN

Licks of fire followed her touch, and Ryan caught his breath. If this was her plan, he was a big fan. It was a close second to strip magic lessons. He nudged his magic into waking as her finger slid down almost to his knee and back up.

It was hard not to reach for her, but he kept his body still. His magic had other ideas. Translucent red tendrils followed in the wake of her hand. He wasn't controlling it, but it didn't seem to be doing anything either. It was just there.

"Put it away."

Ryan glanced up, and she was looking at his face. Her hand kept moving, but her eyes were much more distracting. He tried to call the magic back, to convince it to go back to sleep, but it was obstinate. It wanted her.

He could relate.

"Don't cajole, command. You're in charge. It'll go where you tell it to go."

Her green eyes almost glowed, and if he didn't know better, he'd say she was using magic too. It was hard to resist falling in and letting her take over. The repetitive motion of her hand lulled him. He knew though, that they couldn't go further until he put his magic back to sleep.

Ryan visualized the dark red magic soaking back into him. The tendrils disappeared. The power curled back up in his gut, and he blinked. Zee pulled her hand back into her own lap and smiled.

"Good work. Did you feel the difference?"

Ryan thought about it for a second. "The first time I tried to do the same thing I did to wake it up, and I wasn't sure it would work." Zee nodded. "The second, I had to see it doing what I wanted, and I *knew* it would work."

"What was the change?"

"Motivation. I knew you wouldn't let me do this if I was still glowing red." Ryan leaned forward and curled a hand around the back of her neck, bringing his mouth down on hers. Kissing her was like completing a circuit. She filled the part of him that had been missing, and a current raced through him. Her hands came up to rest on his chest, gripping his shirt.

She tilted her head to give him better access, pressing closer, and he deepened the kiss. He couldn't get enough air, and he didn't care. Zee must have been light-headed too because she pushed him away enough to suck in several breaths.

"This is the most enjoyable magic lesson I've ever taught."

Ryan grinned. "I'm certainly way more eager to participate."

"I like your motivation techniques, but there's more *magic* I wanted you to do today."

He released her and sat back against the cushions. "Fair enough. What's next?"

"More practice." She shifted suddenly and straddled him on the couch. His hands rested on her hips, and he barely kept the groan inside. It was too bad her weight was on her knees instead of where he wanted it. "Wake your magic."

It roared to life with hardly a thought. She leaned forward to put her lips against his ear and he could see his arms were glowing red from the elbows down. His hands slid around to palm her ass, leaving streaks of red along her thighs.

She shivered and her nipples hardened against his chest. "Focus on your intentions. Let the magic free, but don't use it."

He tried to do what she said, but the temptation to get rid of their clothes was strong. He intended to get her naked, but he wanted to do it the old-fashioned way. Her muscles were taut from holding herself up, and he ran his hand down and along her inner thigh. He let his fingers brush the edge of her panty line on the way back up. She arched her lower back, moving a tiny increment closer to his hand. Her breath was warm against his neck as she made a little noise in the back of her throat.

"Pull the magic back. Contain it." Her hands traveled down his chest in slow motion, and it took him a second to process her words. The power was flooding his system, begging for an outlet. He brushed her center again and visualized it curled up inside him instead of coating his hands. The red glow faded immediately, and he was free to focus his intention where he wanted it. On Zee.

He never doubted that the magic would stay docile. She finally let her weight drop fully onto him. "Excellent." Her breathy comment was probably supposed to reference his training, but it sounded like she was happy with their new position. Ryan gripped her ass again and pressed up against her. They both groaned at the long, slow pressure.

He leaned forward and mouthed words against her collarbone. "Any more lessons for today?"

Before she could answer, the door banged opened behind them, and Jake walked in without knocking. Ryan took a moment to be glad he hadn't magicked her clothes away, before he focused on the immediate problem. His hands returned to her hips and held her in place. She was staying right there. Ryan craned his neck to address Jake, who'd stopped a couple steps inside. "Go away."

"You look busy. Hi, Zee."

Zee gave him a little wave with her fingers. "Ryan is getting magic lessons."

Jake raised a brow. "Please tell me this was how you taught Sera." He held up a hand. "Actually, no. Don't tell me. I don't want the truth. From now on, this is how I'm going to imagine it went down."

Ryan's focus was a little fuzzy, but he *did* notice that Jake wasn't leaving like a good best friend should. "You're not going away, are you?"

"Nah, I have some news about Will."

"You couldn't call?"

"I did call. No one answered."

"And it couldn't wait until, say...tomorrow?"

"Nope."

Ryan glanced over at his phone on the side table. Sure enough, there was a missed call symbol. He must have left it on silent when he got back from school. He sighed, resigned, and shifted Zee off his lap. "I regret giving you a key."

"Sorry about this." The glee in Jake's eyes belied the sincerity in his voice.

Zee didn't look any happier about being interrupted, but he could sense she was making a concentrated effort to calm her racing pulse. "What's your news?"

"Right." Jake lost the playful attitude. "We finally pinpointed where he's been staying, but we were a little too late. He and a couple of the developer people were trespassing earlier and 'wandered' into the Wood."

Zee stood up. "What did it do?"

"That's the thing. The Wood didn't do anything, but Will swears he saw the trees move. Something about shadows and branches reaching for him."

Ryan was a little disappointed. If the Wood ate Will or one of the developers, maybe they'd all leave and everything could go back to normal. The thought made him sadder than he expected. Zee drew his attention, still standing but with relief stark across her face. They'd been on the verge of something for a long time, and now that everything had changed, he wasn't sure he wanted to go back to normal. To a life with Zee in the Glade, and Ryan alone in his apartment again.

"I'm glad no one was...eaten, but I don't understand how the situation is a problem."

"Well, it seems Will's mental stability had come into question because of his ranting about ghost shadows and killer trees. They actually had to sedate in the Kilgore hospital under twenty-four-hour watch. Whatever happened, it seriously messed him up."

Satisfaction swept through Ryan. The guy had spent almost two years trying to convince Sera she was crazy so he could have access to her grandmother's assets. It was sweet karma that he'd be the one to end up in a hospital. "I don't see how that's bad."

Jake rolled his eyes at Ryan. "If he's sedated and under watch, how are we supposed to question him about the mysterious people-eating woods where he had a psychotic break? He could be sent home or released before we can find out what he has to do with all this."

"Okay, yeah, that's bad."

"There's also one more minor problem. I went and checked out the place where Will had his episode—"

"What the hell, dude? You know better than anyone not to go into the woods." Ryan really didn't want to have to form a rescue mission to extract Jake from an elemental forest. Especially since they didn't know if said forest was, in fact, eating people or not.

"I didn't have to go in. They hadn't made it very far past the fences. At first, I didn't see anything weird, but when I pulled on Sera's magic, these roiling shadows appeared deep in the trees. Normally when I use her magic, I get swarmed by sprites, but there was no response. I think something's happened to them."

Ryan was considerably less worried about the sprites, but Zee's brows pulled together. "The sprites are gone?"

Jake shrugged. "I didn't do an exhaustive search, but they didn't show up as usual. Now that I think about it, I haven't seen any sprites for a few days. And Sera had another zombie bunny nightmare last night. We tend to wake up with a room full of them at that point. Nothing appeared."

Zee sat on the arm of the couch. "The sprites are native to the Wood. They're physical manifestations of the connection between the various magics. They provide a measure of protection against the magics that formed them."

Ryan held up a hand. "What do you mean by various magics? There's more than one type of magic?"

He could feel her urge to lecture, so he was grateful when she kept it short. "Yes. The one I use is Fae. Yours is human. The Wood is elemental. There are others, but all the magics operate slightly differently. When they collide, sprites are formed."

Ryan sat back against the couch. This was new information to him, and the idea that there was more than one type of magic shifted his worldview. Despite what Sera claimed, he'd always thought sprites were some kind of magical dust balls. Jake looked equally stunned.

"What does it mean if the sprites are gone?"

"That something is very wrong with the Wood."

Jake narrowed his eyes. "Are we sure this isn't Torix? He ran away from the last encounter, but he's not dead. At least, we don't think he's dead. He could've been hit by a bus or something. The world is a dangerous place if you've been trapped in a tree for a century and a half."

Ryan hated Will, but he despised Torix. He'd known Maddie since he'd moved to Mulligan, even dated her for a little bit, and knowing Torix had been in control of her pissed him off to no end. He'd bet Jake felt the same way and then some. They didn't know the full extent of what Torix had made her do because she'd refused to talk about it and then moved to Europe to be near their parents.

Zee tilted her head, thinking. "It's possible, but unlikely. Even if Torix had been caught the way I was, he's powerless to affect the Wood."

"Will's powerless."

"There are other types of power besides magic." Zee sent him a knowing look, and Ryan thought he understood.

She'd been demonstrating her power over him on the couch not too long ago.

Jake eyed both of them. "Right. Well, Sera got the hospital to give her some information. She's still listed as his emergency contact. They've sedated him for his own safety, but will evaluate him again in twenty-four hours. Even if we could get into his room, he'll be out until tomorrow afternoon at the earliest."

"We should come up with a plan to get to him," said Zee.

Jake ran his hand through his hair. "Agreed, but I left Sera alone at the house, and I want to get back."

"Dude, she's not going to disappear if you're gone for more than ten minutes."

Jake flipped him off. "She doesn't want to be alone right now, so I'm going home. We can touch base tomorrow and see what we can do then."

Zee walked over and opened the door for him. "Give Sera my regards. We'll talk to you tomorrow."

Jake waved on his way out. Zee closed and locked the door after him. She met his eyes, and he knew they were both considering picking up where they'd left off.

Zee shook her head slowly. "Magic lessons will have to wait. I need to find more information on what could make the sprites disappear."

She stayed by the door, with the couch between them. Her demeanor told him that the situation needed to be taken more seriously than he'd initially thought. Ryan was disappointed, but he could wait. He had some paperwork from the semester to finish up anyway. It was tempting to linger and try to convince her differently, but she was right. They needed more information. Besides, now that they were done avoiding each other, every day was a new chance. There was no rush.

He nodded, rose, and went to his bedroom, but turned at the door with a little grin. "I can't wait to see what you're going to teach me next."

A slow smile lit Zee's face. "I look forward to it."

"Goodnight, Zee."

"Goodnight, Ryan."

He closed the door between them and adjusted his pants. That smile was going to stay with him all night.

ZEE

ZEE GOT VERY LITTLE SLEEP, but she did find the information she needed for once. She took copious notes for the others and saved the page before passing out on top of the blanket. When she woke up, well past dawn, her arm was asleep from lying on it awkwardly and the light hurt her eyes. She stumbled out of the room in search of donuts and found Ryan making something at the stove.

He looked over his shoulder and grinned. "Good morning."

"No. It's a bright morning and far too early for good."

"I'm making French toast. You want some?"

She grabbed a glass of water and took a seat at the breakfast bar so she could watch him cook. The food smelled amazing, and she could see syrup and butter waiting on the counter. Anything covered in syrup and butter would taste good. She hadn't been hungry when she got up, but she was ravenous now.

"Yes, please." Her voice came out in a croak, so she chugged half the water glass and tried again. "I would love some breakfast. Thank you."

The smell of warm bread, eggs, and cinnamon-sugar wafted over her, and she was thankful once again for Ryan's cooking skills. She reached her arms up and arched her back to stretch. When she finished yawning, Zee found Ryan watching her, his gaze caught on her chest. His eyes blazed, but she was hungry for food first.

"Are you going to serve me burned toast?" She nodded toward the stove where smoke had started to trail up.

Ryan blinked and tried to salvage his cooking. "Damn."

"I'm sure it'll still be delicious."

She'd tried to give him the benefit of the doubt, but he snorted. "It's fine. I'll eat this one. Why don't you grab two glasses of orange juice and bring them to the table?"

He carefully avoided looking at her while she did as he asked. Zee had to smile at his reaction. She was wearing her usual outfit of leggings and a shirt, but this one was a tight tank top with the words "Gamer Girl" written across the chest. It didn't seem like Sera's type of clothes, but it had been in the drawer where she'd put away the piles Ryan kept bringing home.

It was fun to see him distracted, but not at the cost of her breakfast. "I'm safely out of eyesight."

He glanced up to confirm she was sitting at the table, then flipped several pieces of bread onto two plates. She wasn't entirely awake yet, but they might as well stop wasting time and talk about what she'd found.

"I know what happened to the sprites."

He turned and pointed with the spatula. "That's no way to start a morning." He moved the last of the bread. "We're going to eat and enjoy the fact that I'm off of work for the foreseeable future and not mention woods or trees or magic creatures of any kind."

Zee was a little taken aback, she was a magical creature

after all, but the bond told her he needed a break. He strived to be normal, and on his first day off, he'd wanted to have breakfast with her. Not for her position or her power, but because he liked her. She wasn't sure he'd even acknowledged that yet, but the bond didn't lie.

"What do you do when you're not at work or dealing with woods or trees or magical creatures?"

He carried both plates to the table and sat down. "Usually play video games or harass Jake, but today is different."

Zee took a bite and nearly moaned in ecstasy. "*This* is my new favorite food."

"You say that about everything you eat. Yesterday, pears were your new favorite."

"This would be great with pears."

Ryan considered his plate then nodded. "Actually, it *would* be good with pears. Next time."

"What's different about today?"

"I need to go Christmas shopping, and you're going to help me."

Zee nearly choked. "Unless you plan to get everything on Amazon, I'm not going to be much help."

"You're female. Sera's female. My mom is female. I need help."

"Even if your reasoning wasn't extremely sexist, I think a forest that eats people should take priority over gift-giving."

"It's not gift-giving; it's gift-buying. Part of being human is admitting that sometimes life sucks and you have to deal with it, but it doesn't have to consume you. We can put the concerns aside for a little bit and shop for Christmas presents."

"Doesn't that feel irresponsible?"

"Not when there's nothing we can do. Will is going to be

unconscious for a few more hours, and we need him responsive to tell us what he's been up to."

Zee pushed her empty plate away and sat back. He had a point, but he also didn't know what she'd figured out last night. "Let me tell you what I found about the sprites. Then we can decide what to do today using *all* the information we have."

Ryan got up to refill his juice. "Fair enough. Hit me with it."

"Sprites aren't elemental magic, they're a composite of several kinds. They form where elemental magic specifically meets other kinds. A nexus of sorts. My ancestors used the nexus in our Wood to help keep Torix contained. They used their magic, the elemental magic surrounding them, and they tapped into the other bits available to them through the nexus." Zee paused to see if he was following.

"So, you guys trapped a powerful dark Fae, conscious I might add, in a place where even more power converges, which is also the birthplace of sprites?"

She couldn't tell if he was mocking her, but the judgement was quite clear. "I'll say it again. It was before my time. The only reference I could find to sprites disappearing was if the flow of magic was blocked or stopped in some way."

Ryan was quiet for a moment. "When Sera absorbed the barriers, she broke something else, didn't she?"

Zee nodded slowly. "It's the most likely answer, though I can't see how Will and the developers could make it worse. They're a nuisance at worst, but they don't have the magic to touch the nexus. If Sera had done irreparable damage on Samhain, the effect would have been immediate. You all would have suffered the consequences. That leads me to believe it was more subtle and it's been growing since then."

"Okay, but can we agree to not tell Sera it's probably her fault the woods are eating people?"

"Of course, though I don't believe eating is the correct term any more. I found a reference to a shadow realm deep in the Wood, but that particular entry enjoyed embellishing the facts with nonsense for dramatic effect."

Ryan grabbed both plates and took them to the kitchen. "A different realm? Like alternate universes and superhero stuff?"

He sounded so gleeful that Zee almost didn't explain. "Not quite. It's an in-between place, but between magics, not realms. There aren't people or creatures living there. At least, according to the author."

"I have to admit, I'm very disappointed. You got my hopes up with that one."

"How can you be so excited for superheroes with powers when you have power and you want nothing more than to be rid of it?"

"I'm full of contradictions. What does the shadow realm —I'm going to keep calling it that because it's badass—have to do with the Wood eating people?"

"I think the shadows we see are a portal of sorts. When you went in, you entered the shadow realm."

"But...why?"

"It holds the magic in place. In your case, your latent magic triggered it, and it deposited you in the shadow realm to contain you."

Ryan glowered. He apparently didn't like the idea of a magical prison, but that was what she'd found. "How were you able to get me out then?"

"That I don't have an answer to."

"Okay." He nodded. "Let's go shopping."

Zee sighed. "You're very stubborn."

"Take a day off with me."

"What about Will?"

"I talked to Jake this morning. He'll call when Will's awake."

"I don't even celebrate Christmas." It occurred to her that Yule was approaching, which explained the edgy feeling that hadn't completely gone away. She wasn't sure she could sit still for another day doing research when the shifting magic was urging her to do something instead. "Very well. I'll go along, but don't expect me to be helpful in picking out gifts."

Ryan grinned and did an awkward victory shimmy. The answering warmth in Zee's chest made her think his genuine happiness was probably worth a few hours of procrastination.

"You're going to want to change."

Zee inspected her tank top. "What's wrong with what I'm wearing?"

"Despite how much I really like that tank," his eyes lingered on her chest again, before he nodded toward the window. "It started snowing this morning."

She gasped and rushed to look out. Large, fluffy flakes were drifting down in lazy spirals. A couple wearing puffy jackets and boots walked their dog arm in arm with their breath making clouds in front of them. She supposed the temperature would have to drop considerably for snow to form. It melted as soon as it hit anything, but the falling was the beautiful part anyway.

Ryan came to stand behind her and watched over her shoulder. "It doesn't snow in the Glade?"

"No. The weather stays temperate thanks to the protection of the Wood. I've seen snow on the television, but never in real life." Her wonder was tempered by the knowledge that the protection was probably non-existent at the moment, and they couldn't do anything about it. Another item on the list that might be falling to chaos.

Ryan put his hands on her shoulders and gave Zee a gentle push in the direction of her room. "Go put on a couple more layers, and I'll find you a jacket. It snows here sometimes, but usually only once or twice a year."

She had exactly one long-sleeved shirt, so she pulled it on over her tank and added a short-sleeved shirt over that. Her sneakers would have to do. It wasn't very wet outside, so she thought she'd be fine. Ryan was waiting for her in the living room with a hoodie over one arm. She recognized his school logo from the gym, but she'd never seen him wear it. Come to think of it, he rarely wore a jacket either.

Zee slipped the sweatshirt over her head and was surprised when the arms extended past her fingers. She was taller than most humans, and she'd found that a majority of the non-legging pants Sera had provided were too short. The long-sleeved shirt she was wearing under it barely hit her wrists. The soft fabric of the sweatshirt engulfed her. Ryan must have worn it before because the best part was that it smelled like him.

The scent reminded her of when she curled up with her head on his shoulder during the evenings. He'd watched TV, but she'd relaxed and let her mind wander. There weren't a lot of opportunities for her to relax in the Glade. She pulled the collar up over her nose and inhaled deep.

Ryan opened the door. "Ready?"

She let the sweatshirt drop back into place and nodded. "Do you know where you want to go?"

He closed the door behind her then led her down the stairs. "Nope. I thought we'd wander around the shops in town until we got hungry, then we'd grab some food at Rosie's."

"You all keep raving about Mr. Hogan's food, but I've never eaten at Rosie's."

Ryan glanced over his shoulder, his brow furrowed. "What about that time you summoned him?"

"Fae business." His shoulders tensed up, so Zee changed the subject. "He did well in the class for being paired with Sera."

Her gambit worked, and he relaxed then snickered. "Yeah, I didn't expect him to be the warrior princess sort, and Sera did *not* take it easy on him."

Most of the shops in town were on the edges of the park. Ryan's apartment also happened to be on the edge of the park, so they were crunching over frozen grass as Zee blinked snowflakes off her eyelashes. She made sure he wasn't looking, then caught one on her tongue.

"I wish you'd stop calling it a warrior princess class. I'm not a princess. We don't have any concept of royalty."

Ryan sent her a sidelong look. "Maybe not a princess, but you look like a warrior, and the best nicknames are the ones that are annoying at first. There's no going back now, princess."

Zee had to admit that she didn't mind when he called *her* princess, but it made the class seem silly in her mind. At some point, she'd taken ownership of it, and she wanted to take it seriously. She'd searched the phrase on the internet after Sera had used it, and the television show that popped up sounded interesting, even if the armor was ridiculous. There could be worse comparisons.

Ryan stopped short at a shop with an abundance of windchimes in the front. He glanced through the big front window then pulled the door open. Zee followed him inside and almost ran into his back when a small, flowing woman yelled from behind the counter.

"Ryan! Where have you been, you naughty boy." She leaned forward and affected a whisper, but it wasn't any quieter. "Maddie told me all about that night in the reservoir."

Red crept up his neck and ears in front of her, and Zee decided she liked this woman who could make Ryan blush. "Hey, Janet. Sorry I haven't been around, but you know it's hectic during the school year."

She tsked. "That's no excuse. And who is this gorgeous creature behind you?"

Ryan pulled her up next to him. "Janet, this is Zee. Zee, Janet. She owns this treasure trove. Maddie used to work for her before she shipped off to Europe."

10

ZEE

ZEE SHOOK JANET'S HAND, and marveled at the sheer number of scarves the woman wore. Some were cozy, some were sheer and brightly colored, and some she'd tied around her upper arms to make a trailing set of wings. Zee experienced a pang of sadness that she hadn't been able to fly in weeks.

"You remember Henry, of course." She wiggled her fingers at a terrarium in the corner with an iguana sunning himself under a heat lamp.

Ryan nodded, and Zee moved closer. She'd never seen a live iguana before. It didn't look up as she approached, but she didn't expect it to. The ones she'd seen in pictures were all brown, but this one was a beautiful bright green with light blue speckles. She wondered if Janet would let her hold him.

"C'mon, Janet. You said you'd have it by now." Ryan's raised voice drew her attention. Janet had her arms crossed over her chest, and he was frowning. With reluctance, Zee left the iguana in favor of the humans.

"I have no control over when my vendors ship me their goods. I'm as frustrated as you are, but I try not to bring those negative vibes into my shop." She eyed him pointedly, and Zee had to hide a smile. "I'll contact you as soon as it comes in."

"Fine," Ryan grumbled.

Zee put a hand on his arm. "I thought you were looking for gift advice."

"That was for me. I like to shop locally as much as possible, and Janet will order pretty much anything." She beamed from across the counter. "As long as you're willing to be flexible about shipping dates."

Her smile dimmed a little but didn't disappear. "I have some new stock by the front window. An order from that glass artist out in Kilgore. I hear Sera likes dragons."

Zee hadn't known that, but considering Sera's choice of shields, it made sense. She took a closer look at Janet, past the scarves and the positive attitude, and sensed a kernel of magic deep inside her. The power was almost hidden by her personality, and Zee seriously doubted if she was aware of it. At a guess, Zee thought it gave Janet the ability to suss out items people were unaware they wanted. It would explain how her odd little shop seemed to be doing so well.

They walked to the new display, where a dozen glass dragons in varying sizes were suspended from the ceiling. She imagined on sunny days this would light up the whole shop. Even on a snowy day they were magnificent. Zee reached out and ran her finger down the translucent wing of one of the smaller dragons, about the size of her palm. It was a deep indigo with swirls of light green. She looked up, and Ryan was watching her. He understood. She missed her other forms, and her ability to move between them.

Ryan could have dismissed it or ignored it; instead, he acknowledged it. "It's okay to be sad. It doesn't make you weak." He untied one of the larger dragons with golden wings and took it to the front.

She stroked the wing again. The smooth glass was cool under her touch, but warmth blossomed inside her. Yes, she'd lost her wings, but had she gained something better?

Ryan was waiting outside under the awning. "I heard from Jake. Looks like we have another day to plan. Will panicked when he woke up, so they had to sedate him again."

To Zee's surprise, relief won over annoyance. She was enjoying her stolen time with Ryan. He had a paper gift bag in one hand, but when she got close, he reached for her with his other. They held hands and strolled along the sidewalk, stopping occasionally to window shop. Zee liked the feeling of her hand in his and the silence she didn't need to fill.

A few other people were out, but they were mostly moving from car to store and back. The trees in the park shined with a sparkling layer of white, and Zee wasn't sure she'd ever seen anything so beautiful. Ryan dragged her into a few more shops, where he chatted with the clerks but didn't buy anything. Each time, Zee tried to pull her hand back, but he refused to let go. She didn't miss the way everyone picked up on it then eyed her suspiciously. Ryan seemed to be popular and well-known among the townspeople.

The only exceptions to the wary inspections were students from her class. A group of teenage boys stopped her outside the post office to ask some questions about grappling in video games, and two ladies getting drinks hurried out of the coffee shop to thank her effusively for the training. They all wanted to know when the next class would be. Several others she recognized waved as they drove past.

Zee didn't have a good answer for anyone. When she'd agreed to teach Sera some self-defense moves, she'd thought she'd be back in the Glade by now. It wouldn't hurt to do another lesson though. Teaching had been fun, and the time commitment was negligible. She'd have to talk to Sera about setting it up again.

While she'd been musing, Ryan had pulled her into yet another small resale shop. The town was full of them. This one, however, was bursting with books. Zee gasped, diving deeper into the store, and this time Ryan let her go so he could chat with the man behind the glass counter.

The Fae had books, but most of the tomes were meant solely to pass along information. Spell books and history books. These books were flights of imagination. She ran her hand along the spines and grinned at the many feelings of joy that emanated from them. People had loved these books and passed them along for someone else to love.

She pulled one at random and examined the cover. A glinting dagger over a blue and gold background with a single word printed across it. The art was lovely, and Zee thought again that maybe humans had the right of it in some instances. Fae books were always bound journal style with no art on the outside. She flipped it over and read the description. A thrilling tale of fantasy and finding one's truth.

It spoke to her.

She didn't have any money, and it was rude to ask Ryan to get anything more for her when he had already provided so much. But she wanted that book. Zee hugged it to her chest and walked slowly back to the counter, unable to make herself put it back just yet.

Ryan hadn't moved from the front of the store, but he held another gift bag filled with colorful paper. He smiled at the clerk and reclaimed her hand when she sidled up next to him.

"—couldn't believe it. Miller swore it was Big Foot, but it couldn't have been over six feet. You know how he gets when he's been at the sweet tea. All sugar and no brains."

Zee made herself set the book on the counter, and the man switched his attention to her. "You want that book, sweetheart? It's a good one. My little Amelia loved it. Read it through in one sitting."

He scanned it, and Ryan spoke up before she could think of a polite way to say she couldn't buy it. "Put it on my tab, Bill."

"You got it, professor." Zee sent Ryan a questioning look, but he was busy adding her book to his bag. Bill didn't notice, or seem to stop for breath in the conversation. "You two keep your eyes peeled if you're going near the woods, you hear? Strange things are happening in there."

Ryan pulled her toward the door and waved with both their hands. "We sure will. You have a good day, Bill."

The door chimed as it closed behind them, and Zee let him lead her toward their next destination. "Thank you for the book. I didn't mean for you to buy it for me."

"Don't mention it. You were clutching it pretty tightly." Ryan grinned at her.

Zee glanced at the bag, then changed the subject. "Professor? I thought professors taught at colleges?"

Ryan shrugged. "Bill likes to give nicknames. He doesn't understand the first thing about computers. I helped him set up his payment system, and ever since, he's decided that I'm super smart."

Zee smiled. "All brains and no sugar?"

He laughed again. She liked this happy, carefree Ryan. "Something like that. If you have time, it's fun to sit and let him talk for a while because you never know what's going to come out of his mouth."

"I hope he warns everyone away from the Wood like he did us. This town keeps surprising me with the way everyone looks after each other."

"It's a good place."

Zee was surprised to hear him say that. She'd been under the impression that he lived here out of necessity to be close to the Glade. Part of their original bargain was that he had to be available for tasks, but he also had to check in with her regularly so she could monitor the seal on his power. That would have been hard to do if he lived anywhere else. Maybe, like her, his opinions had been changing for the better.

They crossed a small side street and cut across a parking lot. The big sign for Rosie's was lit even though the sun had barely begun to set. The rest of the town must have had the same idea because one by one the Christmas lights wound around the trees and along the buildings came to magnificent life. The sight made her smile and reminded her that Yule wasn't far off. The night when the dark relinquishes to the light. A time of rebirth. Zee let her eyes linger on Ryan. *Rebirth, indeed.*

The smell of pizza wafted past them as Ryan held the door for a woman with her arms full of boxes. Zee's stomach growled, and the wonderful smells made her take more than one deep breath. People filled every spare inch, even standing in the aisles between tables to chat with the ones lucky enough to be sitting down. They pushed their way through to the counter where a teenage girl was cheerily ringing up orders in a Santa hat and a school hoodie like the one Zee was wearing. The girl's eyes lit up when she saw Ryan.

"Mr. Nolan! I didn't think you'd be in today."

Ryan scanned the room. "Yeah, I guess it was the same idea everyone else had. Carrie, this is my friend, Zee. Zee, this is Carrie, one of my better students."

She shook hands with the girl and tried not to grin when Carrie visibly perked up at Ryan's use of the word 'friend'. Despite the fact that she seemed to perceive Zee as competition, Carrie smiled and welcomed her to town. "Mr. Hogan told me all about the warrior princess class. When do you think the next one will be? It sounds fun."

Zee returned her smile. "Sera will let everyone know when we figure it out."

Kindness appeared to run amuck here in Mulligan, a refreshing change from the constant jockeying for position she was used to in the Glade. Carrie yelled to Mr. Hogan that Ryan and Zee were at the counter then moved on to the people behind them. A few seconds later, he came bounding through the double doors labeled Employees Only, wiping his hands on a red-stained white cloth.

"Zee, what a pleasure to see you here. You tell me what you want and it's on the house for my two favorite teachers."

He was much more confident in his own setting, or maybe just when he wasn't on the receiving end of Sera's exuberance. This was the first time anyone had noticed her ahead of Ryan, and it made her inordinately happy. She wasn't an accessory; this man valued her for herself.

"I'd like a calzone with all the vegetables you can fit into it, and extra feta please."

"Make that two," Ryan added.

Mr. Hogan pulled a tiny notebook out of his apron pocket and wrote down their order. "It'll be out in no time. Grab a seat if you can."

He hurried back through the doors, and Ryan pulled her close to whisper in her ear. "I wasn't aware you knew what feta was. Or a calzone."

"I pay attention when people talk. Mr. Hogan was quite proud of his newest cheese addition. He was telling Sera about it while she was trying to break his wrist."

Ryan shuffled them back to a corner where there was a modicum of free space, and they ended up mostly behind a small potted tree wrapped in white lights. Zee leaned back against him with his arm around her waist, content to look around. People continued to come and go, but most appeared happy to linger and talk with their neighbors. Rosie's was clearly the heart of this little town. At one point, an elderly woman got up to leave, and people from two different tables hopped up to hold the door for her.

The two men were struggling to find enough room for both of them to hold the door and still allow the older woman to leave. Zee giggled, and Ryan's arm tightened around her. His lips brushed her cheek as he leaned in again. "That was one of the sexiest things I've ever heard you do."

Tingles of awareness shot down her spine. She wiggled a little and found him hard against her backside. A groan rumbled in his chest, almost drowned out by the chatter surrounding them, and his arm locked her tightly in place. She was torn about whether to call a halt to their flirtation. No one was paying them any attention, and the plant shielded them, but she didn't know how these things were viewed in the human world. Netflix was endlessly contradictory on the subject. Would they perceive him differently if they knew what he was up to?

He nudged her head to the side so he could trail a series of open-mouth kisses down the column of her throat. She pressed her lips together to keep from whimpering. He always knew the exact place she wanted him to touch, sometimes before she did. If he kept it up, she was going to suggest that they forgo dinner in favor of satiating a different hunger.

A couple left one of the smaller tables near the front, but Ryan held her still when she tried to claim it. "We won't be here that long."

She glanced back at him. "Do you have another store to stop at?"

His slow grin was wicked in the best way. "No, but I think we should take our order to go. We'll probably enjoy the food more at home."

Zee licked her suddenly dry lips, and his eyes followed the motion. A curl of anxiety leapt into her chest. She'd come to enjoy her time with Ryan, and she didn't want to do anything that would mess that up. But her next move was going to change things one way or another. *Am I really going to do this?*

In the end, the decision was simple. She ached for him, and she'd never been a coward.

Zee turned in his arms and leaned into him, wrapping her arms around his neck. "We could always cancel the order and go home now."

Before Ryan could answer, Carrie appeared at their side bearing a to-go box and a petulant expression. "Mr. Hogan said you'd want this as takeaway and to let him know how you like the feta." She thrust the box at Zee and pivoted on her heel, short hair flying.

Another giggle bubbled up, and Zee had it under control until she met Ryan's eyes. He burst out laughing, and she couldn't hold hers back any longer.

"C'mon. Let's get out of here." He grabbed her free hand with his and pulled her out into the twilight.

Ryan led her through the park, and Zee shivered as they approached his building. The box smelled delicious, but she hoped she'd be eating it cold sometime later. She'd fully enjoyed their day off together, and she intended to extend it into the evening. Judging by the pace Ryan was setting, he was on board with that plan.

They made it inside and up the stairs in record time. Ryan didn't slow once they were in the apartment, except to toe off his shoes, and Zee followed suit. He dropped the packages on the couch and paused a second to take the food from her and put it in the fridge.

The bond between them was ablaze with energy. Unlike the last few times, Ryan's magic was under control. She could sense it there, but Ryan's mind was preoccupied with thoughts of her. He led her into his bedroom and closed the door behind them. The Christmas lights in the park were the only illumination in the dim room with the sun fully set on the other side of the building. Now that he had her here, she sensed his uncertainty. He wanted her, that much was clear, but he was afraid too.

Zee perched on the edge of his bed and tried to assure her raging hormones that they could wait a little longer. "I told you I'd stay out of your head, so if you have concerns, you'll have to say them out loud."

Ryan paced to his bathroom door and back, stopping in front of her. "I was never supposed to like you."

She cocked her head. "That's not a great beginning."

"Maybe not, but it's *our* beginning. Everything about you

was terrifying, and I wanted to use you to get rid of my magic and be done with it. I was right to think you were terrifying, but you're also generous and loyal and the most badass warrior princess I've ever met."

She swallowed a smile. "Still not a princess."

He crouched in front of her and gathered her hands in his. "You are so much more to me than a means to an end, and the thought of you leaving to go back to the Glade tears me up inside."

Zee nodded and extricated her hands to frame his face. "I know, but I don't belong here."

"You could."

Zee sighed. The longer she stayed with him, the more she wanted to believe that. "If it was simply *my* future, I could, but I have to think of my people. You can have me now, and every day until I have to go back. After..." She trailed off, unsure of what she could promise him. "We can deal with after when it gets here."

He tilted his head and kissed the inside of her wrist. "I'll take anything you'll give me, princess." He met her eyes and nipped her palm, then swiped his tongue along the center, soothing the bite.

The wet touch shot straight to her core. Zee twisted her hand in the collar of his shirt and pulled him up between her legs. His mouth met hers in a rough tangle of tongues and lips and teeth. She shoved his shirt up so she could have access to his chest, and he tugged it off with one hand.

Zee loved the lean muscle he had hidden beneath his shirts. She traced a long, bumpy scar that stretched around his abdomen. If she'd had access to her magic, she could have made it smooth, but she liked the scars humans carried. They were reminders of life and triumph. Whatever made their scars had passed and the person had grown from the danger.

The hoodie, shirts, and tank top came off in one awkward swoop, and left her in a tiny blue bra that had appeared on her bed one day. She didn't need much support, but it appealed to her vanity. Ryan kissed his way down her neck and chest to the top of the cups, and she wished she'd foregone the pretty underthings for once.

Her head dropped back at the feel of his tongue against her breasts, and Ryan helped guide her down until she was lying on the bed. His hands made quick work of her leggings, his pants, and their socks, then his mouth returned to hers. Clad only in thin cotton panties and her bra, Zee wrapped her legs around his hips and arched up. The solid length of him pressing against her center shot electricity through her. She groaned and did it again.

Ryan's teeth nipped her ear as he held her hips still. "I'm a huge fan of your enthusiasm, but I'm not going to last long if you keep doing that."

Zee laughed low and unclasped her ankles. She braced her foot on the bed and utilized the same maneuver she'd used in class to flip him over. "I think you can handle it."

She straddled him and rubbed right where she wanted him, arching her back at the pleasure that coursed through her. His magic flared under her, and her eyes snapped back down to him. A slow, sexy grin curved across his lips as he trailed a hand up her thigh, leaving a trail of crimson magic in its wake. The magic lingered for a moment, warm against her skin, before sinking in and disappearing.

Everywhere he touched, he left tingles in his wake. She stilled, and his hand painted magic across her stomach, up past her breasts, and into her hair. His hand curled around the back of her neck and pulled her down to him. Their lips met in a tender kiss, an exploration. His magic wound down her back and paused at the band of her bra. The clasp gave way.

Zee chuckled against his mouth. "You're getting better. Maybe it's time for a more advanced lesson."

He pulled the straps down her arms and tossed the bra onto the floor. "Like how to remove panties without destroying them?"

She lifted up and slid her panties off. "We don't need magic for that."

Ryan sat up on his elbows and took her in, completely naked. "You're beautiful."

She smiled. Her appearance had never mattered much to her beyond her own ego, but now that she'd lost the ability to change it, she was glad Ryan liked the one she'd picked. "You're still wearing something. That seems unfair."

"See, it would be really convenient if we could magic these off."

Zee took care of it herself, dragging his boxer briefs down with agonizing slowness. His cock sprang free, and she stroked him lightly on her way back up. His length jumped in her hand, and the rest of him collapsed back onto the mattress.

She grinned. "Much better."

None of this was new to her, but the double sensation she was getting through the bond was incredible. She took him into her mouth and could almost feel his eyes crossing. His magic hands were clenched in the blanket, and the bond made it clear how much he was enjoying it. A few strokes were all he allowed before he plunged both hands in her hair and hauled her back up on top of him.

He didn't release her, but held her still while he plundered her mouth. She settled over him skin to skin and reveled in the feeling. He was slick, but so was she, and the sensation had her moaning into his kiss.

She lifted up just enough that he teased at her entrance, but he stopped her. "Do we need protection?"

Zee hesitated. She's never used it before because her magic had protected her, but that wasn't guaranteed anymore. As much magic as Ryan had learned, it didn't seem wise to place the weight of the responsibility on his abbreviated training.

She sighed and shifted to the side, sliding off of him. "I don't know, so I think it would be best."

Ryan jumped up and rummaged in his bedside drawer. A couple of seconds later, he was back. He ran his hand, then his lips down her back, urging her onto her stomach. Zee caught her breath as she heard the crinkle of foil. She'd had plenty of partners, both male and female, but she'd always been on top. There was a certain vulnerability in allowing someone behind her.

The warmth of his magic lingered as he lifted her hips, and his hand curled around between her thighs. He rubbed in exactly the right place, and she pushed back against him. He moved her hair to the side to kiss the nape of her neck, and his heat surrounded her. She couldn't get enough of the new sensations.

His fingers eased inside her and established a slow rhythm. Her heart throbbed in a wild beat. She crested higher, with each stroke of his hand building waves of pleasure. Her muscles tightened almost painfully, and then she tumbled over with his name on her lips. Before she'd fully come down, he removed his hand and thrust into her with a groan.

He was buried to the hilt, with an arm around her waist and his lips mouthing secret words against her neck. They stayed that way for a moment, both acclimating to the feeling of fullness.

She looked over her shoulder, meeting his gaze, and he started to move. Her eyes closed, and she rested her forehead against the rumpled blanket. In the darkness, she moved with him, a quickening tempo that had them both breathing hard. His magic coiled into a cyclone, and she sensed his grip on it slipping as they approached climax.

Blindly, she reached for his hand and pinned it to the bed next to her. With a last bit of effort, she drew a sigil on it and focused their intentions there as she plunged over the edge again. Ryan followed right after her. Several long moments later, his magic settled back into him in a contented ball.

Ryan pulled out of her and collapsed on his side. She only had the energy to turn her head. The sigil on his hand had faded. She knew she'd have to explain that one, but she was too tired and satisfied to do more than lay there.

He roused himself enough to take care of the condom, then he nudged her toward the pillows and pulled the covers out from under her. Zee thought about going back to her own room and frowned. Before she could move, he rolled onto his back and pulled her close, then threw the blanket over both of them. She rested her head on his shoulder and closed her eyes. One arm splayed across his chest, and her leg tucked between his.

She could feel his heartbeat under her cheek as her body relaxed into sleep. Her mind drifted. *Is this what it's like to be human? A trade-off of magic for pizza and art and excellent sex?* Curled up next to Ryan, her body deliciously sore, she decided it wasn't too bad of a deal.

11

RYAN

RYAN WOKE up in a tangle of sheets and hair. Not his hair. Silky dark hair caught in his chin stubble and trailed over his neck. Zee slept with her face tucked into his collarbone, both hands under her cheek. Her breath warmed his chest, but the rest of him was freezing. She'd wrapped herself in the entire blanket and most of the sheets.

Weak morning light filtered through the window, and he didn't have anywhere to be. Ryan smiled because he had one arm curled around Zee, who was lying half on top of him. Her soft, smooth skin pressed against a good portion of his side. Chill be damned, he wouldn't change a thing about the way he'd woken up. It was tricky with a single hand free, but he managed to get under the blanket with her.

The second his cold hand touched her back, her eyes popped open and she sucked in a breath. Her head came up and she took in her surroundings, then she snuggled back down against him. *I regret nothing.*

"Why are parts of you so cold?" Her words were mumbled against his chest, and he had a flashback of her lips locked around him last night. Half-hearted morning wood turned instantly hard, but she wasn't all the way awake yet.

"Because you stole all the covers at some point in the night and relegated me to death by hypothermia." He ran his hand up and down her back, making her shiver.

"Why is your apartment so cold? Don't you have heat?"

He shrugged under her head. "It's set to turn down at night. I usually have blankets to keep me comfortable."

She wiggled closer and slipped her leg between his. Either she felt bad enough to share some of her body heat or she was finally waking up enough to notice his hand was getting lower and lower with each pass. He skimmed over her butt and thigh, then ran his fingers along her center on the way back up. The second time he did it she pushed back into his hand and nipped his collarbone.

"How do you feel this morning?" He kept up the light touches, but he wanted to be sure she wasn't too sore.

Her palm wrapped around his cock and she stroked him up and down before answering. "I feel like this is an excellent way to wake up."

She leveraged up on her elbow and kissed him, long and slow. Last night had been amazing, all frenzy and heat. This was quieter, but he dug it. The low hum of electricity coursing between them built to a crescendo, and Ryan had to close his hand over hers to stop her. He wanted to be inside her again.

She pulled back and grinned, then climbed over him to dig through his nightstand drawer. Clearly, she'd been paying attention. He amused himself by tracing light circles around her nipples but not touching them. Thus far, there hadn't been enough time dedicated to the attention her breasts deserved.

They weren't very big, but he liked the way they fit her toned body and his palms perfectly. He replaced his fingers with his mouth and she moaned low when his tongue finally hit her nipple. She took a deep breath then found the condom she was searching for. He released her and helped her right herself, straddling his lap.

"You are extremely distracting." She tore open the package and sheathed him, and they both moaned when she sank onto him.

He let her take the lead on this one, and marveled at how well they fit together. He matched her movements, thrusting up into her with increasing force. Her hips rolled, and he pulled her mouth down so he could capture the little sounds she was making. They were both close, so he reached between them. A little pressure and she began clenching around him. Her nails scored his chest, but he welcomed the slight pain. His hands went to her hips to hold her steady as he pounded up into her and took his own pleasure.

Spent, she collapsed on top of him, and her hair covered his face for the second time that morning. He smelled coconut again, and he thought it might be his new favorite fragrance. They laid there until their breathing returned to normal, and Ryan dropped a kiss on the top of her head.

Zee was breathing deep, but he didn't think she'd fallen asleep again. The bond assured him she was fine. *More than fine*. He was content to have her splayed on top of him all day, but they had to get up at some point. Will had to be conscious in the next few hours, and Ryan had promised her he'd help with the problems in the Wood.

He trailed his fingers up and down her back again,

unable to stop touching her apparently. There were a lot of things he couldn't stop doing when she was around. Taking care of her. Trying to make her laugh. Protecting her. Wanting her. *Needing her?* His chest tightened with the truth. For once, his thoughts were clear, but he had to be careful to keep them to himself. If Zee knew what he'd realized, she'd pull back, and he'd lose his chance.

He needed that chance to convince her to stay.

SHE DID FALL ASLEEP AGAIN, and after he took care of the condom, Ryan was happy to hold her until she was ready to get up. His mind wandered to the logistics of living with a Fae full-time. If they fixed the Wood, would she get her magic back? Would anything he offered her be enough to keep her? Could he live with her power, knowing how dangerous it was?

It was another fifteen minutes before she stirred and made a sexy little noise in her throat. Her head tipped up, and she kissed the bottom of his chin before levering herself off of him. He made sure his shields were in place and went into the bathroom to shower.

He thought about coaxing her under the spray, that night she'd shared herself with him played on repeat in his erotic dreams, but decided to save it for another time. Zee must have been thinking about it too, or she picked up on his wandering thoughts, because she yelled from the bedroom.

"Don't waste all the hot water. As soon as I can use my legs again, I need to rinse off."

Ryan chuckled and took an abbreviated shower,

allowing Zee to take over. Jake called as Zee shut off the water.

Will was awake.

He and Sera were heading to the hospital and thought Zee might be the best person to ask the questions. Jake said they'd be there in five, and Ryan told him they were ready to go.

The ride to the hospital was charged with tension. Sera stared nervously out the window, even when Jake tried to ease her mind with stupid jokes. She gave him pity smiles, but it didn't seem to help her mindset. Zee had locked down into warrior mode. Her face was serene, but he had a feeling she was prepared to do more than question Will. Ryan didn't give a crap about Will's mental health; he only hoped the guy was coherent enough to give them some real information.

The trees passed in a green blur, and Ryan wondered if the highway between Mulligan and Kilgore wound that way because of the influence of the Wood. As far as he could tell, the road curved through the mundane forest, but didn't come close to the magical people-eating part of it. They pulled up to a squat brown building that could've been a jail in a former life. People usually went to a hospital in one of the bigger cities if they had time, but this place worked in an emergency. They mostly got people stabilized, then airlifted them somewhere else for better care.

Ryan sincerely hoped he'd never need that kind of help because he sure as hell didn't want to pay for a helicopter ride he probably wouldn't remember. Will was on the second floor in a locked wing that required them to sign in and leave all their personal belongings in a box at the nurses' station. The whole procedure reeked of drama for someone who saw some shadows in the woods.

He wasn't sure what Sera had told them, but the staff let all four of them back at the same time with a warning not to agitate Will too much. The tiny room was mostly taken up by a twin hospital bed and a monitor. The lone window had the shade drawn, but bright hospital lights spotlighted Will, who was glaring at the TV suspended in the corner.

"Will?" Sera knocked lightly on the door, but he ignored her. She shared a look with Jake, then moved further into the room. The rest of them stayed back by the door in unspoken agreement.

He'd lost his posh veneer. Red patches marred his pale face under disheveled blond hair. This was the first time Ryan had seen him look anything but perfect. Sera didn't seem fazed. She reached for the remote, but he snatched it away from her.

"It's about time you got here, Sera. Can you believe that drivel? Antonio's accent is atrocious, and his timing was completely off."

She glanced at the TV, then back at Will. "You're watching your station?"

"Of course I am. I have to keep track of the bumbling idiots they find to fill in for me." The channel went to a commercial, and Will shut the TV off in disgust. He tossed the remote to the edge of the bed and finally deigned to look at Sera. "The service here is terrible. It took two entire hours for someone to change the input over so I could check the news."

Sera gave him a shallow smile. "I'm sorry to hear that. We have some questions—"

"I need my phone and my computer. They won't listen to a word I say, so you'll have to get them for me. Once I've checked in, we can get out of here and find a lawyer so you can sign those papers I have for you." Will spoke right over her as if she weren't talking.

He didn't seem to notice that there were other people in the room. Ryan wasn't sure if he was that much of a dick or if there really was something wrong with his head.

Sera lost her smile and crossed her arms over her chest. "You're not going anywhere. If you answer my questions, I'll politely ask the nurse if they can return your phone."

He scoffed. "You always were useless and unable to follow the simplest directions."

She marched back to the group, waving Zee forward. "I'm done. Your turn. I vote for interrogation, preferably the painful kind."

Zee stepped up and waited for him to make eye contact. Will held out for a few seconds, but then he was caught in her stare. "What were you doing in the woods?"

His eyes streaked away from her, and his hands clenched the thin sheets. "I wasn't in the woods. I was researching a potential site for development."

"Look at me. What did you see at your potential site?"

His gaze shot back and stopped on Zee's face again. "I don't want to talk about it."

"What did you see at your site?"

His jaw ticked, but he answered. "Shadows. Demons with horns. Beckoning me forward into the dark."

"Have you been into the woods before?"

"Yes."

"What did you do there?"

He wanted to look away, even Ryan could feel it from across the room, but Zee was in control. Will would look away when she let him look away. "We took soil samples and measurements."

She tilted her head. "What else?"

Sweat broke out on Will's forehead as he fought answering, but Zee was too strong for him. "We tried to stage a sacrifice."

Zee's eyes narrowed. "Explain."

Ryan could see the second he gave in. His shoulders slumped, and his words came out fast. "Sera's grandma was into that crazy witch stuff, so we wanted it to seem like Sera was killing animals or something. Then we could conveniently find it before the court hearing and have her declared incompetent. Once I had control of the land, I could sell it to the developers. Do you have any idea what it's all worth? But we never made it very far. It got dark really fast and Andrew got the creeps so we left."

Zee turned to the others and released Will, who slumped back on the bed with his eyes closed. "That's all he has."

"What did you do to him?"

Zee waved a hand dismissively. "A light hypnosis to make him sleep. It's useful when dealing with the young or injured."

Sera raised both brows. "I thought your magic was gone."

"Not gone. Sealed. But as I keep telling Ryan, that's not my magic." Zee walked past them out the door and down the hall.

Ryan shared a glance with Jake, who'd been silent since they entered the locked ward. Zee was scary powerful even without access to magic.

Sera glanced back once and Ryan thought he heard her mutter, "Sleep is too good for you."

They caught up to Zee in the parking lot. She leaned against the car, staring into the trees. Sera climbed in, but

Ryan stopped Jake with a hand on his arm. "Give me a minute."

Jake looked between Zee and Ryan, then shrugged. "Whatever you need, man." He got in, and cranked up the radio.

Ryan joined Zee leaning against the car. "That wasn't just your mind stuff."

"No."

"I felt it, you know. The pull."

She nodded. "You would have."

"Why didn't you tell me?"

Zee shifted her focus to him. "At first, I wasn't sure it would work. Jake is able to use Sera's magic, but that's not always the case with a bond. Then..." She trailed off and returned her gaze to the trees.

Ryan stepped in front of her and rubbed her arms. "You can use as much of my magic as you want, anytime you need it. I'd give it all to you if I could." He made sure she could feel his sincerity through the bond. The magic would be in way better hands with her anyway. He almost hadn't noticed the tiny drain while Zee was questioning Will. It'd taken him until he joined her in the parking lot to put it together.

She moved closer and slid her arms around his waist. "You're a good man, but I still should have asked first."

Ryan pulled her close and brushed his lips against hers. "Consider this blanket permission."

Before he could do more than tease them both, Sera stuck her head out the window. "Some of us have things to do today."

Zee laughed and released him. "Very well." She got into the car, but her eyes showed him what they'd be doing when they got home. Sera raised her window again, and

Ryan wondered how long before she found some other way to interrupt them.

Sera didn't last ten seconds down the road. "I'm hungry, let's grab lunch at that barbeque place you keep telling me about."

Ryan checked with Zee, who shrugged. They needed to eat. "We're in."

"Good. Let's go before I start gnawing on someone's arm."

Ryan thought Jake appeared inordinately happy considering they'd gotten diddly squat from that visit. "Shouldn't we be discussing Will's utter uselessness?"

Sera sighed. "That's always a fun topic, but yeah."

"I don't think Will or the developers are influencing the Wood," said Zee.

Jake glanced back at her in the rearview mirror. "I agree with you. Maybe if the sacrifice thing had worked, but Will screwed himself."

Sera snorted out a laugh. "They're opportunistic and morally reprehensible, but they can't do anything with the land."

Ryan leaned forward between the seats. "How do you know?"

Jake answered him. "Sera got a court summons. Will tried to file a claim that would make him Sera's legal guardian because she wasn't of sound mind. I immediately went to talk to Kathy, the court clerk. The two developer guys were with him when he brought it in. Unfortunately for them, Will was stuck in the hospital when Kathy put the claim through to Judge Anderson yesterday, who laughed it out of court. She and Evie used to be on the town council together."

Sera smiled. "I was looking forward to finally

confronting him about his abuse in front of witnesses, but the karma here is acceptable too."

Jake reached over and rubbed her thigh. "I've been thinking though. We should do something with the land so that no one else can come after you for it."

"That's a good point. It's not like I ever plan to sell it, so the monetary value is worthless. I should give it to Zee."

Zee dismissed it with a wave of her hand. "I'm not legally a person, but it's an interesting idea."

It *was* an interesting idea, but the way she'd said 'not a person' bothered him. And it made Ryan think about all the legal problems that would come with Zee staying with him. *How illegal is it to forge papers?*

They were all silent for a few minutes. A sign for Old West Barbeque pointed them toward a dirt lot where Jake pulled in. He parked and shut off the car. Zee stared skeptically at the small building.

Ryan had been there a couple of times before. Barbeque wasn't his favorite food, but Jake loved it. He dragged them out here maybe once a year to satisfy his craving. It was a miracle the place was still open. The building used to be an old gas station, but no one besides locals used this road, so it had gone out of business. Leon Walczak bought the place and reinvented it as a restaurant.

Ryan only remembered his name because the guy came out and introduced himself every time they ate there. He still couldn't remember how to pronounce it.

They'd never seen any other employees, and the interior looked like Howdy Doody had exploded in a tragic prop accident. Despite that, it was by far the best barbeque he'd ever tasted.

They piled out of the car, but no one approached the door. Ryan and Jake had been out there at various times of the day and the door was never locked, but they were never sure the restaurant was open either. He suspected Leon lived somewhere in the back, but he couldn't imagine where.

Sera stared for a moment, then eyed Jake. "Are you sure this is the right place?"

"Yep." Jake grabbed her hand and pulled her forward. "Ask Ryan. He'll tell you."

Ryan held his hands up. "Whoa, don't bring me into this."

They all followed Jake into the thankfully dim building and grabbed one of six tables. Low country music was playing, but barely loud enough to make out the words. Sera claimed the plastic-coated menu sitting in the middle of the table and frowned at it.

"Is it all meat?"

Jake leaned over to look. "He has some cornbread rolls and fries too, but I wouldn't bother with the fries. Takes away stomach space better used for brisket."

Sera sighed and asked Ryan, "What do *you* get?"

"Whatever Jake orders for me. Usually meat drenched in sauce with rolls."

She muttered something derogatory about men under her breath, but his focus had shifted to Zee. She looked around the restaurant in awestruck horror. "What do you think?"

"I think I saw this place in a horror movie once."

Leon chose that moment to bustle out of the back with four waters on a tray. Ryan wanted to ask when she'd watched a horror movie, and with who. He knew she preferred Jane Austen to Stephen King, and he had to push down a rising sense of jealousy that someone else had convinced her to try something new. It was a completely irrational set of thoughts, but he was becoming more and more irrational about Zee.

Leon stopped next to their table and smiled, a slight man with wispy facial hair and a heavy Eastern European accent. "Greeting, my guests. My name is Leon Walczak. Ah, Jake, welcome back, my favorite cowboy. Would you like your usual?"

"Sure, Leon." Jake plucked the menu out of Sera's hands and plopped it down on the table. "Could you bring us four of those please?"

"Of course. Do you want four sweet teas too or only one for you?"

"Four teas too."

Leon winked, making an awkward finger gun with one hand. "You got it." He put the four waters on the table and hurried back through the door.

Sera picked up the menu, smacked Jake with it, then put it back in the stand. "I love when you order for me. How often do you come here?" Jake grinned and moved the menus out of her reach.

"It's not his first time," said Ryan.

"Don't you mean it's not his first rodeo? Where's your Texas?" Sera snarked.

Jake shook his head. "No one actually says that."

"I'm going to start saying it. I'm a Texan now."

Ryan made a harsh buzzer noise. "Nope, sorry, still a California transplant."

"What do you know, you moved here where you were seventeen."

"Yeah, but I moved from Austin." He pointed to himself. "Texan."

Sera harrumphed, but Jake's shoulders were shaking with silent laughter.

Zee chimed in. "What does that make me?"

All three stared at her for a second. Ryan finally responded. "I'd say Texan. You were born in the Wood, which is in Texas."

The mention of the Wood sobered them. Ryan had been playing around with Sera's idea in the back of his mind, trying to find a way to protect the land without forging papers for Zee, and he thought he might have come up with an idea that could work.

"What if you turned it into a nature preserve?"

Sera tilted her head, but she followed his train of thought. "Can we do that?"

Ryan shrugged. "It's your land. If you can turn it into luxury housing, I don't see why you can't go the other direction."

Sera nodded as she warmed to the idea. "A nature preserve. I like it. Zee, what do you think?"

Zee stared at him, unblinking. He couldn't read her face, but the bond told him that she was surprised and proud. "I think it's a great plan if your government allows it."

Sera leaned forward and started rattling off ideas for ways to make the preserve work. Jake nodded along, throwing in an occasional comment, but Ryan tuned them out. A sheen of tears had come and gone in Zee's eyes. He reached under the table to take her hand, and she linked their fingers tightly. It felt like she was holding onto more than his hand, and he was surprised by the strength of his own feelings.

The food came out shortly after, along with the absurdly sweet teas, and they threw stupid ideas at each other for naming the preserve while they dug in. Ryan ate with one hand, unwilling to let go of Zee, and she did the same. The meal provided a welcome respite from the stresses they'd been dealing with.

Soon enough, the food was gone, the bill paid, and they were back in the car heading to Mulligan. As usual, Leon had been strange but kind, insisting the ladies take some rolls home with them. Objectively, his barbeque *was* the best around. Sera groaned and rubbed her belly, while Jake laughed.

"Told you it was good."

"I retract my previous snark about you ordering for me. You can order for me whenever you want."

Zee sighed. "The food was delicious, but we've only solved one problem so far today."

"If Will's not involved, then who or what could it be? The Wood has been in the same place since Mulligan was founded, *before* probably, but it's just recently decided to turn rogue?" Sera glared at the trees they were passing.

"There's more information we're missing," said Jake.

Ryan grimaced. "No shit, but how do we find it?"

Zee slipped her hand into his and squeezed. He looked over at her, and she sent a single thought to him. *I have an idea.* He nodded slowly. She clearly didn't want Jake or Sera to know about her use of his magic, and honestly, he was happy to tell them as little as possible about it. He'd spent years cultivating the idea that he was powerless, so it was second nature to hide it.

The three of them brainstormed the rest of the drive, but Zee stayed silent and distracted. Whatever she had in mind, he was all in for it.

12

ZEE

Zee and Ryan got back to the apartment late in the afternoon. She hadn't meant to pull on his power while talking to Will, but it had been second nature to use what was at her disposal. There was something wrong with Will's mind all right, but she'd been able to pull what they needed out of him. Even so, she was concerned with the aftermath.

Ryan kept searching her face on the drive back. He held her hand, but he'd raised his shields, and he was being cautious with his thoughts. Zee's idea pushed the boundaries of their relationship. His magic would play a key role, which always made him uncomfortable, but it might help reunite her with her people. *Which might separate her from Ryan for good.*

The apartment door closed solidly behind them, and Zee twisted her fingers in front of her as she hesitated. Had she thought through all the possibilities? Caution had served her well, but it felt like the stakes had never been so high.

She sank onto the couch as Ryan grabbed his laptop from his room. He slowed as he came back into the living room and cocked his head.

"What's wrong?"

Zee smiled. He was getting better at using the bond. "I think I might have a way to contact my people." She stopped talking out of habit. Never reveal more than necessary. But this was Ryan, and he deserved more than that. "I'd need to use your magic."

He set the laptop aside and sat next to her on the couch. "I meant what I said earlier. Use as much as you need."

Zee met his eyes and searched the bond, but all she found was truth. He was genuinely offering himself up to help her. Her anxiety melted away, replaced with hope. Perhaps she'd exaggerated the risk in her mind. "Okay. It'll have to wait until tonight though."

"Why tonight? Do I get to be in on the plan?"

She laughed. "I think I can use your magic to fuel a dreamwalk with my second, Lana." The laugh died, and she frowned. "If she's willing. We didn't part on the best terms. As for why tonight? She has to be asleep. You and I would have to maintain contact for this to work. I'd depend on you for that."

Ryan reached out and tucked a loose strand of hair behind her ear, then trailed his fingers down her neck over the sensitive spot above her collar bone. "I think I can handle it."

"Contact that won't distract me."

"Well, that's less fun, but still within my capabilities."

Zee captured his hand before it could wander any further. "I'd like to try another magic lesson."

Ryan perked up. "Naked magic time?"

"You are incorrigible." She shook her head, but she was smiling. "I want to teach you how to heal properly."

He sobered instantly. "How are we going to do that if we don't have any injuries?"

She pulled out a pack of sewing needles she'd found buried in the back of the pantry and stuck in her hoodie pocket. "We're going to make injuries."

"You are *not* hurting yourself so I can practice a skill I may or may not have."

Zee shrugged. "Okay, I'm not above making *you* bleed instead."

"Uh-huh, I can feel the concern."

"It's a tiny moment of pain. I've had worse trying to cut an apple in your kitchen."

"Yeah, but that wasn't intentional and for no good reason."

She laid her hand on his arm. "It's a good reason. A little blood now to be able to stop something more serious later."

He was going to give in. She could feel it through the bond and see it in the frustration on his face. His nature was to protect, so he was fighting the logic, but the logic would win. Instead of pushing him further, she got up to sanitize the needles she planned to use and to collect some clean washcloths.

In the end, they both ended up bloody. It was necessary to have him practice on himself to feel the impact his magic had on the wound. She'd learned the same way, with needles and pinpricks. She and Lana had practiced on each other until Zee could perform the basics. Lana was a natural healer. She hadn't needed the extra experience, but she'd done it for Zee.

Ryan learned at almost the same pace as Lana had. His skill as a healer far surpassed her own. When she called a halt, he wasn't tired from the expenditure, and Zee had no pain from the repeated punctures.

She threw the spotted washcloths in the laundry bin in his bedroom and sanitized the needles again before rejoining him on the couch. He stared off into the distance, but she could tell he'd quieted his magic.

"You have a great deal of talent. Natural healers are rare, and you wield the magic with a finesse that I certainly didn't teach you."

He met her eyes and let his distraction fade. "Are you claiming you don't have finesse with magic? Remember, I watched you make Will spill his guts without our friends knowing you were using magic."

"Sera suspected."

"Yeah, but she believed your answer without question. That's smooth right there."

Zee inclined her head. "I'll accept your point, but I've had many years of practice. You've had three sessions, and only one where you used your real talent."

He picked up her hand and played with her fingers. "Maybe you're a good teacher."

"It's more likely you're highly motivated to learn this particular skill."

"Okay, we're both awesome." He pulled her closer and brushed a kiss over her mouth. "How long do we have until you try to invade Lana's mind?"

She grimaced. "More than an hour, and I'd prefer if we phrased it differently. I'm not trying to control her."

"We can call it whatever you want, princess." He kissed her again, lingering longer this time. "Have you factored in the time difference between here and the Glade?"

"I'm under the impression that when the barriers fell,

the Glade's time aligned with the time out here and has followed suit since."

Ryan didn't ask another question. He drew his lips along her jaw and down her neck. Zee sighed as she tilted her head up to give him better access. His hair tickled her face, and she noticed again how long it was getting, past his ears. An image of him with braids in his hair excited her. She wanted that for him. Fae braids for her human warrior.

The hoodie was getting in his way, so he released her hand and pulled it over her head, taking her top with it. Zee smiled at his efficiency. The cool air hit her skin, and she shivered. Ryan tossed her clothes somewhere behind him and pulled off his own shirt. She'd never get tired of touching his chest. Her greedy hands reached for him, but he stalled her.

"I'm all for naughty couch time, but I have plans for you that require more space."

Zee raised a brow, but let him lead her to the bedroom.

———

She missed her hour mark, but it was worth it. They lay naked with Zee sprawled on top of him, tracing designs on the planes of his chest.

"Are you ever going to explain the symbol you drew on my hand?" His voice rumbled under her cheek.

Her fingers stilled. She'd forgotten about that. "You were at risk of losing control of your magic. I gave it a focus."

He tipped her head up so he could see her eyes. "What was the focus?"

She struggled to find the words to explain. The magic had been redirected into him, between them, but without any specific intention.

"Balance," she finally said.

"Okay, can you explain that without sounding like a mystical harbinger?"

She snickered. "Probably not, but I can try. The sigil literally means balance, but it doesn't give any intention to the spell. It's like..." She trailed off as she searched for the right comparison. "Like a holding pattern. The magic waits until you need it for a purpose and then comes forth."

"Balance, huh? So if I'm about to slip on the ice outside, it'll keep me upright."

"No, you'll still fall on your very nice butt. It's a metaphorical balance."

"Why that in particular?"

Zee gave him a dry look. "I was a bit distracted at the time. It was the first thing that popped into my head."

He nodded soberly. "I understand. I can be extremely distracting. Speaking of that, are we still going to dreamwalk with Lana?"

She sank back down and put her cheek against his chest. The idea was exciting because she hoped to finally get some concrete answers, but they'd fought before Zee had left.

THE MEMORY WAS sharp and painful. She'd been in her cottage, putting on her leather armor and preparing to leave to confront Torix. A quick knock at the door preceded Lana barging in without waiting for permission. She'd stopped short when she saw Zee getting suited up and put her hands on her hips.

"What are you doing?"

"Getting dressed. Can you get the last bit for me?"

Lana sighed and expertly looped the catch. "We talked

about this. The humans will stop Torix's servant, Torix will remain behind the barriers, and we'll celebrate Samhain with a little party."

Lana gave a shimmy that sent the glittering strips of fabric at her waist swaying. "We got that cider you like."

Zee put her hand on Lana's bare shoulder. "The others can have a party, but we need to be ready. Torix is making his move tonight, and I don't know if Sera and her group will be enough. As my second in command, you need to take this seriously and armor up."

Lana's face closed down, and she shrugged Zee's hand off. "As your second in command, I'm telling you we need to stay here in the protection of the Glade and let the humans handle Torix's minion. You nearly died putting the barriers back up this last rotation. It was a miracle you made it back here, and now you want to face off against him when he's potentially at his full strength?"

"Yes. It's our duty to protect the people who live in this area, not just ourselves. You think he won't come after us if he manages to regain his power? And what about Evie? Her sacrifice shouldn't be in vain. If we can isolate the servant, we can use their power and connection to him to add another layer of defense. Together, we're stronger than him, but we can't do anything from in here."

Lana took a step back, shaking her head. "No, Zee. Evie made her choice. You've been obsessed with Torix for the last seven years, training incessantly, bringing in new technology, manipulating the humans. It has to stop. He can't break the barriers even if the humans fail, nothing can now that they're renewed properly. We don't need another layer. The worst he can do is unleash a slightly stronger human on other humans. It's time to let it go and enjoy the harvest."

Zee couldn't believe what Lana was suggesting. They'd

worked closely the last seven years to protect the Fae and the humans together, but now she wanted to abandon them? A dull pain ached in her chest as she realized that Lana had been indulging her this whole time. And why not? It had been partially Lana's fault that Torix was able to call a servant in the first place.

Zee grabbed a hold of her anger, pushing the pain away. "I'm disappointed you won't participate in cleaning up the mess you helped make."

Lana scoffed. "Let's be real. Your main concern isn't the humans. It's Ryan."

"What nonsense are you spewing now?"

"I see the way you look at him."

"He's a means to an end."

"He's a distraction, and he has been since you made your deal with him."

Zee schooled her face so her surprise wouldn't show. "What makes you think we have a deal?"

"I saw you with him the last time he was here. The spell is distinctive, though I don't remember there being so much touching in other iterations." Her meaning was clear, and Zee didn't deny it. She'd embellished the spell a bit. Physical contact *did* make it stronger, but she could perform it from across the room if she needed to. At the time, it had been a harmless bit of fun. They renewed the spell once a year, usually just after Samhain, and it gave her an excuse to touch him.

Lana crossed her arms and laughed dryly. "It's hard to keep secrets among us, but you've done an excellent job. It made me wonder what other secrets you've been keeping."

"None." It wasn't a lie. She couldn't lie, but the truth was often a grey area. "And the deal with Ryan has provided us with much needed improvements."

She snorted. "And now the cost comes due. You expect us to throw ourselves into harm's way to protect your pet."

Zee straightened and pulled on her power, letting it flash in her eyes and fill the room. Lana was powerful in her own right, but Zee was stronger. Zee had taken a chance on her after Lana's mistake with Chad, but now she wondered if she'd made the wrong choice.

"I won't make you fight if you're not willing, but you will not undermine me by your cowardice. Go and enjoy the party. Take your fill of the magic offered by the Wood. But remember this night was in part *your* doing. I certainly will."

Concern flashed across Lana's face, but she didn't get in Zee's way. She'd made her choice.

Zee left Lana in the cottage and marched out of the clearing with her chin high. The peak of Samhain was approaching, and she needed to get to Torix's clearing. She called a trod at the edge of the Glade, and stepped onto a path lit by tiny, glowing sprites. An image of Ryan flashed across her mind, dark hair tousled across blue eyes, lean body gleaming with sweat from sparring practice. She steeled herself to remain aloof as always.

There were many truths in any given situation, and she'd still been telling herself that her feelings for him were a passing attraction. *Apparently, she was capable of lying to herself if not anyone else.*

RYAN MUST HAVE SENSED her unrest because he rubbed his hand up and down her back, pulling her out of her memories. Lana had been right. Zee had wanted to stop Torix for good this time, but more, she'd wanted to protect Ryan, and she'd been willing to put her people in harm's way to do it.

She'd do it again in a second if it kept him safe.

He was still waiting for an answer about the dreamwalk. After that disastrous parting, Lana might refuse to speak with her, or worse, not respond at all. That last option that had her hesitating. If she couldn't connect with Lana, it could be because Lana wouldn't let her or it could be that something had happened to her. There was no way to know. They could try again at a later time, but Zee was already anxious.

She took a deep breath and prepared herself for whatever answers awaited her.

"Lana should be asleep by now. I'll put myself into a trance and reach out to her using your magic. I've never tried this using another person's power before, so I'm not sure of the effect it will have on you."

"I'm not worried."

His easy response was a far cry from his usual attitude toward magic, and Zee wanted to rejoice in his openness. He trusted her with the thing he most feared, and not the way he had before when he'd needed her to seal it. She basked in the special gift. He had confidence in the woman who liked donuts and had trouble navigating text messages instead of the warrior princess. She hadn't embraced that part of her until now.

Ryan yawned, oblivious to her realizations. She pressed a kiss to his chest and started relaxing her body parts, one by one. The open bond allowed his magic to rise to her call as if it were her own. She pulled it into herself, a shimmering crimson cloud, and sent herself toward Lana's mind.

For the second time in five minutes, the Glade appeared around her. The hazy, disheveled clearing had changed drastically from the last time she'd been there when it had been tidy and warm. Clouds blotted out the sun, and a cold breeze made her shiver, dancing through a pile of dead leaves near the closest cottage.

Zee peered down at herself, not surprised to see her leather armor over the long-sleeved shirt and leggings she'd been wearing earlier in the day. She reached up and touched her hair. It was tightly braided again in loops and tucks. Lana most associated this vision with her, so it was how she appeared in Lana's mind.

The clearing was empty at first, but she didn't have to wait long. Lana emerged from the cottage and spotted her right away. "Zee, thank goodness." She was dressed strangely in soft pants, almost sweat pants like the ones Ryan lounged around the house in, and a loose tunic. Her blonde braids sagged and came loose at points.

Lana ran over and embraced her. After spending so much time with Ryan, Lana seemed tiny. Her head came up to Zee's chin. Zee put her hands on Lana's shoulders and pulled her away.

"What's happening here?"

Tears gathered in Lana's eyes. "Our magic is sealed. It has been since Samhain. The barriers are gone. Torix is gone. The trods aren't working."

"Is anyone harmed?"

Lana shook her head and pulled herself together. "No. Some minor aches and pains, but no serious injuries. Not yet. Zee, we're starving. We can't harvest without our magic, and we don't have any human food. The forest has provided some sustenance, but it's barely enough. The Wood has cursed and abandoned us. Where have you been?"

"I'm trying to find a way back. The Wood sealed me as well, and the trods won't let me through to the Glade."

Lana snorted delicately. "There's not much of a Glade

to speak of. Without the protection of the Wood, winter set in." She shivered. "I didn't realize it could get this cold."

Zee considered telling her about the snow and the lights in the trees and the joys of real food, but it wasn't a comparison she wanted to make with the dreary landscape around her. Her people had been suffering while she spent her days safe and comfortable. "We need to find out how the Wood was able to do this."

Lana cocked her head. "Don't you mean why?"

"I know why. The barriers were broken, and with them the pact we had."

She shook her head. "I don't think that's the whole reason. Before my magic was sealed, I could tell there was something wrong, an irritation in the Wood. It happens sometimes when the magics are out of balance, but it usually self-adjusts."

Zee frowned. "Why haven't you ever told me about this?"

"It wasn't important. You know magic moves in cycles, it's why we harvest when we do, but it ebbs and flows regularly as well. When something interrupts the flow, it feels like a tiny wound to me, so my inclination is to heal it. I've learned to ignore it though."

Zee stared at the trees, unseeing, and let the new information settle in. It reminded her of the main reason she'd chosen Lana as her second. Her deep reservoir of knowledge. Everything she'd said made sense, and Zee had been blind for not seeing it earlier. Sera's actions could have been a catalyst that offset the flow of magic in a way the Wood couldn't immediately fix itself. But why seal all the Fae and remove all access? And why was the Wood attempting to trap power now? It was an extreme reaction, and unlikely to restore the proper flow.

"Zee?" Lana laid a hand on her arm. "Where have you been?"

Lying naked in bed with Ryan. It was the answer she couldn't say, and the answer she wanted to return to. Lana, for all her knowledge, was bitter about what she thought was an obsession with a human. Zee needed more information. She was missing something, and she wanted Lana cooperative. Obsession or not though, she wished Ryan were there with her, even if it *was* a horrible idea.

It took Zee a moment to realize she was watching Ryan *actually* saunter out of the trees toward them. Her thoughts must have called him into the dreamwalk. Zee's eyes widened as he approached, and Lana turned around to see what had caused that reaction.

He moved past Lana is if she weren't there, and stopped in front of Zee. The heat in his eyes warmed her. "You called."

"It was an accident." *Lana was going to get her answer after all.*

He crossed his arms and smirked. "Even a warrior princess makes mistakes sometimes, huh?"

He looked fierce and strong, and so much more real than the world she'd lived in her whole life. Unfortunately, it was Lana's dreamwalk, and Zee couldn't afford to be ejected.

Lana's gaze swung back and forth between them. "You were with *him*." She shook her head. "I should have known."

"It's not like that, Lana."

"Don't grey area me. I can see the marks on your neck."

Zee's hand rose without thinking and covered the red rash that Ryan had caused. She didn't care if Lana knew she'd been with Ryan. Their relationship was nothing to be ashamed of, but Lana's disdain hurt. She'd dismissed Zee as soon as she'd seen Ryan. Anger clouded Zee's judgement, and she spoke without thinking. "I would never abandon our people for a dalliance with a human."

She felt the moment Ryan heard her. A blow to his chest that echoed into her, locked as deep into his magic as she was. Zee reached for him, intending to explain, but he stepped back away from her hand and kept going all the way to the edge of the clearing. Out of hearing of her argument with Lana, but not enough to pull her home.

Lana didn't notice Ryan's movement as she narrowed her eyes on Zee. "For a random human, no. For *him*?" She raised her arms and gestured around her. "Look at what you've left."

The nearly empty village was devoid of the normal bustle of Fae life. No one was training, animals lay listlessly shivering in the sun, doors and windows were shut tight. It was like a plague had swept through. Zee was torn between trying to help her people and trying to relieve Ryan's pain from her careless words.

"We're starving. We have no magic to protect ourselves, heal ourselves, feed ourselves. We're helpless and exposed without the barriers around us. I had to institute a curfew and tell people to stay in their homes. We've been rationing what food we can find from small groups scouting the forest." Lana's words brought her attention back to the tiny, angry Fae in front of her.

Zee shook her head. "I thought it was only me because I was in the trods when it happened. It never occurred to me the Wood would seal all of us."

A smile tipped up Lana's lips. "Not all of us. Chad was spared."

"Seriously? Chad, out of everyone?"

Lana shrugged thin shoulders, but didn't reveal her thoughts on the matter. "He's not as strong as he once was, but he retained access to a small amount of his power. We can't figure out why. He's been using what little magic he has to help the Glade cope. We all hoped you'd come back, tell us what to do, save us." Her eyes shifted to Ryan, far enough back to almost be in the trees, and back to Zee. "I guess you were busy."

"Dammit, Lana. I *can't* come back. The trods are closed to me. You have to find a way to leave the Glade. I can't come to you without my magic."

She spread her hands. "You're here now."

"At Ryan's will. *You* need to lead our people out of the Glade."

Lana was already shaking her head. "No. It's too dangerous. You know what's out there, and you said yourself that Torix was free somewhere."

Zee closed her eyes for a moment. Lana's innate stubbornness would hamper any attempt to help. If she'd determined that the outside world was a threat to their people, she'd keep them in the Glade at all costs. They needed their magic back. All of them.

"What was Chad doing on Samhain that spared his power?"

Lana's eyes narrowed. "I don't know, and I don't appreciate your insinuation."

Zee took a deep, calming breath and loosely grasped Lana's hands. "You trusted me once. Chad could be the key to unlocking the seals. We need to know what he did that was different."

Pain flashed across Lana's face at the reminder, but she schooled it again. "He told me he was celebrating like the rest of us. He found a private copse of trees and drank his fill from their magic. The next thing he knew, he weakened and returned to the Glade. It became immediately obvious that we were sealed and you were missing, but we didn't realize until several days later that he could still use his power."

She pulled her hands away and stepped back. "That's all I know. If you're not planning to come back to us, I have duties to see to. Tomorrow is Yule, and we're without a harvest."

"Lana." Zee met her eyes. "I *will* return."

Their gazes held for a moment then Lana tipped her head to the side. "I guess we'll see."

Zee was unceremoniously shoved out of Lana's dream. She opened her eyes to find Ryan lying stiffly beneath her, staring at the far wall. His hand had stopped on the small of her back. He was physically there, but she could feel him retreating behind his shields.

She rolled to the side, and he immediately got out of bed. Ryan pulled out clothes, tossed them on the bed next to her, and went into the bathroom. The shower came on, and Zee wilted. She searched her mind for where to begin, but she kept returning to the look in his eyes when she made that stupid comment to Lana.

The bond wouldn't let him hide his pain completely, but he was trying. It still washed over her in waves. They needed to regroup and discuss the Wood, the Fae, Chad, any potential avenues for repairing the damage Sera had done. Lana had reminded her that Yule was approaching, and with it another rush of elemental magic. Zee worried at the Fae attempting to live in an increasingly dangerous Wood when it would be at full power.

Lana's lack of belief burned. She'd given up on Zee the second she'd seen Ryan, unwilling to look past the circumstances to the bigger picture. Without Zee there, the rest would follow her. There'd be no more help from that quarter. Zee's frustration and hurt mingled with Ryan's. The betrayal stung with a particular irony. She'd worked her whole life to help her people, and they'd essentially abandoned her. Zee was determined to find a way to break the seals and return them to their lives, but at this point, she didn't know if she wanted to lead them.

She reeled at the potential loss of the such a large portion of her identity, but the destruction paled in comparison to what she'd done to Ryan. Zee knew better than to be careless with her words, but the mistake had been made. He didn't trust easily, especially among the Fae, and she'd tossed his feelings back in his face. She'd made him feel small and insignificant, and that damage needed to be repaired before anything else.

The running water stopped, and Ryan emerged naked rubbing his hair with a towel. Outwardly, he was calm, but she could feel his hurt growing.

"Ryan, we should discuss this."

He focused on digging through his drawer for underwear. "There's nothing to discuss."

"I warned you I'd have to return."

"That you did."

Zee got out of bed, comfortable in her skin, and came around to where he was searching. "Will you look at me please?"

His movements stilled, and he met her eyes. Anger burned there, and pain, but also longing. All wasn't lost yet. She reached out a hand, but he stepped back out of her reach, like he had in the dream. It hurt more the second time.

"Don't do this, Ryan."

His face went blank. "I'm not the one doing it."

He was wrong. He was the one cutting himself off from her. He was the one shutting down, unwilling to have a conversation. Anger began to heat her blood. Did he think he was the only one with emotions involved? With something to lose?

"I'm still here, right now, instead of helping my starving people. They're my duty, and I'm shirking the responsibility to be here with you."

"Sounds like you shouldn't be here then. If the barriers are all down and the Wood isn't protecting the Glade anymore, what's stopping you from marching into the trees and stumbling onto your hidden fairy village?"

Zee crossed her arms over her bare chest. "I know what you're doing."

His eye flicked to her breasts then back up. "Helping?"

"You're pushing me away because you're afraid."

He laughed and took a better look. She wasn't embarrassed by her body, she'd go to battle naked if need be, but this look wasn't about appreciation. It was staking a claim. His eyes were blue flames when they returned to hers, and she held herself rigid so she wouldn't reach for him a third time.

"I'm not afraid of you, of what you make me feel, of us together. But I *am* pushing you away. You don't want to be here, and I'm not interested in being a dalliance."

Zee shivered at the chill in his words. "Ryan, you misunderstood what I said to Lana."

He pulled on pants. "You can't lie, right?"

"You know that."

"Then I think I understood just fine." He tossed the hoodie at her, and she caught it before it hit her in the face. "Better put that on. It's pretty chilly out there in the woods."

Zee winced at the painful ache spreading through her and slipped the sweatshirt over her naked body. "It's true that I won't abandon our people, but Lana was right too."

"I'm sure she was. I don't care."

"You didn't hear the rest of the conversation."

"I assume you and Lana made up, talked about fairy stuff." His dismissive tone fanned her anger.

She held on to her temper through sheer will. "You could have cut off the flow of magic at any time. If you thought the exercise was so futile, why didn't you?"

"It was what you wanted, wasn't it? The magic. The part you can't live without." He yanked a shirt over his head and moved toward the door.

"I can't live without *you*."

Her words fell softly between them, and Ryan paused with his hand on the knob. He didn't turn around. She'd said them, and she wouldn't back down, but she hadn't realized they were true until then. He'd taken over so much of her life since she'd left, shown her how much more she had to offer, and how much she could feel. A life without him, even one in the Glade, would be empty.

He'd pulled himself so far behind his shields that all she could get from him was a vague sense of anger and pain. As much as she wanted to push deeper to find out more, she'd made a promise to him to stay out of his mind, and she would keep it. The longer they stood there, breathing into the silence, the more Zee wished she'd kept her mouth shut.

Ryan punched the door in front of him, startling Zee. His fist strained against the wood for a second, then he pushed off and faced her again. "Is it fun?"

She expected anger, but his words confused her. "What?"

"Is it fun? Playing with me." He stalked her, his eyes on hers, and she refused to retreat.

"I'm not playing with you." She raised her chin as he stopped directly in front of her.

His eyes dropped to her mouth. He cupped her cheek roughly and traced her lower lip with his thumb. Heat suffused her, burning away the anger and letting the arousal rush forward.

"You let me have your body. You let me in enough to convince me that I might be wrong. About the Fae. About magic. About you. But none of it's real. It's only what you want me to see, as always." He leaned in, but instead of taking her mouth, he brushed her ear with his lips. "I guess I don't care anymore."

She sucked in a breath as his hands palmed her butt and lifted her against him. Instinctually, her arms around his neck to steady herself. His words ricocheted inside her, setting off sparks of pain wherever they landed, but she wanted his hands on her. The future stretched indefinitely, lonely without him, but if this was all he was going to offer, she'd take it.

13

RYAN

RYAN COULD TELL when she surrendered. Not that she was fighting, but the point when she gave up the pretense. There was no future for them. She believed she needed him, but it was his magic that drew her. He turned them so her back was braced against the wall next to the door, and nipped the spot at the base of her neck that she loved. She arched into him and moaned.

His hands were on her bare ass, and he was rock hard against her. At least this he believed. She wanted him as much as he wanted her. If he was going to be a dalliance, he'd make sure it was one she remembered when she was back with the Fae.

Her legs anchored on his hips, which freed up his hands to stroke her into a frenzy. She said his name in a breathy little whisper, and Ryan claimed her mouth in a deep, drugging kiss. He freed himself from his pants and plunged inside her. Zee was hot and wet and urged him deeper.

She gripped the back of his neck, her fingernails digging

into skin, and he embraced the pain. They moved together hard and fast, straining to get closer, until she tightened around him with his name on her lips. That was all it took, and he followed her over.

When the rush had faded, he felt strangely bereft. Her breath came in ragged gasps, echoing his, and though her warmth still surrounded him, he missed the connection. She welcomed his touch, reveled in it, but the bond remained stubbornly silent. Ryan pulled out and released her weight. Her legs slid down to the floor, and she pulled the sweatshirt down to cover herself.

Ryan fixed his pants, and sadness filled him once the heat began to recede. Zee stood silent between him and the wall. He couldn't get a read on her, but he wasn't willing to lower his shields. *Never again.* He stepped back, and tears filled her eyes.

He'd never seen Zee truly cry. She was more likely to destroy whatever was making her sad than let someone see her weakness. The idea that he'd been the one to make it happen tore at him. He didn't want to hurt her, and he couldn't resist her tears.

"Don't do that. Don't." He gathered her close, and she rested her head on his shoulder. The terrible feeling that he was making a mistake welled up inside him. She put her hands on his chest but didn't push him away.

"What are we doing, Ryan?"

He didn't have a good answer for her, so he didn't say anything.

She sighed and shook her head. "Why can't we have a normal discussion?"

"Why can't we keep our hands off each other, you mean?"

He felt her nod. "That too."

"We can't help what, or who, we want."

"What we want isn't always what's best for us." His shirt muffled her words, but he heard them loud and clear.

They were a pointed reminder that she may want him, but she needed her magic. Or his. Any magic would probably do as long as she could control it. He stepped away from her, and shook his head. The situation wasn't going to change, so why did he keep hoping for a different end result?

"You're so sure you know what's best." He couldn't help the bitterness in his voice.

The tears were gone, replaced with pain behind a thin layer of steel. "People depend on me."

And they'd circled back to the same argument. "It looked like they've moved on from where I was standing."

"That doesn't absolve me from responsibility."

"You'll protect them whether they want it or not, huh? Damn the consequences?"

Her temper finally snapped, and she surged up with blazing eyes. "Isn't that what you're doing? We can have sex all you want as long as we're careful to keep our emotions out of it?"

"Oh, I think we're well past that point."

She scoffed. "The second we get too intense, you close off and pull back to protect yourself. That makes it all the more pitiful. Shields conceal, but they don't erase. The emotions and the pain will be there regardless."

He leaned into her, full of fire and fury. "What do you know about pain? You've been stuck without magic for what? A couple of weeks? And that's the worst tragedy you could think of. Your people are starving because they're too stubborn and prideful to leave your precious Glade. They'd rather die than live like humans for a while. And *those* are the people you're going back for?"

"Yes."

The simple answer enraged him. She couldn't see past her own prejudice to the opportunity she had right in front of her. A muscle ticked in his jaw, and his palm slapped the wall next to her head. "Dammit, Zee. Why do you have to be this way?" The worst of it was that he wanted her to stay. Despite everything, knowing her people and her magic would always be more important than him, he wanted her to stay.

The longing emptied him out.

He dropped his head, and pushed away from the wall and from her. Zee gasped out his name, and something about the sound made him jerk his head around. She hadn't moved. Her hand was half-raised as if trying to entreat him, but she was too still. A sheer coating of red magic slowly oozed over her body and across her face.

"What the hell?" He stared down at his hands, at the churning power coming off of him. At some point in their fight, he'd lost control of his magic. Then he'd wished for her to stay.

Zee's eyes pleaded with him, but he didn't know what to do to fix it. Panic started to rise. He rushed back to her, but stopped before making contact. He knew how to recall magic if it was inside him, but this seemed like a separate essence now. A presence pushed against his shields, and he recognized Zee trying to talk to him. He relented enough to let her in, and she brought calmness and clarity with her.

I can't redirect this. You need to break it yourself. Reach into the spell and insert your power into it again. When you feel the connection, pull it back into yourself. You can do this.

Ryan didn't waste time responding. He touched her

cheek where the magic was slowly expanding. His magic felt strange from the outside, familiar and yet not. He didn't have to do much once he connected. His magic reached for the spell, and the two separate chunks of power linked together like they were completing a circuit. The spell reversed with barely a thought, and his magic retreated back inside of him.

He had to resist the urge to seal it tight like he had the last time. Clearly, he couldn't be trusted around Zee when his temper was up. Without magic, she couldn't defend herself, and he wasn't willing to put her in danger again. His only recourse was to keep as far away from her as possible. For her own protection, whether she wanted it or not.

In the end, they weren't so different after all.

***

ZEE

ZEE HADN'T PREPARED for him to use his magic against her, albeit accidentally. He released her from the spell, but didn't let her go right away.

"Are you all right?" His eyes searched hers, but the momentary fear had faded almost before she'd registered her reaction.

She didn't know how to respond to him. Her temper had calmed the second she'd felt the spell hit her. Out of habit, she'd centered herself and dealt with the magic first. His anger at her seemed to be gone too, but his shields remained impenetrable. "I'm fine. That's a powerful spell to know."

His hand dropped, and he shook his head. "Maddie did it to me once before. At the time, I thought I was going to die." He glared at his hands. "I'm sorry, Zee. I thought I was getting the hang of it."

Zee missed his touch, but she could only reach out so many times. "It's common among those who are novices."

"Yeah, but I'll bet those people have a mentor who can take control nearby, someone with power."

She didn't think he meant it as an insult, but it hit her all the same. He was right. Novices were trained by people who could take control if a spell failed or went haywire. Clearly, she couldn't do that.

The day had been emotional and tiring for both of them, but she couldn't easily forget his accusations. *Why do you have to be this way?* They couldn't seem to stop hurting each other. Better to focus on the immediate problem.

Zee could feel Yule approaching, and knew the burgeoning elemental power often interfered with control. "Ryan, this means you need to keep practicing. Keep learning."

He was shaking his head before she'd finished her sentence. "No. It means I'm dangerous without a leash."

"You're not a wild animal. Magic is a natural part of—"

"No, it's not," he yelled. He paced to the bed and back, making sure to stay well out of reach. He clung to his obvious frustration and wouldn't let her in to help him. "It's not natural to me."

She'd reach one more time. Zee took a chance and placed her hand on his arm. He twitched but didn't shake her off. "I know you'd never hurt me."

"Yes, I would. I've hurt people before."

His certainty pained her. "How? You've been sealed for years."

"Before I met you."

She moved closer and framed his face with her hands.

He let her, but wouldn't meet her eyes, staring over her shoulder instead. "Will you tell me?"

He waited so long she thought he planned to refuse. Zee stayed planted in front of him. She could be patient when she needed to be.

Eventually, he closed his eyes and spoke. "I started having issues when I was seventeen. Weird stuff happening sometimes. A red glow that I could see, but no one else could. I thought there was something wrong with me, but when I told my dad, he blew me off. We were driving to visit his folks, and I got so angry. He'd always said we could tell him anything, but when I had a real problem, he didn't want to hear it."

Zee could feel the raw agony coming off him in waves, even through his shield. This was an open sore that he'd never tried to heal. The warrior in her urged caution. His vulnerable state made him unpredictable, and like he'd said, she couldn't stop him from truly harming her with his magic. The woman in her ignored the warning.

She slid her hands around his waist and hugged him. He held himself stiff for a second, but quickly curled forward, locking his hands behind her back. He needed the comfort, and she'd never deny him.

"I wanted him to pay attention. I wanted him to stop the car and listen to what I was saying. And he did. He stopped mid-sentence talking to Mom. His hands froze on the steering wheel, and when the road curved, we kept driving straight. Right through the ditch and into a tree at fifty-five miles an hour."

She pulled back so she could see his face, but his eyes were clenched closed. "It wasn't your fault."

He wasn't listening, too caught in his memories to hear her. "Mom and I were wearing seatbelts, but Dad always hated them. He said they got in the way in an emergency. Mom broke her left leg, I had a concussion, but Dad didn't make it."

"I'm so sorry, Ryan."

"We moved here because Mom wanted to be closer to her family." He opened his eyes and their gazes locked. "And I met you."

"That's why you were so adamant," she whispered.

"You helped me. All these years you've helped me. I need you to help me again."

Her heart hurt for him, but his way wasn't the answer. "I can't, Ryan. Even if I could use my magic, I couldn't remove yours. I told you that then. Locking it away will only hurt you in the end."

"We have a deal."

She nodded and hoped she could make him understand. "You want me to seal your magic for good, and I have an idea that will work indefinitely, but it comes at a high cost."

"I don't care."

She wanted to shake him. "I do. You can learn to control it."

His face softened, and Zee thought he might give in. That he might trust her and believe in her enough that he'd be willing to learn. "I'm not going to risk it."

Her hope drained out of her. She remained a means to an end to him. Disappointment ran through her, and she didn't bother to hide it. She wanted him to understand how she felt about his decision. About choosing fear over her.

He shook his head as if she'd said something, but he was reacting to her emotions. "Is that all that matters to you? My magic?"

"No. You matter to me, but you refuse to hear that. You won't be the same person after."

"Maybe not, but I won't run the risk of killing anyone I care about."

She growled in frustration and let him go. "Very well. Have it your way, but we need to deal with the Wood first. I think one of my people may know something or have something to do with all this."

"I said I'd help, but not tonight."

"Ryan, this is serious."

He backed away as if she'd caught fire. "I'm done talking about this. The apartment is yours as long as you need it." The door opened and closed silently, and Zee was left in his bedroom alone.

She leaned back against the wall and slid to the floor. He'd left. Zee'd never thought he'd actually do it. Deep inside, she'd always believed that Ryan would hold. The apartment door closed quietly in the other room. Her mind circled around and around to the same thoughts. He was afraid. He didn't trust her. He hated himself. She didn't want him to leave. *I don't want to leave him. Magic or no, I'd stay with him.*

Tears fell silently down her cheeks. She knew she should get up. Put on clothes. Go back to her research. Her head dropped to her knees. Fatigue pulled at her, and her heart hurt like he'd ripped out part of her and taken it with him. *Because he had.*

The loss of her magic had been traumatic, but she'd adjusted. She'd learned she could live without it if she had to. This feeling was worse. The loss of Ryan, of seeing him every day, curling next to him on the couch, waking up to his warmth, that devastated her. She'd begun to believe that her future could be different than the one she'd always seen for herself. But Ryan didn't want that future. Pain lodged in her chest and made it hard to breathe.

She'd thought he might want the same thing she did, but he valued the seal far more than her. As painful as that was to admit, she also knew it was because he wouldn't risk the people around him. He would pay dearly to be rid of magic, of her. She understood his need to protect, but this wasn't the way.

She wiped her cheeks and got up, but instead of getting dressed, she crawled into Ryan's bed. The dreamwalk and the fight had drained her. The bond told her that Ryan was somewhere safe for now, even if that somewhere was away from her. She resolved that she'd rest and then she'd leave. Ryan wouldn't return as long as she stayed; he'd made that clear. She'd take her ancient cell phone and venture into the shadows. They'd done enough talking and research, it was time for action.

ZEE WOKE up alone in the apartment. She'd gotten used to the different feel when Ryan was home, and he obviously hadn't returned. The memory of last night slammed into her as she noted his absence. He wasn't coming back. Tears threatened again, but she'd already wasted enough time crying. She threw off the covers then paused in the middle of the room. The hoodie she still wore smelled like Ryan, but the previous night's activities had left her sticky and sore. She needed a shower and clean clothes, but after, the hoodie would accompany her into the Wood. A memory and a warning to remember where his priorities were set.

Forty-five minutes later, she raided the pantry, dressed for a walk outside. Thick leggings, her sneakers, and two layers of shirts under the hoodie. There was a large tender spot inside of her that she avoided thinking about, but every once in a while, the bond with Ryan flared and the spot twinged. She could call Sera and have her remove the bond, but Zee wasn't ready to sever the connection.

She'd taken the time to rebraid her hair, and she felt more like her former self than she had in weeks. Her leather armor would have been nice, but Zee imagined it had returned to her cottage in the Glade. Zee still didn't understand why the Wood would change her clothes while exiling her. The armor would have been nice to have while traipsing through a shadow realm made by an elemental forest. The symbols inscribed into the leather gave her some magical protection, and Zee worried she'd need it.

She stilled while stuffing her pack with food. *Magic imbued her leather armor.* The Wood had kept the leather because it couldn't counter the inert symbols. That magic couldn't be sealed. The shadows appeared for people with some active magic in them, luring them in. She'd bet the purpose was to neutralize the magic.

Her people were all too stubborn to leave. Ryan had been right on that front. The Wood let them stay because it had sealed all their magic. Except for Chad. She tilted her head and stared at the box of granola bars in her hand, her mind far away. How had Chad avoided the same fate as everyone else? She knew from experience that they couldn't stop the neutralization. The Wood vastly out-powered a handful of Fae.

She shook her head. It was frustrating that she couldn't contact anyone else in the Glade. Lana was the only person whom she had enough of a connection with to make the dreamwalk work. Without being in physical contact with Ryan, she wouldn't pull that much magic anyway. His reaction could be volatile, and he was already running scared. She didn't need to give him another reason to fear.

The granola bars went into the pack along with her cell phone, a flashlight, a bottle of water, some oranges, and a package of gummy dinosaurs labeled in small, neat handwriting. She wanted to be prepared for what lay inside the shadows, but she'd reached the end of her limited options. The bond with Ryan should maintain across the distance, it had when he'd disappeared inside accidentally, so she'd be able to reach him if something went horribly wrong.

Her lips flattened together. Then again, if something went horribly wrong, she had no intention of encouraging him to run to her rescue. She could rescue herself, and he could stay safely in the human world exactly as he wanted it.

She left his apartment, but backtracked to grab the book he'd bought her and stuff it in the pack with her provisions. If she wasn't going to return, she wanted to keep this reminder of her hopes for a happier future.

Despite being mid-morning on a Sunday, people bustled about from store to store like hummingbirds. Wrapped in brightly colored scarves and hats, they slowed down to window-shop as the cold turned their faces pink.

No one paid Zee any attention as she turned away from the center of town and strode down a side street that would lead her to the Wood. She walked the opposite direction from Jake and Sera's house because she didn't want to run the risk of either of them seeing her, or of Ryan being there. The bond indicated that he was in that direction, but she didn't linger on the connection long enough for him to sense her or her intentions. He was more adept than he thought at using his magic and reading the bond. She didn't want him to get any idea of what she was doing and follow her. Luckily, the Wood circled the town on three sides. Any of those three directions would get her where she needed to go.

A brisk wind blew through the bright, sunny day, and Zee could feel the rising power in the Earth under her. Yule had arrived, after all. Tonight marked the longest night, when the energy shifted from dormancy to growth. An influx of power through the tainted Wood would make things interesting. If she was right, she needed to find the root of the taint before that power flooded the Glade.

Zee stuffed her hands into her pockets and let the pack slap against her back as she walked. Her mind kept flitting back to Ryan, then jerking away again when the pain set in. Walking through his town made it hard not to think of him, especially surrounded by his scent. Harder not to reach for him. She had no intention of offering herself up as a sacrifice to an angry elemental forest, but the forest might have other ideas. The possibility sobered her. She knew, even after their fight, maybe especially after, that Ryan would be by her side in a second. He understood the importance of calming the Wood, and he had a deep-seated need to protect her.

His lack of faith in her ability to protect herself stopped her from calling him.

Zee realized she'd clenched her hands into fists and forced them to relax. She was terrible at not thinking about him. A small car that reeked of sandalwood pulled up next to her on the road and honked. Zee stooped and peered into the window to find a bright green iguana staring back at her. She jumped back a step, then realized that the woman behind the iguana was waving her around the car to her open driver window.

With the window open, the sandalwood scent nearly overpowered her, but Zee schooled her face into a polite greeting. Janet, scarves dangling everywhere, smiled and pointed to the backseat.

"Need a ride?"

Zee glanced into the back of the car, expecting it to be full of marmots or something ridiculous, but it was perfectly clean. The wind gusted against her face, and she shivered hard. Stinking of incense was a small price to pay for a ride. "Yes. Thank you."

Janet waited until she'd buckled her seat belt before putting the car back in drive. "Where do you need to go?"

"The woods at the edge of town."

She squinted in the rearview mirror. "It's a little cold to be hiking today, isn't it?"

Zee stared out the window at the slowly passing scenery, but kept an eye on Janet. "Yes, but it had to be today."

"I understand." Janet nodded sagely. "The universe decides what it will, we must simply trust the timing."

Flinging oneself into an unknown, potentially dangerous conclave of powers certainly required trust. Zee trusted herself, and she trusted that the Wood remained neutral at its core. Whatever insidious magic was at play could be countered if she could find the source. After that, maybe she'd let the universe decide.

Janet tapped the steering wheel in a quick rhythm, drawing Zee's attention back to the eccentric woman. "What better time than now to start anew?" *Maybe Janet did understand.*

14

ZEE

JANET DIDN'T HAVE to drive far to reach the end of town. The road ended at a dirt driveway leading to a rundown house with a boarded window. Zee thanked her and shouldered her pack, stepping off the hardened mud and into the wild growth that preceded the forest. Janet waved with her whole body as she turned the car around and drove away.

What a strange woman. She'd even rigged up a seatbelt for the iguana's tank in the front seat. Zee shook her head. Strange, but kind. In town, the buildings had created a bit of a windbreak, but out past the clearing only the trees to shield her. Television, and living in a magical Glade where elemental magic controlled the climate, had led her to believe that Texas was temperate. Zee didn't have gloves or a hat, so the cold wind became a problem. She'd pulled her hood over her hair, but the air zipped in and out of it with abandon.

Zee hoped that whatever the Wood did with other magic, it was in a temperate place. If she remembered correctly, the Wood started a few feet into the trees out here. No paths appeared, and the usual shadows lurked under the canopy of pine branches. As had happened last time, the Wood wasn't responding to her.

The wind whipped her hood off again, and Zee wished she could use even a modicum of magic to counteract the December air. She picked her way carefully through the trees and the underbrush, grateful for the weak light filtering through the needle-covered branches. The snow that had fallen had already melted in the trees, or had never reached the ground. She wasn't well-versed in snowfall, but she knew it melted into water, and mud would have made the trip much worse.

After several minutes, Zee came to a stop next to a small group of boulders. She should have been well into the Wood by now, but she didn't sense any magic. The walking had helped a bit with the temperature, but she'd lost feeling in her nose. Second thoughts began to creep in. She knew she wasn't wrong about the borders, but what about the rest of it? Maybe the Wood simply didn't see any value in her anymore and had cut ties. She suspected Lana had done as much, and Ryan was well on his way to eliminating her from his life. What interest would a non-sentient elemental forest have in her?

She leaned against the boulder and took a swig of her water. Her hand brushed the book as she replaced the bottle, and her stomach tightened. Everyone of import to her had decided that she wasn't worth their time. It was a rough lesson in guarding her heart, and she'd learned it too late.

Her magic had always been a valuable part of her, but she'd never realized how much other people valued her based on it. She couldn't even do anything as simple as capturing the attention of the Wood. Ryan had succeeded with zero effort.

She sighed, faced with her answer. She needed to borrow his magic again to entice the shadows.

He'd notice. She'd hoped to complete this mission on her own and return to the Glade without seeing Ryan. He'd search her out there so she could fulfill her end of their bargain, but she'd have some time first. If he sensed her pull, he'd follow the magic. With the bond still connecting them, she couldn't mask her location.

Zee didn't want him in danger, but she also needed some space. Her wounds were raw, and having Ryan in her vicinity would make it that much harder to put their ill-fated relationship behind her. Zee tried drawing several sigils against the boulder, the trees around her, directly in the pine straw and dirt, but none of it had any effect. She needed magic. *She needed Ryan*.

Zee stood up straight and brutally quieted the voice. Ryan had made his choice clear, and she needed no one. His magic provided a means to an end. She wouldn't be able to pull very much at this distance, but she had a feeling it would be enough.

Her eyes drifted closed as she followed the bond with her senses. It stretched out between them, shuttered and silent. Both of them were wrapped tight in their shields, unwilling to open to the other person. At the other end, she found Ryan's dormant magic. Zee took special care to only take a tiny amount. A tendril of warmth snaked through her. She smiled for a moment at the familiar feel, and opened her eyes.

In front of her, purple shadows burst into existence. This close, they resembled dark roiling clouds more than shad-ows, but it didn't particularly matter. A doorway was a doorway. She didn't want to let go of Ryan's magic in case they disappeared, but she could tell he'd taken notice of her meddling. If she moved fast, maybe she could finish her mission before he showed up. The bitter wind blew against her back, and Zee stepped forward through the entrance.

The sunlight disappeared completely from one moment to the next. Zee searched the flat black sky. No stars or clouds on this side. Her eyes adjusted quickly to the dim light, but when she examined the area, she couldn't see any source for it. There were no shadows to mark where she'd entered, and she wondered what would happen if she released the magic she'd borrowed. She kept the idea as an unlikely backup plan for emergencies.

The shadows had deposited her in a clearing, and after a moment, she recognized where she was, the edge of the Fae clearing where Torix's tree had stood. The tree, which Sera had destroyed along with everything else, had marked a nexus of power that helped shore up the barriers, and Zee had been there many times to renew their power. She'd been heading here when she'd gotten lost in the trods before this mess had started.

Zee walked slowly to the center and crouched down to brush needles off of the flat stone embedded in the ground. They'd never discussed it, but Sera's battle with Torix had taken place on top of a font of power. Zee had always thought putting Torix there was an unnecessary risk, but she's been born well after he'd been punished. Her finger traced the faint symbols etched into the stone and worn smooth by time.

A sharp edge bit into her skin, and Zee sucked in a breath. She shifted around and brushed more debris off of it. In the darkness, she hadn't seen it immediately, but a long crack with sharp, new edges stretched from one end to the other. Her finger throbbed, and a few drops of blood oozed out of the cut.

Her brows drew together. The stone was largely symbolic, but nothing should have been able to crack it as a marker of the Wood. Then again, nothing should have been able to bring down the barriers. The old magics were fluctuating, and the Fae would need to adapt. Zee wished for a moment that Ryan were there. The tiny bit of magic she'd claimed whispered across her skin and through her body, giving her a faint red glow. It wasn't enough to manifest Ryan, but it wanted an outlet.

The air nearly crackled with power. Zee backed away from the stone and peered into the trees. A few feet from the clearing, they simply faded into darkness. The peak of Yule wasn't far off, and from what she could tell with the cracked stone, *something* had interrupted the flow. Elemental magic was gathering in the Wood, and she stood in the nexus of a system with a hole in it.

As dire as the situation was, it didn't explain why the Wood would be seeking out power and sealing it away. She'd barely finished her thought when to her surprise, a trod opened next to her in the trees. Zee rolled to the balls of her feet to move away, but hesitated. She could try to take the path herself and risk being trapped in the trods again or she could face whatever or whomever was going to emerge.

She didn't want to risk a second chance at walking for all eternity with no destination, so she shifted back closer to the trees behind her. One of the pine trunks was almost big enough to mask her, so she slid behind it and waited.

It wasn't entirely a surprise when Chad sauntered into the clearing, but she'd hoped her suspicions were wrong. He approached the stone and rubbed his hands together. Zee shook her head. He wasn't even taking basic precautions. All signs pointed to him retaining his magic, but he hadn't used it to sense around himself as he'd been taught. She scowled. Probably because he never thought about anyone but himself. She'd definitely be choosing a new lieutenant when this disaster ended.

Chad crouched down and murmured something she couldn't make out from her hiding spot. Sound traveled strangely in the clearing, as if the Wood suppressed it. His head fell back, and she sensed magic flowing into Chad.

Her anger drained away, and she crept closer to get a better look. Ryan's magic would come in handy after all. She took a tiny bit and used it to enhance her perceptions. With the boost, she could clearly see what she'd suspected. Chad's magic was sealed like the rest of them. He was using elemental magic.

RYAN

AFTER LEAVING Zee in the apartment, Ryan hunched his shoulders and hurried down the stairs before he could change his mind. She made him pissed and scared and aroused all at once. He couldn't be around her and act like a normal human without jumping from one extreme to the next. A hefty dose of shame poured into the mixture when he thought about how he'd frozen her in place. If he was capable of doing that to her based on an errant thought, what would happen when he really got angry?

The walk across the dark parking lot to his car cooled down his temper significantly. It was damn cold outside, and he'd left without his coat. He refused to go back for it now, so he'd just suffer through. Better than another go-around with Zee. She had this skewed opinion of magic that counted the good parts, but not the bad. He'd told her, hadn't he? In the wrong hands, it was dangerous.

His were definitely the wrong hands.

Ryan started the car and let it idle. He wasn't sure where he should go, anywhere away from Zee and all her temptations. Jake's house seemed like the obvious choice, but he didn't want to put his friends in danger either. For that matter, should he even be driving?

He breathed in deep and took stock. The magic had settled down again, quiet and inert. Zee's lessons had paid off in that he could control the power as long as he didn't panic. The memory of Zee straddling his lap while she gave him orders lingered. He wouldn't be forgetting *that* lesson any time soon.

A crushing pang squeezed his chest when he thought about spending his nights alone, without Zee curled up next to him. Without her bossing him around or challenging him or delighting in learning a new skill. *It was worth it.* He had to keep telling himself that over and over. *It was worth it to keep her safe.*

Ryan drove to Jake's house on autopilot. The lights were all off when he got there. He parked on the street and debated waking them up. They'd let him sleep on the couch and give him breakfast in the morning, but he wasn't ready to explain himself yet. To hell with it. He'd sleep in the car.

When he woke up the next day at almost noon, his neck hurt from sleeping upright. The night rushed back to him. He had to fight the urge to reach for Zee through the bond, to make sure she was okay. The knee-jerk impulse convinced him he was doing the right thing. Jake's truck in the driveway didn't really surprise him since Jake split his time among several of his crews on any given day, but Sera's car in the driveway reminded him to knock.

Several minutes went by with Ryan shivering on the porch, and he almost went next door to Evie's place. Jake finally opened the door, and Ryan didn't wait for an invitation. He barged into the warmth of the living room and collapsed on the couch.

Jake nodded and closed the door. "Come on in."

"I'm in a bit of trouble."

"And this is new how, exactly?"

Ryan rubbed his hand over his face. "For real this time. Can I stay here for a while?"

Jake glanced at the stairs and sighed. "Of course you can. Anything you need. Where's Zee?"

"That's where the trouble comes in."

"Is she okay?"

"She is now that I've left."

Jake tilted his head. "I'll admit I was preoccupied when you knocked, but I'm paying attention now. Explain."

Ryan stared down at his hands. He'd never told Jake about how his dad had died. He'd never even shared that he had magic inside him, though that secret had come out in October. His deal with Zee had been between them, but now everything was fucked up and he could really use some advice.

"I'm dangerous when my magic is free."

Jake sat down next to him on the couch. "What do you mean free?"

"I've been going to Zee since I first moved here to have her seal my magic. Once a year. In exchange for my help in other ways."

"Well that explains why you always hated when Zee called."

Ryan nodded. "I felt like a servant, but there was always a little thrill, you know?" He glanced at Jake's face and saw understanding.

"You had to do her bidding or whatever, but you got to see her."

Relief flooded him that he didn't have to explain every little thing. "Yeah. It wasn't a big deal until these last few weeks. Zee's here. My magic is unsealed. And I can't control it when I'm around her."

"What'd you do?"

Ryan's jaw clenched, and he had to force himself to respond. "We had a moment. I was...mad. Then I accidentally froze her in place because I didn't want her to leave."

He waited for the recriminations, but Jake was silent. When he looked over, Jake shrugged. "That's all?"

"I magically forced her to do something against her will. Against *my* will. What if she'd been doing something that required her to focus? Or move?"

"Was she?"

"No, but that doesn't make it okay." Ryan stood up and paced to the fireplace and back. "When my magic first appeared, I accidentally froze my dad while he was driving and that's what caused the accident that killed him."

"Oh shit, man. I'm really sorry." Jake was silent for a few beats while Ryan continued to pace. "Does your family have magic?"

"No. It just came out of nowhere, and I had no idea what was happening." Ryan roughly ran his hands through already disheveled hair.

"And then you moved here and had Zee seal your magic."

"Yeah. I'm not safe, and now I've done it again. I panicked. I couldn't fix it until she told me what to do."

"But you did fix it, right? You didn't leave her there all stiff?"

He glared at Jake. "Of course not. She talked me through it, and we got it fixed."

"So now you know how, and even if it happened again, you'd know what to do?"

"Yeah. I told you, she taught me how to undo it." Jake's mouth twitched, and Ryan knew he was trying not to smile. "What?"

"I'm not going to lie. I'm getting a whole lot of pleasure out of you having girl problems for once instead of me."

"It's not girl problems. It's magic problems."

Jake tilted his head. "Are you sure? You've had access to your magic for what...a month and a half? I haven't seen you do anything that wasn't on purpose. It sounds like you're using it as an excuse to run away from something else. I'm sorry about your dad. You have to know that, right? But you had no training and no warning. You were a kid. That's not the case anymore. Even though something unexpected happened, you got freaked and came here. You didn't exile yourself away from the world, only Zee."

Ryan stopped pacing to stare out the window toward the trees. Damn straight he'd exiled himself away from her. He could hurt her. His emotions went crazy around Zee, so he needed to stay away from her specifically, at least until his magic was sealed for good. By that point, she'd be back with her people and her own magic. She wouldn't need him anymore.

Ryan sucked in a breath at the pain from that thought. "Maybe it's both. Either way, until Zee is back in the Glade, I gave her my apartment. I'll help her as much as I can from here."

Jake joined him at the window. "Why do you sound so broken about this?"

"Because I'd much rather be with her than with you."

"Then why are you here? You had a little mishap, but you guys were able to work through it together. It sounds like you're better off with Zee than apart from her if you're going to be having magical breakdowns."

Ryan wanted to argue the solid point, but he couldn't think of a logical comeback. His mind kept returning to the suspicion that the separation wasn't protection for her, it was protection for him. He didn't want to be around when Zee decided she didn't need him anymore without his magic. "It hurts too much to be around her, okay? She thinks she wants me, but really my magic is just a handy replacement for hers."

"Did she say that?"

Ryan played back their fight and something Zee said finally penetrated. *You matter to me, but you refuse to hear that...I can't live without you.* "No. She said she wanted me, not my magic. But—"

Jake held up a hand. "Let me get this straight. She can't lie. She told you, straight out, that she wanted you, not your magic. And you, in all your great and powerful wisdom, decided that she was confused and you knew better. Based on absolutely no evidence whatsoever. Actually, in the face of all the evidence. In addition, you think you're better off avoiding her because in all her years of experience with magic, she doesn't know as much as you."

Ryan growled in frustration. "You don't understand."

Jake lost his jovial tone. "No, *you* don't. You're running so hard in the other direction that you're not thinking this through logically. She's hot. You could take what she's offering and move on when she does. Why do you think that option tears you apart?"

The realization dawned slowly, but it became obvious once he stopped making excuses. "I love her."

Jake clapped him on the back. "There you go. I knew you'd get there eventually."

Ryan's eyes widened. "I'm a jackass."

"And there's the second half."

Sera came down the stairs with her shirt buttoned wrong and offered him a wan smile. "Ryan, what a pleasant surprise that didn't interrupt anything important at all."

Jake grinned. "He figured it out."

Her features went slack with shock, and she sent Jake a look that Ryan couldn't read. "It?"

"Zee. He figured out he loves her."

Sera breathed out in relief. "Oh. Right. Yeah, well, it's about time."

Ryan narrowed his eyes as he watched them. They were keeping a secret, poorly, but he supposed he deserved it for his own years of silence. Jake met Sera at the bottom of the stairs and leaned in to whisper in her ear. A gentle tug from Ryan's middle got his attention. Zee had pulled some of his magic through the bond. He tensed up, expecting to have to settle the rest of it down, but everything stayed calm. The bond buzzed with power, but his magic stayed centered.

What is she doing? Ryan turned toward the direction of his apartment, but that wasn't right. The bond reached in a different direction. Toward the Wood. He cursed, and Sera jumped.

"It's not the end of the world, Ryan. Being in love can be awesome."

Ryan blinked, then his brain caught up. "It's not that. I'll deal with that barrel of issues later. Zee went into the Wood."

"Like...*into* the Wood. With the scary shadows and silence? Could she be taking a walk?"

Ryan shook his head. "She just used my magic, and she's *in* the Wood."

"I don't suppose she shared any kind of plan with you?"

"No. We were, ah...a little busy."

Jake nodded and opened the coat closet. "Time to suit up."

"Suit up? What are we, the Avengers?

"Here, take one of our extra coats. It's cold as balls outside."

Ryan caught the way too small, bright pink puffer that Jake threw at him and raised a brow. "I'd rather freeze to death than wear this."

Sera speared Jake with a look. "Stop trying to give away my coat." She reached past him and pulled out a bigger puffer in a respectable black. "This one should fit your massive shoulders."

Ryan frowned and shared a look with Jake. He had no idea what she was talking about. He and Jake were about the same size, and they'd barely had time to work out lately what with nonstop magical emergencies happening all of a sudden.

"Look, you guys don't have to go with me." Ryan put on the coat because it was there, and Jake was right about the cold. "Zee and I have some issues to work through, but I can do it myself."

Sera walked by and patted his cheek. "Aww, you're so cute when you're making stupid decisions. You may be worried about *your* magic, but *mine* is under control."

"You heard that?"

She shrugged. "Sound travels in here. Also, I was half listening at the top of the steps. Why would Zee take off into the Wood on her own?"

"Probably because of some things I said that I now regret." His mind insisted on running through their fight again, and one of the things she'd said stuck with him. "She thinks there's something going on with one of her people. Some asshole named Chad."

"Her third in command? That Chad?"

Could there be more than one Fae named Chad? Ryan felt the sharp edge of panic. If he'd listened to her before instead of his own fears, they'd have been able to come up with a plan. Together. He wasn't even sure they'd be able to find her, let alone what they'd be up against. What was to stop the Wood from sealing all of their magic?

"Sera, maybe you should stay here."

She stopped shoving snacks and water bottles into a backpack and put her hands on her hips. "We've already covered this. I'm not letting you and this one," she pointed at Jake, "go on a rescue mission with untested magic and a gut feeling. If the Wood is going to eat one of us, it's going to eat all of us."

He shook his head. Sera practically glowed with fierce confidence. He couldn't believe Will had ever been able to bully her. "What if all our magic gets sealed?"

She went back to stuffing. "Then we find our way out without magic. After we retrieve Zee."

Her nonchalant tone made losing her power sound like a minor inconvenience. Maybe he'd been clinging too tightly to his idea of how other people reacted to their magic. Jake tossed items to Sera and didn't seem the least bit worried. He must have sensed Ryan's eyes on him because he looked up.

"What?"

Ryan shook his head a little. "I was wondering how you do it. How do you accept that Sera might be doing something dangerous and go along with it?"

Sera glared but stayed silent.

Jake sighed. "I go with her. I trust her to take care of herself, and me if it comes to it. I remember that closing her out is like cutting off a piece of myself. Do you think Zee is in the Wood right now, cowering, waiting for you to come riding to her rescue?"

Ryan's smile came and went. "No way in hell. She'd fight to her last breath. That's what scares me."

"There's danger everywhere. You can't keep her from living, even if you wanted to, because she'd probably kick your ass and go live her life anyway. I've seen you guys spar."

"Hey!"

"Can't argue with the truth. Besides, you're stronger together than either of you is apart."

Ryan stood in the whirlwind of their preparations and finally listened to Jake's advice. They *were* stronger together. Neutering them both on the off chance something horrific happened with his magic again reeked of stupidity. Something horrific might happen anyway, and he'd rather face it with Zee next to him.

Jake ushered them out of the house, but Sera made them wait for a second while she grabbed a small baseball bat that Ryan had seen somewhere before out of the umbrella stand by the door. She tucked it into her pack and strode out into the sunlight with the handle sticking out through the zippers.

Sera squinted into the sun and slipped sunglasses onto her face. "Let's go give your warrior princess some backup."

15

RYAN

FOR SOME REASON, Ryan had thought it would be easier to get eaten by the Wood. The last time had taken no effort. He stood inside the tree line with Jake and Sera, across the street from their house. The shadows appeared for him, for Sera too, but Jake couldn't see them. All Jake got was underbrush and sunlight, nothing dark.

"I thought you said Zee couldn't see it either. How did she get in?"

"Good question," muttered Ryan. He could feel her, beyond his reach, but close. She'd widened the connection by using his magic, and it reminded him that like Zee, Jake didn't have any magic of his own.

"Jake, use a little bit of Sera's power. I think that's what Zee was doing. She had to use my power to get access."

He shrugged, and a second later, his eyes widened. "Whoa, that looks like some end of the world shit."

Sera tilted her head. "You're sure you didn't see any zombie bunnies or anything in there?"

"Those weren't zombie bunnies. We've been over this," said Jake.

Sera shuddered.

They all stared at the swirling shadows for a moment, but a bad feeling urged Ryan to rush forward. He clenched his jaw, trying to see past the fact that Zee was in there somewhere on her own. They didn't know the situation on the other side. The Wood could send them to the same place or spread them all over.

Ryan didn't want to lose anyone else. "We should hold hands."

For once, they didn't argue or make snarky comments. Sera reached out both hands, and Ryan took the lead. Jake kept Sera sandwiched between them. They only had to move a couple of feet to pass through to the shadow realm. Sera's hand clenched Ryan's tightly, and when he looked back, Jake followed closely behind her. Ryan breathed a sigh of relief. At least one thing had gone right.

The moving shadows disappeared, but the darkness beyond Jake made it seem like the forest simply ended in nothing. Ahead of them, the trees got sparse then opened to a clearing. Ryan wasn't ready to let go of his connection to Sera yet, and Jake must have felt the same way because he edged closer to wrap an arm around her. A weird feeling started at his legs and worked its way up his body, leaving him tingling and hyper-focused as if he'd had too much caffeine.

Sera whispered behind him. "Can you feel that too? It's like what happened at Samhain. There must be another surge of power tonight."

Ryan spoke over his shoulder, not ready to move forward. "Zee mentioned something about Yule coming up."

Jake pointed past them at the opening. "Isn't this Torix's

clearing?" They both gaped at Jake, and he shrugged. "I spent a lot of time creeping through the woods that night."

Ryan wished he'd paid a little more attention when Zee had been talking about her research. He'd thought he'd been listening, but he couldn't remember a single thing about those nights except that Zee fit really well against him.

"So we've returned to the scene of the crime." Sera's voice sounded strained, and he saw Jake drop a kiss at her temple in his periphery.

"It wasn't your fault, Sera."

"We're here because I broke something the last time. Maybe I can help fix it."

A golden glow started to emanate from Sera's hands, but then sort of fizzled out. She gasped, and dread churned heavily in his gut. "What's wrong?"

She shook her hands then looked at Jake with panicked eyes. "I can't make my magic work. It's still there, but I can't touch it."

Ryan could feel his own magic responding, and he had no problem accessing it. "Mine's fine. Why wouldn't the Wood seal me?"

Jake's brows shot up. "You're not Fae, or even half-Fae. Sera's magic is different than yours, so maybe yours is allowed?"

Ryan gazed around at the trees that existed literally in the middle of nowhere, and considered their options. They didn't know how to get back, and now Sera was effectively powerless. "Okay, you guys are now officially emergency backup. Keep your shields up and stay hidden unless it looks like one of us is dying."

Sera's face fell. "Yeah, sure."

Ryan shared a look with Jake. Sera could be unpredictable, but he knew Jake would follow through. He wanted them safe.

The bond was stronger here, maybe because of the magic tingles, and he could sense Zee ahead of them. Probably in the clearing. He walked gingerly toward the opening in the trees, careful to stay in contact with Sera. Their muffled steps sounded loud to his ears, but as he got closer, he noticed that everything was muffled, like he'd changed altitude and needed his ears to pop.

They'd made it to the edge of the trees, but not into the open, when Zee spoke into his mind.

Go home.

ZEE

ZEE KNEW the moment Ryan entered the Wood. She didn't react outwardly because she didn't want to draw Chad's attention, but when he moved closer, she lowered her shields enough to send him a message.

Go home.

She didn't know why Chad was there or how dangerous he was, and she didn't want to be distracted if she needed to defend herself. Ryan was the ultimate distraction. She hoped he listened, but she wasn't going to issue a second warning. Her shields closed tight, and she shifted to get a better view of whatever Chad was doing.

He smiled and patted the broken stone. When he'd entered the clearing, she hadn't noticed any outward signs of his power, but now he practically glowed. She had to tread lightly because with that much magic at his disposal, he could be extremely dangerous.

Her people couldn't normally wield elemental magic. The power was too volatile to be safe, and it had the potential to be addictive to the few who could access it. Chad had never given much respect to the rules and traditions of their people though. Case in point, he was kicking dirt back onto the stone instead of treating it with the reverence it deserved.

Zee wondered how long he'd been siphoning power out of the Wood directly instead of harvesting it from the trees. A new ache joined the others in her chest. *Does Lana know? Have I been a fool all along?*

Chad smirked as he brushed dirt off his hands and turned back to the trees. He must have been about done with his thievery, but Zee wasn't ready to let him leave without some answers. Only Lana knew about her being sealed, so she could probably use Chad's lack of knowledge to her advantage. She pulled her shoulders back and strode into the open.

"Hello, Chad."

He jumped and spun around. "Zee? You're back? What are you doing here?"

She managed to keep the smile off her face, but he wasn't so confident anymore. "A better question is what are *you* doing here?"

His eyes darted right and left. "The Wood is acting strangely, so I came out here to see what I could find."

He couldn't lie any more than she could, but he could tell plenty of half-truths. She'd taught him that skill. She tilted her head and stepped closer. "That's interesting. I'm here for the same reason."

"Lana said your magic was sealed." So much for her advantage.

She let a small smile surface. "Lana told me yours wasn't.

It's odd though. Your magic seems to have changed since the last time I saw you."

His eyes narrowed. "Maybe you're not remembering right. It seems like you've had a lot going on lately. How *is* Ryan?"

She shrugged and feigned arrogance, though her heart beat loud and fast in her ears. He didn't know Ryan watched from somewhere behind her in the trees, and he didn't know that they'd cut all the ties they could. His wild jab happened to land in an open wound.

"I wouldn't know." She was growing weary of the thinly veiled back and forth. They could do this all day, but if the buzzing magic under her was any indication, they didn't have that much time. Yule was approaching faster than she'd thought.

"I know you've been stealing elemental magic, Chad."

Panic flashed across his face, but he didn't give in to it. "It's not stealing if it's leaking out already."

"Semantics. It's not your magic, yet you're brimming with it. How did you even find the break?"

His shoulders curved in, and he took a step back toward the trees. "You told me to come out here and renew the barriers. I was only a few days late, but they'd already been done. You could have told me that you'd already done it, you know. I tripped as I was leaving and landed on the stone. It wasn't my fault that the magic was flowing in my face."

"That was years ago. And you didn't come tell me? Or Lana? You kept it a secret all this time...what, so you could get a little boost at the cost of the Wood? Why?"

He dropped the façade of subservience. "Because I don't want to live the rest of my life trapped in that backwoods village. Some asshole used his power against humans a long time ago and I'm supposed to pay for it because I happened to be born here? What kind of bullshit is that?"

Zee spread her hands. "You never had to stay. There are other communities that would welcome you."

He waved those aside. "None of them have Wi-Fi, not that it works here anymore. It doesn't matter anyway. The crack kept getting bigger, so I could pull more out. After the Wood sealed everyone's magic, I had to pull more so I could keep *your* people from starving. And now *I'm* the only Fae out here with magic, so it looks like I made the right decision."

Sera's relief that it wasn't her fault burst out of the trees, and Zee nearly cursed aloud. *Ryan brought back-up.* Chad had noticed too. His head snapped up, and his gaze searched the trees behind her. Zee used a bit more of Ryan's magic to gather the dirt and needles covering the stone into a mini tornado and sent them winging into the trees in the opposite direction of her friends.

"You're not the only Fae out here with magic."

Her gambit worked. Chad's attention swung back to her. "What do you care? You got what you wanted."

"I care because your selfishness is poisoning the Wood and starving our people." She moved closer to him and gestured to the stone. "What was your plan when this broke completely? You can't possibly hope to contain that much power."

He shrugged. "Who cares? It's not going to break any time soon."

Zee had to take a second to center herself because his idiocy was making her feel particularly violent. "Everyone but you, apparently." She squatted next to the stone and held her hand over it to judge the amount of damage he'd done.

As soon as she opened her shields to it, she could sense the elemental magic seeping out. It felt wrong though. She dug her other hand into the earth next to the stone and searched for the difference. The power under her was clean and strong, but the power coming through the crack in the stone was tainted. Chad shuffled closer, and Zee sent him a warning look. His hands were in the pockets of his pants, but his gaze was locked on the stone.

"We need to cleanse and close it." Zee had her suspicions about what was wrong with the stone, but without more power, she couldn't confirm them. Ryan had ignored her order to leave, but he hadn't barged into the clearing yet. With her shields lowered significantly, she was getting snippets of his mind. Anger that she'd come on her own. Worry that something would happen to her. An occasional flash of her facing off against Chad. The constant images disconcerted her, and made her glad she hadn't taught him how to speak to her mind yet.

Noticeably missing was the intent to protect her from himself. That had shifted to the intent to protect her from everything else. She wondered what had changed during the course of the day.

Zee focused so heavily on Ryan's mind and the power running through the stone that she almost missed Chad pulling the knife from his pocket. He slashed it near her face, and Zee tumbled back away from him and the stone.

"We're not closing shit."

Ryan came barreling out of the trees, but she pulled hard from him. He stumbled, and Zee sent him an apology as she flung a spell at Chad. He flinched as it hit his shield, but instead of falling to the ground stunned, he grinned and took a step closer.

"Looks like someone found their own magic battery.

Pretty ballsy of you to preach at me about stealing from the Wood when you're stealing from him. At least the Wood doesn't feel it."

Zee stood, and the mystery suddenly became clear. The Wood wasn't sentient, but it wasn't inanimate either. Chad had taken a minor wound that probably would have healed itself like Lana had said and made it a thousand times worse with his magic. *Fae* magic. The Wood was responding by trying to eliminate the threat. That's why it had sealed all the Fae magic but not the other types, and why the confluence for the sprites had disappeared. The Wood was trying to protect itself.

They had to heal the injury.

Chad stood in front of the stone, holding the knife loosely in one hand. She recognized it as the one Lana had given him years ago. The rowan wood handle had worn smooth with time, and the blade, roughly the length of his hand, curved to a wicked point. He balanced on the balls of his feet, and Zee knew his skill with that particular weapon. She wished again for her leather armor.

Ryan caught up to her alone, and Zee spared him a glance. He was pale, but steady. She could still sense Sera and Jake in the trees, but if she wasn't mistaken, Jake was doing everything in his power to hold Sera back. Surprisingly, Sera let him.

To Ryan's credit, he didn't try to shove her behind him, though she could feel how much he wanted to. She dropped the shields between them and was startled to find that he was braced for her to use more of his magic, even if it brought him to his knees. Even more shocking was the way he held himself wide open to her. The bond swelled with warmth and love.

Zee let the emotions wash over her, a balm to her battered heart.

She wouldn't reach for him physically, Chad might see that as a potential weakness, but she let him feel how much he meant to her. Let him see that she'd come into the Wood for him. If Chad had paid more attention in training, he would have easily been able to spot their distraction and make use of it. For once, Zee appreciated his lazy work ethic.

With the bond fully open, she shared her plan with Ryan.

Chad shifted his weight slightly left, more to Ryan's side. The asshole assumed Ryan was the bigger threat. Zee wanted so badly to prove him wrong, but if they were to help the Wood before the full influx of magic from Yule, Ryan would need all of his power. She dropped her pack at her feet and decided to give Chad one more chance.

"You don't have to do this, Chad. We can fix this."

He laughed. "I don't see anything that needs to be fixed." He'd made his choice. *Very well.*

"Okay then, see if you can keep up." She released all but a tiny bit of magic back to Ryan and used that bit to boost her speed.

Chad flipped the knife to a reverse grip and swung out wide, quicker than she remembered. She leaned back to avoid the blade and used his opening to kick him in the stomach. He grunted, but absorbed the impact and brought the knife down fast. Zee narrowly avoided being stabbed and slid back to sidestep around him.

He moved with her, but stayed stubbornly over the stone. She closed again, low, ready for the strike. He was skilled, but predictable. Another swing, and she blocked and trapped his knife arm. Zee pivoted intending to disarm him and toss him into the dirt, but a blast of magic against her back dislodged her grip and knocked her forward.

She rolled with the force and hopped back onto her feet. Chad smirked, but he'd moved away from the stone. Behind him, Ryan got close enough to touch it and started channeling his magic through the edges of the tear. Elemental power was building and putting pressure on the crack though. Ryan would need more time.

"Too afraid to fight me without magic?" she taunted.

Chad scoffed. "I'm not stupid. You're gimped right now, otherwise I'd already be unconscious. But yeah, fighting you *with* magic...that's a great idea."

She dove to the side as the knife zipped past her wrapped in his magic. It spun neatly and tried to impale her again as it flew back to him. Instead of dodging, she reached out and grabbed the knife out of the air. The second her fingers wrapped around the hilt, she realized her mistake.

The knife had been a distraction.

Chad's arms wrapped around her middle and his weight drove her into the ground. They hit hard enough to knock the breath out of her. His hands locked around her wrists and squeezed. Zee could sense Ryan's anger at Chad, but he didn't waver from his work. He believed absolutely that she'd handle Chad, and healing the wound in the nexus needed his full attention.

In a slightly more advanced move than the ones she'd showed her class, Zee twisted her wrists and brought her elbows tight against her body. Chad followed, unwilling to let go, and she slid a leg between them to kick him off of her.

He lost his grip as he tumbled to the side. She jabbed the knife out toward his stomach, but he pulled his shield up in time for it to deflect harmlessly. As long as he was using the elemental magic from the Wood to reinforce his shields, she couldn't do any damage. Zee leapt to her feet as a flood of frustration slammed into her from Ryan.

She forced herself not to look at him, but her mind busily scrabbled to find the source of his impediment. Her connection with Ryan allowed her to scan the break, and she found a small spell, hidden among the rushing currents, holding it open. Ryan's confidence wavered and his fear rose. She could feel the Wood beginning to reach out for him. Without faith, the Wood would see Ryan's magic as another irritant.

There's another spell in the way. You have to remove the block first. Like you did with me. I can't defeat Chad without you. You have to fully embrace your magic, Ryan. Anything less and the Wood will seal you too.

Ryan's concentration faltered, and Zee knew full well what she'd just told him. She'd given him a choice between getting his most fervent desire or her. He didn't hesitate. A surge of magic pushed through the blocking spell, and a thought like a caress touched her.

Love, overwhelming in its chaos, engulfed her for a moment, and Chad moved closer in her distraction. He used his magic to yank the knife from her grip and into his hand. With blinding speed, he ripped a gash across her upper arm.

Zee hissed in pain, as her blood flew out in an arc from the tip of the knife. She brought her other arm up to block the second swing which left another long slice on her forearm. Rage from Ryan pounded into her at about the same time he tackled Chad and Jake and Sera erupted from the trees.

Chad didn't seem to notice them. Or he didn't think two humans were much of a threat. Probably the second. Zee felt Sera pull on her magic but nothing happened. Unfortunately, if the Wood had sealed Sera, Chad was right. They weren't a threat.

Zee sent a message to both Jake and Sera as she sprinted toward Ryan and Chad. *Stay back until the last second. When the Wood is healed, you'll get your power back. Throw a shield around Ryan as fast as possible.*

She didn't wait to see if they listened. The two men grappled back a few steps then Chad tossed Ryan over his hip. Zee cursed as fear surged through her. The bond assured her he was alive, but he wasn't moving.

Ryan, you need to get up. Finish healing the Wood. No matter what happens, finish it.

Chad grinned at her and spun the knife in his hand. "Your boy toy is out of practice."

"I'm not." Zee came at him with a high kick he easily dodged, but it worked to back him further away from the stone. Fury and determination powered her. Without sucking Ryan's magic away to use as a shield, she needed to keep Chad's dagger out of arm's reach. And he sure as hell wasn't getting close to Ryan again.

Blood dripped down her arms, and the cuts ached, but the elemental power under her was building to a crescendo. *Move, Ryan!*

Ryan groaned from the ground, but he crawled over until he crouched over the stone again. Zee felt the magic begin to flow, but she didn't take her focus off of Chad this time. They circled each other, feinting and testing.

"You put a spell in the break to hold it open. All of this is your fault." Zee only needed to keep him occupied a tiny bit longer but his sly smile put her on edge.

"What was I supposed to do? Starve in the filth and cold?"

Chad brandished the blade at her once, twice, then

without looking, he whipped the dagger at Ryan. Time slowed, and Zee used the last of her speed to throw herself between Ryan and the dagger. She curved her body around him, and the blade sank into her shoulder.

Zee grunted and slumped to the ground, but she pushed Ryan to focus through the pain. *Finish it!*

Chad charged them with a guttural cry, but he'd moved too late. Three things happened at once.

Ryan sat back with a satisfied grin and a sigil glowing on his hand, Chad bounced hard off a faintly glowing golden bubble wrapped around both of them, and the seal inside her dissolved in a wave of power that rolled out from the center of the clearing. Zee gasped and her head lolled back as magic shot through her limbs. Bolts of pleasure and pain raced through her until her magic settled, tingling under her skin.

The darkness around them melted away to reveal a bright and temperate winter forest. Her ears popped, and sound returned to normal. Wind rushed through the branches, ruffling her hair, and she'd never been so glad to be warm. A smile spread across her face as she wiggled her fingers and woke her magic.

Zee sat up and gingerly looked back at her throbbing shoulder to see most of Chad's dagger sticking out of it. If she breathed shallowly and didn't move, the pain settled down to a barely manageable level.

Chad lay on the ground whimpering a few feet away. Where the power had refreshed and renewed her, Chad looked like he was having one hell of a magical hangover. She guessed that his magic had also returned, and the resulting mix with the elemental magic swimming inside him had not gone well. It was probably overkill to freeze him in place, but she'd had about enough of his bullshit. And it simply felt good to use her magic again.

The spell would keep him still until they decided what to do with him, but his need for more and more elemental magic would never go away. His future loomed as one of many tough decisions she'd have to make.

Sera and Jake rushed forward, but Zee held up a palm to keep them back. Ryan spun from his position and nearly growled when he saw all the blood. Anger beat at her. He reached out, but then hesitated, and her heart dropped. Was he upset he'd lost his chance to seal his magic? After everything they'd been through, would she lose him anyway?

The bond pulsed solidly between them, but the needs of the heart weren't always strong enough to overcome the dictates of the head.

Zee reached for Ryan with her good arm, shoulder be damned, and leveraged herself up to kiss him. After a moment with no response, she began to pull back, but then his hand slid up her neck to cup the back of her head, and he angled the kiss to take it deeper. She poured all her conflicted emotions and pain and joy into the kiss and let him make of it what he would. Zee forgot they were in the Wood, forgot Chad was motionless next to them, forgot the Fae and the humans and magic. All she cared about was him.

When they came up for air, Zee felt a lot less conflicted. Jake and Sera ignored them, quietly arguing with each other, and the façade of privacy gave her a much-needed moment with Ryan. He pulled her into his lap and rested his forehead against hers. "I'm sorry, princess. I can't heal you. I'm drained."

Relief made her weak. His anger wasn't for her. A new voice made her jump. "It would be my honor to heal her."

Zee looked over to see Lana coming out of a trod across the clearing from them. Jake and Sera had grown quiet, and she knew they were listening. Ryan's arm tightened when she attempted to get up.

Lana squatted to the side of them, took in the damage, then met Zee's eyes with her own full of regret. "With your permission?"

Words stuck in her throat, so Zee nodded.

"Deep breath now." Lana grasped the dagger, pulled, and replaced it with her other hand in one smooth motion. Zee tensed as a wave of agony threatened to knock her unconscious, but soothing warmth quickly replaced it. She sighed as Lana's welcome magic seeped into her, and Ryan eased her head down to rest on his shoulder.

Everyone waited quietly while Lana eventually moved from her shoulder to her arms and then backed away.

Ryan didn't waste a moment. He tilted his head and nuzzled her ear. "Stay with me."

Zee lifted her head so she could see his face. "I wasn't the one who left."

He winced. "I'm sorry. I was a jackass, and I can't promise to not be a jackass in the future, but I promise to never walk away from you again."

She leaned back and saw fierce sincerity in his eyes. He meant what he said. "I have to go back to the Glade—"

"Then I'll come to you."

She could feel his determination pushing at her. He wasn't letting her go without a fight. Tears pricked her eyes, but she smiled through them. "You'd give up your life in your world?"

"In a second. You're my life."

Part of her tried to insist that she couldn't ask that of him, but she told that part to shut up. Instead she leaned forward and kissed him, then spoke against his lips. "And you're mine. We'll figure something out."

"You don't have to," interrupted Lana. Zee had almost forgotten she was there.

"What do you mean?" Ryan asked.

Lana's eyes lingered on their embrace then she sighed. "I wanted to think it was a fling. Some momentary fascination. But I was wrong. I was wrong a lot. I hope you can forgive me, Zee."

Zee nodded slowly. "You didn't know about Chad."

"I knew something weird was happening, but I was so focused on you that he was able to take advantage. I'm not nearly the leader you are."

"But you will be. Mistakes are part of learning."

Ryan grumbled, "Killer fairies seems like a serious mistake."

Zee pinched his side.

A fleeting smile swept across Lana's face. "I'm glad I haven't lost your confidence completely. If you trust me to run things in your absence, the trods are open again, and while the barriers haven't returned, the protections have. The Wood seems to have forgiven us. You can easily travel between Mulligan and the Glade."

"There goes the neighborhood," muttered Jake.

Hope filled her. She could stay with Ryan and still do her duty, but if she allowed herself that level of mobility, the other Fae would follow her lead. Ironically, Chad's interference had secured freedom for all of them. Except him. Zee decided she'd had enough of him. She'd send him back to the homeland in Europe. Let someone else decide what to do with him. As a matter of fact, maybe the time had come to let someone else be in charge altogether.

Ryan didn't pressure her, and in the end, she made the

choice with no regrets. "Lana, I'm stepping down. You're more than capable of leading the Fae, though I plan to act as one of your two traditional advisors for the time being." Zee met Ryan's eyes. "I love you, and I want to be with you. As long as you keep me supplied in donuts."

A wicked grin lit up his face. "I'll get you donuts in exchange for more magic lessons."

She remembered the way she'd taught him to control his magic and heat crept up her cheeks. "You don't want me to seal you?"

"No. I love you, and I trust you to help me control it. And I have some interesting ideas for the next lesson."

Heat raced in a taut line to her core, and she let him see some of the ideas she'd had.

A pained expression passed over Lana's face, and she clasped her hands behind her back. "I have an idea for the other advisor."

Reluctantly, Zee throttled back the images and listened. Lana's choice reinforced Zee's impression that she was ready to lead. Sera elbowed Jake and muttered something about a plan coming together, then drew Lana closer to grill her with questions. Though Zee would've loved to spend the rest of the day rolling around in the dirt with Ryan's hands on her, there was damage control to handle.

Sera, Jake, and Lana discussed logistics, while Ryan glared down at Chad and Zee checked his pockets. "Would you think less of me if I kicked him while he was down?"

"Yes," she said without looking up.

"Might be worth it anyway. That knife looked serious."

Chad's pockets were empty, so Zee picked up the knife Lana had dropped and wiped the blade on her leggings. It would need a real cleaning later. "He was never going to win."

"Oh, *that* I know." He pulled her close for a quick kiss, careful of the sharp blade in her hand. "But I wish you hadn't taken a hit for me."

She kissed him back. "Not your choice, and I'd make it again every time."

The others approached them, seeming to have come to an agreement. Zee carefully stowed the knife in her pack. She should probably give it back to Lana, but something odd in the feel of it made her tuck it away instead. Chad must have used it to channel magic at some point, but Zee couldn't pinpoint a specific kind, which was highly unusual.

Sera, as usual, had questions. "Someone explain to me, in small words, what happened."

Ryan linked his fingers through Zee's. "Something or someone, I'm going to go with Torix, made a hole in the Wood many years ago, cracking the stone over there in the middle. Chad found it and was sucking magic out of it, making the hole a little bigger each time. Eventually, his leech impression wasn't good enough, so he tainted the hole with a spell to hold it open, which slowly made the Wood sick. " He sucked in a breath and continued. "When the barriers fell, the Wood responded like it had a virus and began aggressively trying to get rid of Fae magic since that was the cause of the infection. I healed it with my super amazing healing powers. You were here for the last bit. Thanks for the shield by the way."

She grinned. "All part of the plan. He looked super pissed. Why didn't Zee just knock him out or something?"

Ryan opened his mouth, but Zee beat him to it. "The stolen elemental magic protected him. I could distract him so Ryan could do the healing, or I could use Ryan's magic to stop him, but there wouldn't have been enough to fix the Wood. I chose distraction. It worked because we each trusted the other to hold up their end." Jake cleared his throat, and Zee smiled. "With some outside help thrown in."

Lana shook her head. "I'll be glad when this is over and my most pressing concern will be keeping the humans unaware that they're not at the top of the food chain."

Ryan tilted his head. "The way you described that is extremely disturbing."

Lana shrugged, unconcerned. "I'll take care of Chad. Let me know when you're ready for the ceremony." She inclined her head at Zee and dragged an immobile Chad into a trod. "Never should have vouched for you, you mewling quim." Zee smiled at Lana's muttering as the trod closed behind her.

Jake turned to Sera. "Why are we always having life or death experiences here?"

She shrugged too. "I've always maintained that fairies are assholes, and my opinion hasn't changed one bit now that I know I'm half one of them."

The magic in the clearing slowly returned to normal levels as they finished cleaning out the last of Chad's influence, and sprites began drifting out of the trees. Zee lifted her face to the warm air and smiled. Balance had been returned.

EPILOGUE

ZEE

Ryan was *very* inventive in finding new ways to use their magic.

It took nearly a week to organize the Fae and bring Lana's idea into fruition. Zee made the formal announcement that Lana would be taking over as leader, with herself and one other acting as advisors. She'd expected some push back, but it wasn't until they revealed who the other advisor was that the residents started grumbling.

Zee stood with Evie and Lana in the center of the Glade. She raised a hand for silence, and most obeyed.

"Evie has been a friend to our people for many years now, and she's sacrificed more than most for our future. Times are changing, and we need to change with them. Isolation is no longer necessary, and we don't want to be left behind. Evie will help us better integrate with the human world now that the barriers are gone."

A spattering of applause followed her words. Her people were slow to trust, and they'd been through a lot lately, but

Zee knew they'd come around. Especially once she brought in some rugs and faster internet. She hugged Lana and Evie, then joined Ryan, Jake, and Sera at the rear of the crowd.

Ryan wrapped his arm around her waist and pulled her back against his chest. "How long before chaos sets in?"

Zee draped her arms over Ryan's and relaxed into him. "A week or so, but then they'll handle it."

Lana spoke for a few minutes, then Evie. They explained, to the best of their ability, what had been happening the last few months. Zee overheard some angry murmuring about showing Chad what it meant to betray his people, but Lana had already sent him back to the homeland to be dealt with by the high council. The Fae were mostly tribal, but all villages followed the rules set out by the council.

When they finished, the crowd dispersed. Many people came by to wish Zee good blessings on her future. She could tell Ryan was grinning behind her, but she thanked every person with the same solemnity they gave her. It elated her to know so many cared so much.

Evie waited until all the Fae had left before approaching the group. "I feel a bit like Bilbo Baggins going off into the West."

Sera rolled her eyes. "Please. You'll be running this place in no time."

"Don't sass me, girl. I know you've been worried about my future, but I hope you'll relax now. I'm where I'm meant to be. Besides, you shouldn't be stressing with a baby on the way."

Zee took a closer look at Sera. Her strong shields hid a trace of new magic inside her. Evie was right.

Sera blushed and glared at Evie. "We were waiting to tell everyone."

Evie shrugged. "And now you have." She took Sera's hand. "Don't worry, honey. We Allens come from strong child-bearing stock. Good hips."

Tears gathered in Sera's eyes. "Gah, stupid hormones. Thanks, Evie. But don't tell anyone else, okay?"

Evie raised a sardonic brow at Zee. "You mean all the people who think I'm dead? I'll be sure to keep my mouth shut."

Zee winced. She had a feeling Evie would milk that particular miscalculation for a long while to come. As the Glade returned to its normal bustle, Evie invited them into her new cottage for tea. Zee and Ryan declined, but Sera and Jake followed her, with Sera arguing about the chances the baby would have magic. Zee didn't think it was the right time to tell Sera she was definitely going to need lessons on raising magical offspring.

Ryan leaned forward to whisper in her ear. "How long before we can go home?"

Zee turned in his arms and linked her fingers behind his neck. "We should be good now. Speaking of home, I have some ideas."

His eyes lit up. "I like your ideas."

She laughed and tugged him forward to brush her lips against his. "Not those kinds of ideas, but I like your thinking. How do you feel about turning the second bedroom into a workout space so I can plan more classes?"

"Princess, you can do whatever you want with that bedroom." He nuzzled the sensitive spot under her ear, and she shivered.

"Still not a princess." Her voice sounded breathy as she tilted her head to give him better access.

"I love you no matter what you are. Warrior, princess, mooching Fae, whatever, as long as you're mine." His words were sweet, spoken against her neck, but the image he sent her was extremely naughty and made her wish they lived closer to the Wood. She called a trod, and he bit down lightly. Her hands threaded through the braids in his hair and pulled his head up. He took her mouth hard, the way she wanted, and his magic curled up her neck in a warm band to ease the sting. His lessons really were paying off.

Languid heat softened her muscles, but Zee backed away and took his hand to lead him out of the Glade. She didn't want to put on a show for everyone peeking out their windows. Sprites floated by, lighting the path with their golden glow, and Zee took one last look over her shoulder.

Ryan grinned as the rustic cottages disappeared behind them.

I've always been yours, she told him, and the truth echoed through their bond.

———

Continue the adventure with Maddie and Aiden in Treacherous Magic!

———

If you loved Insidious Magic, please take a moment to leave a review on Amazon, Goodreads, or Bookbub.

———

Can't get enough of snarky magical heroines? Get a fun short story with all new characters set in the Modern Magic world when you sign up for my newsletter, Muse Interrupted!

A Note from Nicole

Readers are the best thing that ever happened to me. You give me the opportunity to do a job that I absolutely love, and I hope you get a story you love in return. My favorite heroines to write are strong women who learn to value more than strength. Zee let me play in her world for a while, and I can't wait to go back.

Thanks, as always, to my fabulous beta team and my editor. Special shout out to Amy and Kelly for keeping me sane and answering weird questions about armbars in the middle of the night.

Want to see what happens when Maddie is forced to face her past? Torix isn't done with her, but her secrets might be enough to keep her safe. For now. Her story continues in Treacherous Magic. Buy it on Amazon.

Join Muse Interrupted Romance, my Facebook group, for daily shenanigans and sexy man chest pictures. Sign up for Muse Interrupted, my newsletter, for first access to new releases plus extra content, giveaways, sneak peeks, and first look at new covers.

If you have time, would you mind leaving a review on Amazon? Goodreads or Bookbub would be amazing too! Readers help other readers like you find books they love.

I appreciate you, and because I do, I've included an excerpt from the next book, Treacherous Magic right here for your reading pleasure. Turn the page to get started on Maddie and Aiden's adventure.

~Nicole

TREACHEROUS MAGIC

MADDIE

WHEN MADDIE THOMAS IMAGINED DREAMWALKING, she pictured a tropical island with beautiful shirtless cabana boys bringing her fruity umbrella drinks. Instead, she blinked at the glare of neon beer signs in an unfamiliar bar that smelled of whiskey and regret.

Dark wood paneling and dim lights cast shadows across most of the booths. The giant Texas flag hanging on the wall told her she'd traveled a long way from the little room in Wales where she'd fallen asleep. She looked down, unsurprised to see the leggings and tank top she'd gone to sleep in, but her knee-high boots were a new addition to the outfit.

Maddie shrugged. Strange occurrences happened every day for her. None of the patrons paid her any mind, and the bartender ignored her when she settled onto a cracked vinyl barstool. Country music played from the speakers, and Maddie winced at the twangy noise. She'd never liked the sound, despite growing up in a tiny town in East Texas.

There was no one else sitting at the bar, so she cleared her throat. The guy with the big belly drying glasses didn't look up. Maddie sighed and glanced around. What had brought her here?

Her eyes skipped past a familiar face in the far back booth, then jumped back with a shiver. He was looking down at a phone, so she couldn't be sure, but his profile seemed right. Maddie suddenly felt very exposed by the lights over the bar. The stool squeaked as she slid off of it, and the bartender finally looked up. His brow furrowed as he stared at the seat where she'd been, then he went back to drying.

He hadn't seen Maddie. Yep, dreamwalking. Too bad she'd been unceremoniously yanked into a nightmare.

Despite her throat closing up, she calmly walked to the shadowy corner on the far side of the room and leaned back against the wall with a good view of the booths. The man glanced up at the door, and she had her confirmation. Torix was in the bar with her. Or she was in the bar with him. Her heart sped up with fear, but he ignored her just like the bartender.

The door opened with a rush of cold air, and a disheveled man in a topcoat came in. Maddie had seen him before too, but it took a moment for her to place him. Sera's ex-husband. The creepy one who'd followed her to Mulligan last year. The last time she'd seen him, he'd looked like a movie star, but since then, he'd lost weight and grown a ratty beard. There was no doubt in her mind why he'd shown up, and after a quick survey of the room, he made a beeline to Torix's table.

The mild annoyance on Torix's face transformed into a welcoming smile. Maddie couldn't hear what he said, so she chose a booth closer to theirs—behind Torix's line of sight —that allowed her to see his profile and listen in.

"I'm glad you could make it, Will. We have much to discuss."

"You said you had a solution to my problems." Will looked around the bar and frowned. "This place is a dump."

A muscled ticked in Torix's jaw, but Will didn't seem to notice. "A temporary meeting place, nothing more. You wish to take revenge on Sera and her ilk for what they've done to you."

Will's eyes shot back to Torix. "What do you know about that?"

Torix tilted his head. "I know a great many things. You were once successful, powerful, the master of your world."

Torix's smooth voice coated her nerves in a hypnotizing calmness. Her fight or flight response worked overtime to convince her she needed to leave. Now. Nothing good could come from Torix and Will working together.

Will sat up a little straighter at each of Torix's words. "Yes. I was the master, and that bitch, Sera, took it all from me. They did something to me. Made it hard to think." He shook his head roughly for a second. "I see things that weren't there before."

"I can help you. You can be powerful again."

Maddie didn't know Will, but she wanted to tell him to run far away from that offer. Memories tried to blind her from her own time with Torix, but Maddie pushed them away to focus. Sera had taken all of Torix's power over a year ago, so Maddie wanted to know how Torix planned to fulfill his end of the bargain.

Will nodded, greed in his eyes. "What do I need to do?"

Maddie closed her eyes and shook her head for a moment. The idiot didn't even ask any basic questions. She opened them again in time to see Torix pull a pouch and a tiny knife from a bag sitting next to him on the bench. "We share blood. Like unto like. Only a few drops into the pouch and we'll work together to destroy Sera and her mate."

Will's hand clenched into a fist when Torix mentioned Sera's mate, and a new fear filled Maddie. She loved Jake more than anyone. Her brother had saved her last year while helping Sera stop Torix, and mate was definitely the right term for his and Sera's relationship now. In all the time that had passed since then, Maddie hadn't considered that Jake might be in danger.

Her fingers tapped silently on the table. She wanted to stop the ceremony, but she wasn't really there. Knowing Torix, these events had already happened.

Torix sliced a shallow cut across his own palm with the knife and raised his brow. Will didn't hesitate. He extended his own hand, palm up, and Torix made a matching slash. He held both their hands over the open pouch so the blood could drip into it. Maddie's nose wrinkled as the smell of sulfur drifted to her, but no one else seemed to notice.

Will gasped, and a wave of magic shot out from the booth. Maddie couldn't see it, but she felt it like electric tingles covering her body. She shuddered. Years ago, she'd felt the same tingles, but this time, she experienced the sensation from the outside. Will didn't know it, but he'd doomed himself.

"It's done. You'll return to your room with the bird to await further orders."

Maddie's eyebrows winged up as a pretty little songbird hopped out of the bag and flapped up to land on Will's shoulder. He didn't react to the new addition. In fact, all the personality had drained from Will's face, like he'd been replaced by a mannequin. Man and bird got up from the booth without a goodbye and headed for the door. Torix watched Will walk out of the bar and smiled. Maddie considered trying to follow him to see what would happen, but to her surprise, Torix turned and offered her a slow appraisal.

"You look well, my dear."

Maddie's breath caught in her throat. He shouldn't be able to see her, unless she'd been in his head the whole time. Her heartbeat pounded in her chest. She got a stranglehold on her panic and shoved it down hard. "What do you want?"

He tsked and sent her a charming smile. "That's no way to greet an old friend."

"You were never my friend." She spit the last word at him, and his smile dimmed a bit.

"It seems we remember things differently. All that time spent together, causing mayhem." Torix leaned toward her, and his tongue snaked across his lips. "I've missed the taste of your fear."

A cold chill skittered up her back, but Maddie refused to retreat. "Leave me alone."

His eyes sharpened, and his nostrils flared. "I'm afraid that's not possible. You've hidden yourself well, but the time for patience is over. It seems you have something of mine."

Maddie reminded herself that Torix was powerless. He couldn't touch her, but with what she'd just witnessed, she had trouble believing the adage. "How did you trap Will?"

He tilted his head at her like he was studying an interesting bug. "I don't believe I'll tell you that." He closed the pouch and tucked it in the bag.

Torix had pulled her in for a reason, ostensibly to show her he'd made a Will-zombie, but why would he want her to know that? Maddie wondered about the bird as well, but other aspects of this little visit took precedence. "You're back in Mulligan."

He nodded once. "You'll come to me, but will it be too late to save your brother?" He shrugged as his smile grew. "Perhaps I'll come to you instead. Wales, is it?"

Maggie snapped her shields closed tightly, cursing herself for reverting back to a scared little girl and forgetting her training. He'd been manipulating her, as usual. Misdirecting her, providing irresistible bait, and using her distraction to fish for information on her location. Maddie frowned when Torix didn't disappear. As long as her shields were closed, he shouldn't have had access to her mind.

Fine. She'd separate them the old-fashioned way. Torix may have been controlling things until now, but it was *her* dream. She straightened her shoulders and stood. When he would have followed suit, a low growl from beside her had him narrowing his eyes instead.

A speckled, grey and white wolf had appeared next to her. His huge body came up to her waist, and his lip curled back revealing very sharp teeth pointed at Torix. Maddie spread her fingers in the coarse fur along his back, glad to have backup, no matter how unexpected.

Torix raised a brow and disappeared. The bar began to slowly fade around her, and Maddie took a full breath for the first time since she'd seen him. Seventeen months. She'd been hiding for seventeen months. Training, yes, and reading every scrap of magical information she could get her hands on, but in the end, her fear had trumped all.

The wolf stopped growling as soon as Torix disappeared. He settled back on his haunches and stared at the now empty booth. The two of them together might have scared Torix off, but she didn't think that was the case. Either way, she could have handled it herself.

Maddie crouched down in front of the gorgeous animal, meeting his golden eyes.

"I know you're not a wolf," she said quietly.

He held her gaze for a moment, then she woke up in her bed in Wales. Maddie sat up and ran her hand through her long, tangled hair, pulling it away from her face. The weak predawn light of the room revealed her backpack and little else. In those seventeen months, she'd learned to travel light and always be prepared. When Jake and Sera had told her Torix had escaped, she'd known the danger would return. Fear and resolution fought for dominance, but Maddie refused to let fear win again. She threw the thin blanket off and began collecting her belongings.

Torix had threatened Jake to force her back to Mulligan, and she'd do anything to protect Jake. Even deplete her savings. Maddie slung her pack over her shoulder and pulled out her phone. The international airline booked her on a flight that day for the cost of a small car. Without more information about the setting of the dream, she couldn't afford to wait for a better deal.

With trepidation fluttering in her chest, Maddie left her boarding house and waited for the bus to Cardiff. She'd wasted enough time hiding.

CHAPTER 1

———

MADDIE

MADDIE HADN'T SEEN her family in almost a year. To be fair, her family hadn't really seen *her* in much longer than that. She stood down the street from the house that she'd grown up in, which like Mulligan, had changed very little. Cars lined the street, and people gathered outside despite the chill in the air. She'd known about Jake and Sera's christening party, but as usual, she'd declined the invitation. As far as her family knew, she had no plans to leave Europe. A visit from Torix provided great motivation.

Her dad had the grill going in the back, and Maddie could smell the brisket from where she'd stopped walking. The scent urged her forward, making her mouth water. She hadn't had a good brisket in months. The party made her nervous, but it also probably meant Torix hadn't made his move against Jake yet.

The bright sun made up for the fog and rain she'd left in Wales. She slid her sunglasses into her hair and squinted at the party. Jake and Sera would be there with baby Amber. It was their house after all, but so would Ryan and Zee. Her steps faltered. She hadn't had much dealing with Zee, a few conversations after the events of last year, at Sera's insistence, but if her experience had taught her anything, it was that Fae couldn't be trusted.

A cold gust of wind made Maddie shiver in her thin sweater. Her pack slapped against her back as she abruptly stopped in front of Sera's old house next door. Maddie hadn't been spotted yet. She ducked into the side yard between the properties and settled behind a couple of leafless trees. Her dark clothes blended with the shadows, and she crouched down to make herself smaller.

Laughter drifted to Maddie, and she felt a pang of longing. She wanted to be there with her brother and her parents. Her niece was five months old, and Maddie'd never met her. Jake and Sera emailed her pictures, but it wasn't the same. They treated Maddie as if the events last Halloween hadn't happened, and the guilt nearly drowned her.

Wisps of blond hair escaped her braid and blew into her eyes with the next breeze. She tucked them away and watched Jake come out the back door with Amber on his hip. Her shoulders sagged in relief at the proof that she wasn't too late. Torix knew exactly what to say to get her to act, but after seven years, she'd gotten good at reading between his half-truths. He intended to kill her brother, but he wanted her first. And he wanted her in Mulligan.

Jake had a beer in one hand and a huge smile on his face. He stopped at the grill to talk to their dad, then

strapped the baby into a swing set up in the yard. Amber
smiled big, like her dad, and kicked her legs at anyone who
walked by. Sera came out of the house next, and Jake pulled
her close. He said something to her that made her shake her
head and dropped a kiss on her forehead.

The whole exchange was exactly how she imagined
their life. Easy and wonderful now that she couldn't cause
trouble. Maddie rubbed her chest where an ache spread.
They'd tried to incorporate her after Halloween, but it had
quickly become clear that she needed distance. The things
she'd done for Torix, as Torix, haunted her. She couldn't
forget when every time she saw Jake the images of him
unconscious on the forest floor flooded her. Maddie didn't
fool herself that she deserved the happy ending.

Jake said something to make Sera laugh, then went back
into the house. A couple of people stopped to chat with Sera
as she made her way to the baby, and Maddie wondered
what would happen if she crashed the party and announced
Torix was back.

Probably everyone would welcome her with open arms
and patronize her while they tried to handle it. As if Torix
were a minor annoyance or something. They'd more than
likely get themselves killed. Maddie shook her head and
adjusted to a more comfortable position. She'd gotten bitter,
but then, she had a pretty good excuse. Seven years of servitude would do that. Apparently, a year of freedom didn't
provide a better mindset. Still, she should be thanking Sera
instead of watching in the shadows like a creeper.

Even now, Maddie couldn't make herself walk over to
her family and warn them. She'd come back for that express
purpose, but crossing the distance proved harder than she'd
thought it would be. Maddie considered emailing Sera the
information to avoid any questions, but she didn't want

them searching out Torix. He may have lost his own power, but he'd clearly found another source.

The baby waved her arms, but all Sera did was rub her little tummy and say something to Maddie's dad. He nodded, and Sera turned to look directly at Maddie.

The trees and shadows hid her well, but Sera was half-Fae. Maddie was surprised her hiding spot had lasted this long. Sera strolled through the brush at the property line and came to lean against a tree with her back to Maddie.

"Why are you hiding in the yard?"

"It seemed like as good a place as any."

Sera sighed. "There's food and drinks in the house, and I know your mom would love to see you. Janet too."

"I know." Janet had sent her a healing crystal, though she hadn't known that Maddie even needed healing. It was strange and sweet, and nearly crushed Maddie with guilt for how she'd treated her former boss.

As for her mom, every day since leaving for Europe, Maddie got an email containing a run-down of anything that happened to anyone in Mulligan. Maddie knew her parents weren't planning to stay much longer, there were adventures to be had, but Amber was their first grandchild and they weren't going to miss the Fae naming. Maddie understood the sentiment.

"How did Mom take finding out about the Fae?"

Sera shrugged. "The usual, mostly. She skipped the denial phase and went straight to excitement. Did you know she'd always thought there was something strange about the Wood?"

Maddie chuckled. "Yeah. She's believed in the fantastic her whole life. Having a part-Fae grandchild must be the greatest thing that ever happened to her." She couldn't keep the sadness entirely out of her voice, and Sera picked up on it.

"She wishes you were there, Mad. Her greatest wish is to have her whole family together and safe...and for Thor to descend from the heavens in nothing but a kilt, but we're pretty sure that was the wine talking."

She snorted out another laugh. "That, I believe."

"Come to the party, Mad. Let us help you heal."

"I'm not interested in healing."

It was the wrong thing to say. Maddie couldn't see Sera's face, but the disapproval came through clearly in her stiffened shoulders. Years ago, *Sera* would have been the one hiding while Maddie coaxed her out. Coming into her magic had given Sera confidence that age hadn't. Maddie was only a year younger than her, but she felt much older.

"Jake looks happy." The subject change worked to get Sera's focus off of Maddie. "When are you two going to get married?"

Sera shrugged. "We're not in a hurry, but it would make things easier when we finally sell Evie's house."

"You know I'll be there, right?"

"I know. Jake knows too, but he'd be happier if his sister came home for good."

"I can't do that, Sera. I'm not sure I can ever move back to Mulligan. There are too many bad memories."

"I understand that. You know I do, more than anyone else, but running isn't the answer."

"I'm not running. I'm preparing. Torix will be back."

"He's powerless, Mad. He can't hurt you anymore."

Maddie shook her head, even though Sera couldn't see her. The moment had snuck up on her. All she had to say was *Torix is back, and he has a Will-zombie*, but the words were stuck in her throat. "Will was powerless. That didn't stop him from hurting you."

"That's true." She was silent for a moment. "We're worried about you and we miss you, but it's your life. You get to decide what you need out of it. Promise me you'll be careful?"

"I'm always careful now." Released from the pressure to make an appearance, Maddie could breathe again. The baby started to cry, but before Sera could push away from the tree, Jake came out of the house to calm her down. "You guys need to be careful too. Don't underestimate Torix and Will."

Sera nodded, but the baby was distracting her. Maddie needed to make her understand.

"I mean it, Sera. He's dangerous, even without his power, and Will is under his thrall."

Sera spun around, and Maddie could feel the wave of magic she used to check the area. "Are you sure?"

"Yes. I saw it in a dream."

Sera relaxed. "You had a lot of nightmares after we freed you. Maybe something you were doing in Wales triggered another one."

Maddie wanted to shake her. "It was real." She couldn't claim any more than that because Torix could have been manipulating the situation. At the very least, she knew for certain that Torix had outside magic at his disposal somewhere near Mulligan.

Sera smiled and took her hand for a second. "Okay. We'll keep our eyes open then. Maybe Evie or Lana have some more information about Torix's whereabouts. I know where Will is living. I'll go by and check on him."

Maddie gripped Sera's hand. "No. Please don't, Sera." The whole situation suddenly felt like a trap. Could that have been Torix's plan all along? Use Maddie to lure Sera and Jake into danger? "Please promise me you'll stay away from Will. Even if he calls you or something. I know you'll keep it if you promise me."

Sera grimaced. "Okay, if it makes you feel better. It's not like I hang out with him."

"I need you to say the words."

Maddie felt prickles of magic crawl up her arms as Sera met her eyes. "I promise to stay away from Will to the best of my abilities."

The prickles faded, and Maddie sighed in relief. "Thank you."

Sera glanced over her shoulder to Jake and the baby. "I have to get back."

"Don't tell them I was here. It'll just make everything worse."

Sera speared her with a look. "I won't lie to Jake. Besides, he knows I'm over here talking to you."

"I don't want you to lie. I just don't want you to bring it up."

She nodded and tilted her head. "Are you sure you don't want to come meet Amber?"

Maddie stared past her at the happy baby that Jake was bouncing around. She *did* want to come meet Amber, but too much darkness followed her. "I can't yet. I love you guys."

Her voice cracked at the end, and Sera pulled her into a quick hug. "Be safe."

Sera jogged across the yard toward Jake, who never took his eyes off of her. She said a few words, and his gaze shifted to Maddie's hiding place. He sent her a sad smile then gathered his family and went back into the house. A cloud drifted in front of the sun, and the breeze made Maddie shiver again. She had to stay as far away from them as possible. Torix enjoyed playing twisted games, and until Maddie knew the rules, she needed to take every precaution to keep them safe.

Maddie stayed in the shadows and circled the house until she was out of line of sight of Jake's place. The neighbors didn't worry her. Evie had left for the Glade months ago, and no one else would care that Maddie had returned. She'd spent a lot of time in the last few years severing connections. If she couldn't control her actions, she'd at least be able to limit the amount of people hurt by them. Torix had allowed it because it amused him to see her in pain.

The for-sale sign and the empty feel of the house made her sad. Even under Torix's influence, she'd spent a lot of good hours there practicing magic with Evie. Maddie hated what she'd done to her former teacher, and the time Evie had spent trapped ate at her. For a second, she considered going to the Glade and throwing herself on the mercy of the Fae, but they weren't well-known for their mercy. She'd heard Evie had tempered that a bit, but the idea of putting another person in charge of her fate again made her itch to run away as far and as fast as she could.

Maybe not the Glade, but the forest had always been her safe space. Maddie shouldered her pack and walked toward the trees across the street. She'd slept on the flight and the drive up from the airport, but she hadn't had a chance to stretch her muscles.

Maddie had taken worse strolls through the woods on a crisp January day. Her mind wandered as she wove between full pine trees and walked over crunchy leaves. Torix had engineered her presence in Mulligan. He'd known she wouldn't be able to ignore a threat to her family.

Torix said he'd been searching for her, and she wasn't ready for him to find her yet. Best case scenario, he'd get what he wanted and leave her more of a broken mess than she already was. Worst case, he killed her and everyone she loved. Maddie frowned. Mulligan was a small town, and by evening, everyone would know she was back. How could she keep away from Torix if they were both frequenting the same nine square miles?

She'd warned Sera and Jake; she could go back to Europe. An image of Amber kicking her feet in her swing popped into Maddie's head, and a fiery anger filled her. How much of her life was she willing to sacrifice for Torix? He'd stolen seven years. Was she going to give him another decade while she hid from him? She kicked a rock into the underbrush and looked up at the sliver of bright blue sky visible between the trees. He had to be stopped. *She* had to stop him. Everyone else had responsibilities, and none of them knew him as well as she did.

Fear threatened to overtake her, freezing her muscles and closing her throat, but she'd learned to move around it. Torix used fear to control, and she was done being controlled.

A clearing opened up ahead of her, and Maddie shook her head. She hadn't meant to walk there, but old habits died hard. It was bigger than she remembered, and full of tiny glowing balls of light. Sera had decimated the old dead oak, but the sprites and the circle of pines remained. She walked to the center and found the stone etched with ancient markings. Torix had called it a nexus. A place where several magics converged. And a place he'd spent several generations trapped in a tree.

She'd considered it the heart of the Wood, and considered the Fae stupid for trying to imprison a powerful force there. In the back of her mind, she'd always wondered if Torix hadn't manipulated that outcome as well.

A wind moved the tops of the trees, but the nexus stayed silent. The blue sky had faded as if the sun had gone down, but Maddie recognized the in-between space. At some point, she'd crossed from normal forest to magical trod. Maddie hadn't been able to make any paths since Sera had freed her. She'd tried. The trods hadn't responded before, but the Wood apparently wanted her here now.

Her stomach growled, and she remembered that she hadn't eaten anything since the questionable egg sandwich at the airport. Maddie cursed her issues for keeping her from the food at the party. She *really* missed brisket.

Maddie scrounged through her pack for a granola bar, but stopped when she felt someone watching her. She lifted her head and looked around. A quarter of the way around the clearing she spotted the wolf sitting in the brush. His dappled coat blended with the shadows. He looked relaxed, but his ears were perked up. She moved further into the circle, and his golden eyes followed her.

The last time she'd seen him, not counting the dream, he'd been as trapped as she'd been. Sera had removed Torix's hold and dismissed him as an errant wolf, but Maddie knew better. She dropped her gaze to her pack and pulled out her last two granola bars.

"You might as well join me. I have enough for both of us."

He didn't move right away, and when he slunk closer, he made no noise among the leaves. She sank to the ground and tore open one of the packages. He'd stopped a few feet away, and when she offered him the bar, he stayed where he was. It would be smart to fear him, but Maddie simply didn't. She sighed and tossed the food to him, then opened her own.

He ate the bar in three neat bites, but his eyes never left her.

Maddie tilted her head and stared back at him as she ate her late lunch. "Why do you stay in that form after everything he made you do?"

His ear twitched, but he didn't answer her. Not that she expected him to.

"You know he's back. That's why you're here. I get that part. What I don't get is if you're here to stop him or help him."

His shape blurred, and she felt magic dancing along her skin. Survival instinct said she should back away because if it was the latter, she was in trouble. Curiosity kept her still. His change fascinated Maddie, but watching him was probably rude. In all time she'd known him, she'd only seen the wolf. During the nearly instantaneous change, her eyes couldn't focus on him. One second a large wolf sat in front of her, the next, a large man crouched there.

He propped his arms on his knees, and Maddie raised a brow at his clothes. Honest to God leather pants tucked into high boots. At least they looked like leather pants, maybe suede, some kind of supple dark brown material. She had the urge to touch them and find out for herself. On top of that, his thigh muscles might have been bigger than her head.

He cleared his throat, and she realized she'd been basically staring at his crotch. A warm flush flooded her cheeks, and Maddie looked up. Broad shoulders, dark hair tied back from his face, a smirking mouth, and the same golden eyes. She'd expected him to look older, more grizzled, but the smooth angles of his face made her glad she'd been wrong.

He couldn't have been much older than her. When had Torix had managed to capture him?

He quirked a brow, and Maddie was drawn back to his eyes. Wolf eyes, but not. He watched her like a predator, and a shiver went down her spine, but not from fear. If she ran, would he chase her? The thought sent a thrill through her, and she fought to shake off the effect. She had no time to be attracted to whatever he was.

Her mouth opened to question him, but her brain hadn't caught up with her common sense yet. "You look ridiculous."

He glanced down at himself. "How so?"

His rich, deep voice echoed inside her, and Maddie struggled to remember what she'd said a second ago. "No one wears leather pants unless they're going to a club."

"I'll keep that in mind the next time I'm in combat."

He didn't sound annoyed by her critique, which was fantastic because *Maddie* was annoyed with it. *What was wrong with her?* A sinful face and a sexy voice shouldn't be enough to completely shut off all rational thought.

She mentally shook herself and tried to focus on his relationship with Torix. The most likely scenario played out with him as a victim, like her, but people were crazy. Who knew what the effects of enslavement had been on him? "So, good guy or bad guy?"

"Neither." He didn't take his eyes off her, but he sat down in the pine straw, which made her feel a little better about his intentions. "But I'm not working with Torix. You?"

Considering her reaction to his human form, his response relieved her. She also appreciated having her instincts confirmed again. This time, they'd said he wasn't there to bring her back to Torix, and she'd learned the hard way to listen to herself first.

"No. I'm here for a different reason." She wasn't being coy; she wasn't sure why she'd ended up in the nexus.

He watched her a moment longer, then broke the tension by looking around the clearing. "Things have changed. I like it better this way."

She stifled a laugh. "You mean without the super powerful, psychopathic Fae controlling everything we did from inside a damn tree?"

His smile was quick, then it was gone. "Yeah, and being human again has its perks."

She sobered. "You couldn't change?"

"No. His hold was absolute, and he wanted the wolf."

Maddie nodded. She knew all about Torix's hold. "I'm Maddie Thomas."

"Aiden Morgan." He extended his hand, and she shook it. His warm, gentle contact settled her better than his words had.

Maddie drew her hand back reluctantly. "If you're not here to serve Torix, what *are* you doing here?"

"I'm here to kill him." The words were matter of fact, and Maddie respected his bluntness.

She nodded again. "Me too. You were in my dream."

He grabbed a handful of pine needles and stared weaving them together. "I was following Torix. He pulled you in; I pulled you out."

Maddie couldn't look away from his hands. The motions were delicate and precise. "How is that possible? I understand Torix and I are still connected, which theoretically lets him pop in, but how were you able to affect anything?"

He shrugged. "There must be more connecting us than indentured servitude."

Maddie wasn't so sure, but she didn't have a better idea.

He worked a small circle in his hands, and she could see the beginnings of a tiny knot design forming. "You're not Fae."

"No." He didn't look up from his crafting.

He wasn't human. His magic felt like something...else. Not to mention she'd seen him shift from wolf to man. Most humans couldn't do that. "Werewolf?"

He chuckled. "You think the stories are true?"

"I think anything is possible at this point."

"Not a werewolf."

"Will you tell me if I guess it correctly?"

His eyes raised to hers, and she felt that tingle again. He fell quiet for a moment, intense, as if searching her for something. "I don't know."

At least he'd given an honest answer. "I'm going to keep asking."

His smile returned. "I know."

Maddie didn't usually go for the cryptic, know-it-all routine. She wanted direct answers to her questions, but she couldn't fault him for wanting to keep his secrets to himself. It's not like she was being all that forthcoming. Maybe she should ask a question that required a more complicated answer.

"Why a wolf?"

"Better than a dragon."

"I'm going to disagree with you on that one," she muttered.

A small crash and a thud came from the trees, interrupting their peaceful interlude. Both of them sprang to their feet. Aiden moved with an easy grace, despite being much taller than her. He scanned the area, turning in a slow circle, but didn't reach for any weapons. She didn't relish the idea of fighting side by side with Aiden in his human form.

As a wolf, she knew what to expect from him, but men sometimes reacted in stupid ways.

He looked up at the darkening sky as if he'd seen something, and a flash of movement streaked out of the trees at them. Maddie didn't have time to think. She threw herself between Aiden and the creature. Her hands came up as if drawing a sword, and a blade of shimmering silver magic took shape.

She swung at what looked like a white lizard that was roughly the size of a cat. It dodged around the magic and leapt at them with bared fangs. Maddie jerked back and bumped into Aiden. One arm came around her waist from behind and spun her to the side. The lizard missed her face, but managed to sink its teeth into her shoulder.

Her breath hissed out between her teeth as fiery pain shot down her arm. Aiden grabbed the creature around its neck, and it disappeared in a puff of warm smoke. Blood trickled into her shirt as the trees started to slowly spin. She released the magic, and the blade disappeared, but she was having trouble keeping herself upright. Aiden's other arm slid under her knees, and he lifted her without much effort.

"Put me down. I'm fine." Maddie's weak voice embarrassed her as she tried to push against his chest. The guy was solid muscle.

"You're not fine, but you will be. It's okay. I'll take care of you."

She wanted to laugh at the idea, but her eyes drifted closed. He tightened his grip, which jostled her arm painfully. She must have made a noise because he shifted her until her head rested on his shoulder with her wound tucked between them. It should have been terrifying to let him handle it, but she was strangely okay with it. Her arm had gone numb, and instead of trying again to handle things on her own, she pressed her face into the softness of his shirt and marveled that he smelled like warm cotton instead of dog.

Treacherous Magic
Buy it now!

ALSO BY NICOLE HALL

Modern Magic

Accidental Magic

Insidious Magic

Treacherous Magic

Impulsive Magic

Rebellious Magic

Chaotic Magic

ABOUT THE AUTHOR

Nicole Hall is a smart-ass with a Ph.D. and a potty mouth. She writes stories that have magic, sass, and romance because she believes that everyone deserves a little happiness. Coffee makes her happy, messes make her stabby, and she'd sell one of her children for a second season of Firefly. Her paranormal romance series, Modern Magic, is available now.

Let Nicole know what you thought about her sassy, magical world because she really does love hearing from readers. Find her at www.nicolehallbooks.com or Muse Interrupted Romance on Facebook!

Want to find out when the newest Nicole Hall book hits the shelves? Sign up for the weekly Muse Interrupted newsletter on her website. You'll get a welcome gift, the *Modern Magic* ebook, plus new release info, giveaways, exclusive content, and previews of the new books especially for fans.

facebook.com/nicolehallbooks

instagram.com/nicolehallbooks

amazon.com/author/nicole_hall

bookbub.com/authors/nicole-hall

Printed in Great Britain
by Amazon